3

D0837974

Praise

"Ms. Richards possesses
a magical way with words."
—*RT Book Reviews*

"Richards's ability to portray compelling
characters who grapple with challenging
family issues is laudable."
—*Publishers Weekly,* starred review, on *Fox River*

Praise for Janice Kay Johnson

"I can't wait to read more of [Johnson's] books."
—*Dear Author* on *Bone Deep*

"Johnson wonderfully depicts
her characters' emotions."
—*RT Book Reviews*

Praise for Sarah Mayberry

"This very talented writer touches your heart
with her characters."
—*RT Book Reviews*

"Reading [*All They Need*] was like finding a
twenty-dollar bill in your coat pocket, then
unfolding it and finding a fifty wrapped inside.
It started out great and just kept getting better."
—*USATODAY.com*

AUBURN HILLS PUBLIC LIBRARY 50
3400 EAST SEYBURN DRIVE
AUBURN HILLS, MI 48326
(248) 370-9466

DISCARD

EMILIE RICHARDS's

many novels feature complex characterizations and in-depth explorations of social issues, a result of her training and experience as a family counselor, which contributes to her fascination with relationships of all kinds. Emilie, a mother of four, lives with her husband in Florida, where she is currently working on her next novel for the Harlequin MIRA line.

JANICE KAY JOHNSON

The author of more than seventy books for children and adults, Janice Kay Johnson is especially well-known for her Harlequin Superromance novels about love and family—about the way generations connect and the power our earliest experiences have on us throughout life. Her 2007 novel *Snowbound* won a RITA® Award from Romance Writers of America for Best Contemporary Series Romance. A former librarian, Janice raised two daughters in a small rural town north of Seattle, Washington. She loves to read and is an active volunteer and board member for Purrfect Pals, a no-kill cat shelter.

SARAH MAYBERRY

lives by the bay in Melbourne in a house that is about to be pulled apart for renovations. She is happily married to another writer, shades of whom can be found in many of her heroes. She is currently besotted with her seven-month-old Cavoodle puppy, Max, and feeling guilty about her overgrown garden. When she isn't writing or feeling guilty or rolling around on the carpet with the dog, she likes reading, cooking, shoe shopping and going to the movies.

EMILIE RICHARDS

JANICE KAY JOHNSON
SARAH MAYBERRY

THE
Christmas Wedding
QUILT

HARLEQUIN® ANTHOLOGY

If you purchased this book without a cover you should be aware that this book is stolen property. It was reported as "unsold and destroyed" to the publisher, and neither the author nor the publisher has received any payment for this "stripped book."

ISBN-13: 978-0-373-83781-6

THE CHRISTMAS WEDDING QUILT

Copyright © 2013 by Harlequin Books S.A.

The publisher acknowledges the copyright holders of the individual works as follows:

LET IT SNOW
Copyright © 2013 by Emilie Richards McGee

YOU BETTER WATCH OUT
Copyright © 2013 by Janice Kay Johnson

NINE LADIES DANCING
Copyright © 2013 by Small Cow Productions Pty Ltd

Recycling programs for this product may not exist in your area.

All rights reserved. Except for use in any review, the reproduction or utilization of this work in whole or in part in any form by any electronic, mechanical or other means, now known or hereafter invented, including xerography, photocopying and recording, or in any information storage or retrieval system, is forbidden without the written permission of the publisher, Harlequin Enterprises Limited, 225 Duncan Mill Road, Don Mills, Ontario, Canada M3B 3K9.

This is a work of fiction. Names, characters, places and incidents are either the product of the author's imagination or are used fictitiously, and any resemblance to actual persons, living or dead, business establishments, events or locales is entirely coincidental.

This edition published by arrangement with Harlequin Books S.A.

For questions and comments about the quality of this book, please contact us at CustomerService@Harlequin.com.

® and TM are trademarks of Harlequin Enterprises Limited or its corporate affiliates. Trademarks indicated with ® are registered in the United States Patent and Trademark Office, the Canadian Trade Marks Office and in other countries.

HARLEQUIN®
www.Harlequin.com

Printed in U.S.A.

CONTENTS

LET IT SNOW

Emilie Richards

PROLOGUE

Jo Miller was sure she liked her next-door neighbor. There was no reason not to. She and the other woman were both in their early thirties, both professionals. Any number of mornings in the three years Jo had lived in her San Diego condo, she had noticed the other woman downstairs in the parking lot, leaving for work decked out in tailored suits and gotcha heels.

Of course if Jo really liked the petite blonde with the friendly smile, why couldn't she remember her name?

"So I told the UPS man I would keep it for you," the neighbor said of the package she had just presented to Jo. "I hope that's okay? I know how hard it is to track down a delivery once they take it back to the warehouse, especially in December, when they're so busy."

Jo realized it was now her turn to speak. "That was so nice of you."

"Of course, I didn't realize you would be gone so long. I hope nothing spoiled. It looks like a gift."

Jo glanced down at the package newly resting in her arms, set there before she and her suitcase could escape into her home and close the door. She was so exhausted she could hardly make out the spidery writing. She squinted, then her heart threatened to stop midbeat. "Oh..." She swallowed.

"I'm sorry, I hope it's not bad news."

"No, no..." Jo clutched the package to her chest. "I'm

just back from Hong Kong. I…I…" She shook her head. "I'm exhausted, that's all."

"No wonder. I thought I'd call out for pizza in a little bit. Would you like to share? My treat? I bet you don't have a bit of food in your fridge."

Jo shook her head, a reflex that was her standard response to invitations. "I need sleep more, I'm afraid. Maybe another time?"

The blonde smiled, but without conviction. In three years she and Jo had never crossed each other's thresholds.

"Sleep well, then." She opened the door that was only two feet from Jo's own. "And I'm Marian, Jo. Marian Parker. In case you change your mind."

The door closed behind her, but not before Jo glimpsed soft peach walls, a slipcovered sofa, and a Christmas tree with twinkling lights in the corner.

She stood staring at Marian's door for a moment, then fumbled for the keys she had slipped into her pocket during the limo ride from the airport and unlocked her own.

Pulling her suitcase behind her, she stepped into a room that was a mirror image of Marian's, but only in layout. Here the walls were a gloomy taupe and the furniture sleek black leather with chrome armrests. The only pop of color vibrated from a pillow on the sofa with geometric designs of chartreuse and shocking pink.

Right after Jo had signed the lease here, her mother had decorated the condo as a surprise. Jo had opened her door after another business trip to find it the way it was now.

The surprise had come during Sophie's interior decorator phase, which had been sandwiched between her

jazz singer phase and landscape photographer phase.
Jo's walls were dotted with out-of-focus black-and-white
photographs of Point Loma and Venice Beach, framed
in more chrome. Thankfully a year had passed without
additions. These days Sophie was busy channeling a
spirit guide named Ocelot Lee, who was slowly revealing the secrets of the universe in exchange for large in-
fusions of cash to the medium who arranged his visits.

The decorating scheme made it hard not to think
about her mother, but right now Jo wanted to think
about Aunt Gloria, who had sent the package.

Gloria Harrison had been a constant presence in Jo's
life, first when Jo's father was alive and the extended
Miller family spent large portions of every summer together in the family summer cottage at Kanowa Lake in
western New York. Then later, too, after Harry Miller's
death, when Sophie had moved Jo to California, where
she could have her daughter to herself. Aunt Gloria
had continued to call frequently, and send birthday and
Christmas cards, making it clear in her own sweet way
that Jo would always be a Miller, and neither distance
nor the death of her father changed that.

Now Aunt Glo was gone, and with her the last real
link to the Millers. There was still plenty of family
around. Jo had distant relatives as well as three first
cousins, women close to her in age. Once upon a
time the four had been as intimate as sisters, but time
changed so many things.

Of course time had been helped by Jo herself, who as
an adult had been too busy to keep in touch. Her cousins were now strangers.

Like her next-door neighbor.

Gloria had died two weeks ago while Jo was in Hong

Kong. Sophie had emailed the news, generously offering to find out if Ocelot Lee could pass on a message from the departed Gloria, an unusual offer in more ways than one, since Sophie had never wanted to share her daughter with her father's family.

Jo wished she could have flown home for the funeral. She had owed Aunt Glo that grueling trip and more. But leaving Hong Kong in the middle of tense negotiations would have been as good as throwing up her hands in defeat. In the end, with so much riding on her presence in China, she had wired a huge arrangement to the funeral home and made a donation to her aunt's favorite charity. She had sent a card to her cousin Olivia, Gloria's daughter, and told herself she would call Olivia when she returned.

Except for the sadness, she had expected that to be the end. She had not expected to receive a package from her aunt, a package that had obviously been sent just before her death.

Jo realized that somehow she was now perched on the sofa, picking at the tape along the edges of the box. Sophie's granite coffee table didn't yield anything as practical as a drawer for scissors, so Jo rose and took the package into her study. At her desk chair she carefully sliced the tape with a letter opener and tugged it apart.

Inside lay two smaller packages wrapped in tissue paper. She opened the smaller of the two to discover two pieces of jewelry—a brooch in the shape of a fan, studded with red and silver rhinestones and tiny seed pearls, and a thin silver chain with an enameled locket.

A note in the same tentative handwriting read:

These belonged to your grandmother. I wanted you to have them.

Jo blinked back tears. As Aunt Glo was dying she had still been thinking of Jo. Her quickly failing health was clear from the handwriting, which was a shadow of her formerly robust script.

Moments passed before she remembered the second package. She carefully set down the jewelry and unfolded the paper.

For a moment she couldn't put a name to the object she was holding. Then she realized that the fabric in her hand had been carefully folded and padded so it wouldn't crease. She unfolded the first layer, slipping out more tissue paper until a large square was lying across her lap.

The fabric was the beginning of a quilt, a beautifully appliquéd folk art rendition of Hollymeade, the Miller family cottage on the shore of Kanowa Lake. It was eighteen, maybe even twenty, inches square on a royal blue background with one silver star shining directly over the house. The house itself, with its wide front porch and its second story turret—where she and her cousins had formed a secret club the year she was ten—was decorated for Christmas. The century-old holly trees that gave the house its name were also embroidered with ornaments of red and gold, and strings of lights that seemed to twinkle. A bright green wreath adorned the front door, and snow covered the ground.

Jo looked closer. There were two snowmen, or more accurately a snowman and a snow-woman, to the left of the house. The snowman wore a shiny top hat and tails. The snow-woman was dressed as a bride, with a long veil and a bouquet clutched in front of her.

She whistled softly because suddenly she understood what she was holding. "Olivia's bridal quilt."

Jo knew her cousin was getting married at Christmastime next year. She had expected to be invited and expected to be too busy to attend. She hadn't expected to receive a portion of the bridal quilt that her aunt had been making for her only daughter.

There was a note here, too, although this one was typed. She scanned it quickly, then read it slowly out loud, so she could absorb it.

"Dear Jo,

I know this will come as a surprise to you. I've been sick for some time and have known for weeks now that I probably won't live to see Olivia and Eric's wedding. If they had been given a choice, they would have moved up the date, but of course, they couldn't, not with Eric serving in Afghanistan. I had hoped to live long enough to make a bridal quilt, but I know now that this first block is the most I will be able to finish.

I've thought about what to do next, and I've come up with a plan. I don't have the strength to discuss it with all of you, so I am going on faith. You see, I am praying that you, Ella and Rachel will finish the quilt for me.

Do you remember the fun all of you had when you learned to quilt at Hollymeade? All those lazy summer quilting lessons with your wonderful grandmother? You, of course, were a natural, a serious quilt-maker from the beginning, just like I was at your age. I still remember the way you measured everything twice and restitched every seam that wasn't perfect.

I know you haven't quilted in years. But I don't think you will have forgotten how.

Do you know what a round robin is? Here's another quilt lesson you will need. A round robin quilt begins with one block in the center. Then the center is passed to another quilter, along with some of the fabrics that were used in the center, and the second quilter stitches a border, combining the shared fabric with some of her own. The quilt and more fabric are then passed on to another quilter until the final border is completed.

I hope you will add a border to this block, then pass it to Ella and finally to Rachel. Perhaps the three of you will reunite with Olivia to quilt the finished top before the wedding, so she will have it to display at the ceremony. Wouldn't that be perfect?

You'll see that some of the fabric I've enclosed isn't new. In fact these are pieces of dresses Olivia wore as a little girl. I'm hoping that you or your cousins will work them in to make the quilt that much more meaningful.

I know this is a project you probably wouldn't choose. But please do this for me. I know this quilt will be in good hands, Jo. You always try to do the right thing without complaint, sometimes to your detriment. But this project may have surprising results. I hope it will bring you closer to your cousins. I know Olivia will need her family once I'm gone.

I have always loved you, Rachel and Ella like you were my daughters, too. I know you loved me, as well. Never worry about that.

With love,
Aunt Glo"

Jo clutched the letter to her chest as tears threatened to spill down her cheeks, then reality began to intrude. She, who hadn't quilted for a decade and a half, who at her most creative had only managed to sew pillow tops, was supposed to add a border to this gorgeous quilt block. Her aunt had won prizes for her needlework. The rendition of Hollymeade was in every way perfect. The stitches were invisible. The colors were glorious. The design was detailed, yet cheerfully rustic.

She couldn't do it.

Yet hadn't her aunt chosen well? Gloria had known Jo couldn't possibly say no, and that furthermore Jo would feel responsible and make sure that Ella and Rachel did their parts, too. Not that they wouldn't, of course, or at least that was Jo's guess, because she hardly knew her cousins anymore. She couldn't even remember the last time the four of them had been together.

Her next thought was that she could pay someone to do the border for her, someone experienced and expensive. Who would ever know?

Except Jo herself.

Carefully she folded the block and took out the small pile of fabrics that had been folded in tissue, too. There, on top, was a square of fabric she remembered, a bright red-and-white check with tiny Scottie dogs sprinkled among the white blocks.

One summer the four cousins had all worn dresses made from this fabric. Their grandmother, Margaret, had sewed the sundresses for each of the gap-toothed, skinny little girls, and they had insisted on wearing them whenever they went anywhere together that summer. She knew this was a piece of that original fabric, saved over the years by her sentimental aunt.

For just a moment she held the fabric to her cheek.

"You really know how to stick it to me, don't you, Aunt Glo?"

With a sigh Jo refolded the checked fabric carefully and thumbed through the rest of the pile. There were Christmas prints in red and green, some of the fabrics that had been used in the center block, some new ones, a stack of oddly shaped patches that had probably been part of Olivia's childhood wardrobe.

The truth was right here, written in brightly colored fabric. She couldn't say no. She couldn't hire a surrogate. She couldn't disappoint the woman whose funeral she had been too busy to attend.

She didn't have time for this, but even now, with fatigue washing over her, she wondered why not. She had just spent a month in Hong Kong, living in hotel rooms, eating late-night room service and sandwiches at the conference table. She had pulled out all the stops for her employer, and the negotiations had still ended badly. On the trip from the airport she had read only a few of a long list of emails her boss had sent during her flight, blaming her for a failure that had nothing to do with her. In the end she had missed her aunt's funeral for no good reason.

At what point in her life had she decided that work was more important than family? When she'd started using her job as a shield to ward off her overbearing, flighty mother? When she had vowed that as an adult she would have the financial security that had disappeared after her father's death?

When the man she loved broke their engagement and with it her heart?

Of course the quilt and memories of her childhood were a reminder of that man, one Brody Ryan. She wondered if he still lived in Kanowa Lake. His name had never come up in conversations with her aunt, but then Aunt Glo had never known how serious Jo and Brody's relationship had been. Was he married now with a houseful of kids? He was definitely a houseful-of-kids kind of guy.

How strange that her aunt's death would open doors to her past she had sealed long ago.

A border. How hard could it be? She would go to the internet and the local quilt shop, do research, make a plan. Maybe she didn't have time to do this, but could she afford not to? This was the Christmas season. Didn't she deserve a little time off?

The moment had come for a long winter's nap, but when she woke up, she would email Ella in Seattle and Rachel in far-off Australia. Considering time zones, email would be the best way to communicate. Surely she had their addresses somewhere. She would tell them what she had received and make sure they were on board.

She hoped they remembered who she was.

She rose, but after a few steps she turned around, took out the quilt block again and carried it with her. She fell asleep with the block draped over the foot of her bed so that Hollymeade would be the first thing she saw in the morning.

CHAPTER ONE

From Rachel@mailoze.com.au: Still the overachiever, Jo? New York seems like a long way to go to find old baby clothes or whatever of Eric's to work into the quilt with Olivia's dresses. I remember taking a long walk around the lake with you one summer because you had to find the perfect wildflowers to make a bouquet for Grammy Mags. By the time we got back they were all wilted and I wasn't speaking to you anymore. Good thing baby clothes don't wilt.

"YOU'RE NOT FROM here, are you?" The teenager manning the cash register at the gas station twenty-five miles from Kanowa Lake looked up, and his cheeks flushed. "I just mean, you know, I haven't seen you around."

Jo glanced at her watch. Could it really be getting dark? It was only three-thirty, yet a curtain was drawing closed over what had passed for sunshine just half an hour earlier.

When the boy cleared his throat she looked up again. "My family owns a summer house over on Kanowa Lake, but I haven't been back in years."

"Bad night to visit. You ought to stay here."

She cocked her head in question.

"The weather, I mean." He cleared his throat again. "Bad storm coming."

For the past twenty miles the skies had been spitting snow, but Jo wasn't worried. She had paid the extra bucks for a rental car with four-wheel drive, and now she had topped off the gas tank. She was prepared.

"Doesn't look that bad," she said.

"It'll be a dumper. You better get where you're going fast and settle in."

When she smiled he flushed again. Jo had that effect on men, although she never played it up. Right now she was wearing jeans and fringed suede boots—the closest thing to winter boots she owned. Under her suede jacket a rust-colored cashmere sweater flattered her chestnut hair and amber eyes, but the only makeup she wore was a little lip gloss.

"I'll be fine."

He didn't look convinced. He was maybe sixteen, broad-shouldered and skinny. He probably couldn't eat fast enough to keep up with his latest growth spurt.

"You might want to stock up on a few groceries, just in case," he said. "Snow hits, you won't be going anywhere for a while."

Five minutes later she left with a small bag of everything edible that the station's sparsely populated shelves had offered. A box of cereal, the last quart of milk in the cooler, two cans of corned beef hash and three chocolate bars. The chocolate bars were three for two dollars, and her teenage admirer had suggested she take advantage of the sale.

The snow was falling harder now, and she grabbed a few guilty moments in the parking lot, arms flung out like a little girl's to embrace it. Since moving to California at thirteen, she'd only seen snow at ski resorts, where it always seemed professionally staged. This was the snow she remembered from her childhood in the small Pennsylvania town where her physician father had run an emergency clinic until his own emergency, a brain aneurism, had ended his life.

By the time she pulled onto the road the snow was a thin sheen, but the asphalt was still clearly visible. Four-wheel drive or not, she took her time, not sure if ice had formed under the snow. Three miles down the road she realized that the road and the shoulder now seemed to be one. She could barely discern where her wheels should go, and unfortunately no one had yet come this way to mark the path with tracks.

She slowed even more and set her wipers up a notch, because the snow was falling faster. Fortunately her tires weren't losing their grip, and signs helped her gauge where she ought to be. According to the rental car's GPS she had twenty-two miles to go, and once she got to Hollymeade, all she had to do was find the key under a vase beside the door and settle in. She guessed there would be a few staples left from the last Miller to use the house. The great-uncle who had told her where to find the key had also assured her the power and water were never turned off, and the house and grounds were checked periodically. The house would be livable, and she would be welcome but alone. Nobody else was scheduled to visit until late January.

Now, as she gripped the steering wheel and gingerly guided the car through deepening snow, she tried to imagine that kind of freedom, that silence. Nobody but Rachel, Ella and her great-uncle, Albert, knew she was here.

Well, that wasn't *quite* true. Eric Grant's parents, who spent winters in Florida, knew. Eric's mother, Lydia, had given her permission to rifle through the Grant's lake house attic in search of Eric's old baby quilts. In a flash of sentiment Jo had decided that incorporating Eric's childhood into the quilt, along with Olivia's, would make it even more meaningful. His mother had promised that anything Jo found that was too far gone to save for a grandbaby was fair game for the bridal quilt, and Lydia had promised not to breathe a word of the plan to her son or her daughter-in-law to be.

So Eric's mom knew, but not her own. Jo had stretched the truth a bit and told Sophie she was on a spiritual retreat and not allowed to reveal the location. That was close enough to the truth that she didn't feel she'd actually lied.

As for her boss? The only thing Frank Conner knew was that over the Christmas holidays Jo was taking some of the many vacation days the company owed her and would be available by email, but only for emergencies.

The last part was a gamble, but Jo had finally faced the fact that her skills and talents were largely unappreciated by her boss. And wasn't some of that her own fault? For too many years she had taken Frank's abuse without comment. It was time he realized how hard it would be to run his consulting firm without her. Even during the holidays, when work tapered off.

She came to a crossroads and slid to a stop, her heart thumping wildly until the wheels stopped spinning. She took a deep breath and carefully made the required left turn, fishtailing just a little, but straightening as she picked up speed.

Twenty minutes later the GPS promised she only had sixteen miles to go. At home sixteen miles meant something less than sixteen minutes, but here she was barely crawling. The same clouds shoveling snow over the landscape had now completely blocked the sun. She saw occasional lights from houses or businesses along the road, but no sign of driveways to reach them.

She wasn't scared. Not exactly. The road wasn't a major byway, but eventually there would be traffic. If the worst happened she could pull over—if she hadn't already run off the road—and wait for a plow or state police car.

An hour later, after skidding three times and one time spinning wildly, she arrived at the turnoff to Hollymeade. At least that was what the friendly GPS was telling her. The only signs of a road were the ridges beside a slightly lower area that might well be the long winding driveway. She wasn't sure she would recognize the turnoff in bright summer, but she *had* seen a sign to Kanowa Lake a mile back.

What choice did she have? There was a shape lurking far in the distance, like a monster waiting to pounce.

"Welcome to Hollymeade," she whispered, as she turned into what she hoped was the driveway.

She was parked in front of the house before she took another deep breath. She couldn't believe she had made it through the drifts of snow piling higher and higher. But here she was, the familiar old house just waiting for her. She had fought the elements and won. Memories of her childhood summers were in reach. She couldn't wait to go inside.

Of course part of the reason she couldn't wait was that cold was already seeping into the car, and the air wasn't getting any warmer.

She reached for her jacket again, the warmest she owned, and wished she had taken the time to buy a better one. She leaned forward and shrugged into it, zipping it to the top before she opened the door and stepped outside.

Snow immediately filled her boots, which hadn't been designed for blizzards. She pulled on lightweight leather gloves and grimaced as she opened the rear door and reached for her suitcase and groceries. She wondered how long she could make the three silly candy bars last.

Lifting the suitcase to keep it above the snow she trudged to the front steps, feet already turning numb. By the time she arrived she was winded but cheered. In a minute she would be inside, where she could take off her boots, turn up the heat and make herself a cup of something warm. Then she could explore to her heart's content, choose a bedroom, make the bed and settle in for the night after a meal of corned beef hash or a bowl of cereal.

Gray canvas awning swaddled the wide front porch to keep the snow outside. She unzipped the doorway and hefted the suitcase in with her, zipping it behind her. Then she rolled the suitcase to the door and leaned it against the wall with her purse and grocery bag.

The vase where the key was hidden was farther from the door than she had anticipated, and the tented porch was so dark she had to feel her way along the wall with one hand to stay steady. But she reached it and lifted the vase.

No key.

She squatted, stripped off her gloves, and searched the floor with her fingertips. Only a cobweb wrapped itself around her fingers in welcome.

"Yuck." As she stood she wiped her hand on her jeans. She was out of the wind and the snow, but cold was still her enemy. The temperature was probably in the twenties, and her clothes and feet were soaked.

No key, no light. While it was dark outside, it wasn't

this dark. She went back to the door and unzipped it again, tying back the flaps to let in what light she could. Then she carefully walked the length of the porch, lifting various knickknacks, a row of concrete ducklings, a plant stand, checking each for the key. She felt along every shelf on an empty book case at the end, opened the drawer on a small end table between two shiny metal chairs.

No key.

Now she was shivering. She pulled out her cell phone to call her great-uncle for advice, but there was no coverage. Either because of the storm or the rural location, she was on her own.

The town of Kanowa Lake lay beyond the house, perhaps three miles farther. There were other houses around the lake, of course, but most of them were summer cottages, many without heat. Now they were tented and locked tight, pipes drained and electricity turned off until warm weather brought them back to life. Without suitcase or groceries she trudged back down the steps, muddled through a snowdrift and peered into the distance, making a slow circle. Not a single light was visible.

Pushing down panic she considered her options. There were so few, and she was so cold, the process didn't take long. Only one possibility made sense. She needed to get back up the driveway while she could. If she was lucky a snowplow would come by soon and she could follow it toward town. But that window of opportunity was quickly closing. She wasn't sure she could turn around, and even then, she wasn't sure she would make it back down the drive.

She donned her gloves and returned to the porch for her suitcase, groceries and purse, then, when the car had been packed again, went back one more time to snatch a snow shovel leaning against a wall.

The tracks from her car were already filling with snow. She certainly couldn't back out of the driveway. She saw what looked like a turnaround just ahead of where she'd parked. If it was what it seemed, she could circle and head back up the driveway. But when she got in the driver's seat and tried to inch forward, her wheels spun. She put the car in Reverse and rocked back a bit, then tried to move forward again. This time she made a little headway, but not enough.

She was about ten feet from the turnaround, which was about ten feet wide and ten feet long. Slamming her palm against the steering wheel she took a deep breath, then got out, grabbed the shovel from the backseat and went around to the front of the car. Her feet felt like they were on fire, and even with gloves, her hands felt cold enough to freeze to the shovel handle.

She worked as quickly as she could, shoveling the snow in front of both front tires. Then she started a track to the turnaround for one set of wheels. The snow was light enough, but she tired quickly. She'd had a long flight from California, a long drive from Buffalo, and now this. Rested and appropriately attired, she would have been more successful. But exhausted, with body temperature plummeting, every shovelful was a Herculean task.

At the turnaround she leaned on the shovel and bowed her head. Even if she was able to finish, would it do any good? Her tracks were almost invisible now. If she was able to move the car and turn it around, would she be able to make her way up the driveway? Then what? The road was probably piled with snow.

She hadn't heard so much as a car passing, but as

she tried to figure out the best option, she heard a distant rumble. Was it a plow? If she floundered through the snow up to the main road could she flag down the driver, explain her predicament, perhaps even get a ride into town?

The rumble deepened and grew louder. Dragging the shovel behind her, in case she needed it, she stomped up the driveway, stopping only for her purse. Ten yards later, ten grueling, numbing yards, she stopped again. Because suddenly she was no longer alone. A snowmobile was coming down the driveway with a lone, helmeted driver.

She wanted to cry from relief until she realized she was in the middle of nowhere in a blizzard with a stranger, and almost nobody knew she was here. Relief turned to apprehension.

The snowmobile pulled to a halt, and the broad-shouldered driver, clothed in appropriate gear, turned off the engine before he hopped down. For a moment he didn't move; then he reached up and stripped off his helmet to reveal a wool stocking cap beneath it.

"Hello, Jo."

This man was no stranger, although he was capable of causing a great deal of distress.

She didn't know whether to laugh or cry. The last time she'd seen Brody Ryan, he had carefully and unemotionally explained the reasons why they couldn't get married. Now, as then, she didn't know what to say. She stared speechlessly for what seemed like forever, assessing the way the world seemed to be tilting on its axis. At last she settled for the obvious.

"Brody."

"I guess 'long time no see' is a cliché."

"What are you doing here?"

He smiled, a smile she remembered too well, creases that were almost dimples in his cheeks, laugh lines fanning out from green eyes.

"I guess I'm rescuing you. Looks to me like you might just need it."

CHAPTER TWO

As BRODY TENDED a fire in the living room fireplace, the shower on the second floor screeched to a halt. Jo must be getting out at last.

He tried to put that image out of his mind.

He was glad he had arrived when he did. By the time he'd managed the driveway Jo had been one stick short of a Popsicle, and by the time he'd unlocked the door to let her inside, she had been shivering uncontrollably. There had been no time to talk. He'd sent her right upstairs to shower and put on warm clothes, and he'd busied himself starting the fire, followed by a pot of coffee. There were few provisions in the Hollymeade pantry, but he'd scraped just enough grounds out of a canister for one pot. He knew Jo had brought next to no groceries with her, because once the fire and coffee were going, he'd retrieved her suitcase and a flimsy plastic bag from the car.

Now the suitcase was resting in the hallway outside the bathroom, and the pitiful groceries were resting on the kitchen counter.

His work was done. Jo wouldn't freeze, and she wouldn't starve. Yet somehow, he was still in the house, adding kindling to a fire that was already blazing merrily.

He heard footsteps on the stairs, then a voice behind him. "Thanks for bringing in my things."

When he turned he saw she was wearing fleece from neck to ankle, something soft, warm and a pretty shade of green. He was glad she'd had the good sense to bring at least *some* weather-appropriate clothing in her sleek little suitcase.

"You look a little warmer," he said.

"I think I've stopped shivering."

"I made coffee. It's in the kitchen."

"Perfect. May I get you some?"

He heard the stiff formality in both their voices. *How nice of you. Thank you. What can I do?* He knew better than to sigh, because what had he expected? That the woman who had been pathetically grateful when he called off their engagement all those years ago would throw herself into his arms tonight?

"I take it black," he said.

"You never used to." She immediately looked chagrined, as if remembering a simple preference opened doors.

He examined a speck on the wall to avoid her eyes. "I don't have time to pretty it up anymore."

"I guess…well, it's obvious you still live in the area."

He wasn't surprised she hadn't known. From what he'd heard, she hadn't been to Kanowa Lake in years. And whenever he had casually asked about her, nobody in the Miller family seemed to have news. Clearly she had *never* asked about *him*.

"In the house where I was raised," he said.

"Your father still has vineyards?"

He took too long to answer. She didn't know *that,* either, but—he guessed for a number of reasons—this time he was grateful. "He died. I care for them alone now."

"Oh, I'm so sorry."

He thought she probably was. His father had liked Jo, and so had his mother. He was pretty sure the feeling had been mutual. Of course nobody, not his parents, not her family, especially not her mother, had ever known how serious they were about each other, how they had planned to marry after they finished school, how they had chosen universities close enough that they could spend long weekends together.

That in his senior year the whole flimsy house of cards had tumbled to the ground.

"So I stayed a local boy," he said. "What about you?"

"After I got my master's degree I moved back to California. I'm a systems analyst with a consulting firm in San Diego." After clipping the words as short as a boot-camp haircut, she left for the kitchen, and he gave the fire one more poke for good measure before she returned with coffee, handing him the mug, handle turned for him to grasp.

"I couldn't get inside," she said. "When I arrived, I mean. That's why I was shoveling the driveway, so I could turn around. The key wasn't where Great-Uncle Albert said it would be. I was about to head to town."

"The key's been in the same place as long as I can remember. The concrete vase by the back door."

"Back door." She shook her head. "I missed that part, I guess."

"You never would have found it. By now that vase is probably buried. I doubt anybody expected you to arrive in a blizzard."

"*You* seem to have expected it."

"I heard you were coming. I manage a bunch of properties around the lake in the wintertime, and I thought I ought to check, just in case you didn't know any better than to ignore a storm warning."

She didn't seem to take offense. "It's a different world here in the winter. But I should have known better. I just wanted…"

"To be here?"

"It's been a long time."

"I heard about your aunt. I'm sorry she's gone."

"Me, too."

Brody realized he hadn't taken a sip. Instead he had been drinking in Jo's lovely, familiar face. Her hair had been longer the last time he'd seen her. Now straight and shiny, it just touched her collar. The oval face, dark brows and lashes and straight nose were the same. So was the wide mouth that once had smiled so easily.

Not so much anymore.

"You probably need a good night's sleep." He held up his mug. "And I probably can't drink this fast enough. Maybe I ought to just go."

Instead of answering she settled on one of the love seats flanking the fieldstone fireplace and motioned him to the other.

"I still have to warm up hash for dinner, and I'm on California time. Keep me company a few minutes, unless somebody at home is expecting you?"

He thought she had managed that neatly. Was there a wife? Kids?

"In the winter I'm here alone," he said. "Mom goes to Arizona to stay with Kaye. She and her family live outside Phoenix. It gets Mom out of the cold, and she loves being there."

"How are they? Your mom and Kaye? Kaye was only, what, sixteen when—" She stopped herself. "She must be, what, twenty-six or so, yes?"

"Happily married, with a two-year-old and another

on the way. Mom babysits while Kaye's at school. She teaches third grade. How about your mom?"

She seemed to relax a little, even smiled. "Still wacky after all these years. Sophie's on her third marriage, but my stepfather is remarkably patient, adamant she stay on her meds, and madly in love with her. Plus he has money, which means she'll try harder. I think this one might stick."

"Does that let you off the hook a little?" He realized how personal the question was, how much it said about how *well* they had known each other, but it was too late to call it back.

"I'm allowed to have my own life, yes."

In for a penny, in for a pound. "Does that include a family?"

"I'm not married, if that's what you're asking."

He had always liked the way Jo laid her cards on the table. Of course in contrast, there was another part of her that carefully played the rest of her hand close to the chest. Anything really important stayed deep inside her, but that habit had suited him, since he operated the same way. For survival she had been required to keep a part of herself from her mother. Brody's traditional upbringing and parents had been very different, but as a boy he had realized that they had many burdens and didn't need his, as well.

"So why did you come back?" he asked. "At Christmas, too. There must be a hundred better places to spend the holidays."

She launched into a story about her cousin Olivia's bridal quilt, her own desire to get away for a while and work on her part of it in peace, and a desire to see if she might find some baby quilts or clothing of Eric's in the Grants' attic.

She finished up on that note. "If I was going to do this, I wanted to do it right. I thought the quilt would be that much more special if we had some of Eric's childhood quilted into it, too. Lydia says there are boxes in their attic I can go through. Once I'm settled I'm supposed to call her about a key. Then I'll go through them until I find what I'm looking for."

"I have the key. I look after the Grants' house, too."

Jo leaned back. "Well, you're a busy boy, aren't you? Nothing to do in the vineyard this time of year?"

"I have a bargain with the owners. For a nominal fee I watch their houses in winter, and in the fall they come to my place and pick grapes. We make quite a party out of it."

"You don't have machines for that?"

"We harvest the juice grapes by machine, but these are more fragile. Vignoles grapes for wine."

"I always loved seeing all those acres of grapes."

"And eating them. The summer we met."

She had been smiling, but that died now. "You know, Pacific time or not, I really am wiped."

He had been dismissed, so he stood. "The snow's going to continue through the night. You have some staples in the pantry, a little flour, sugar, salt, that sort of thing, along with some canned soup. But not a lot else. It might be some time before you can shop. I'd ration."

"Uncle Albert said somebody plows the driveway after it snows."

"That would be me. But not until the snow stops long enough for it to make sense."

She uncurled her legs and gracefully rose to follow him to the door. "Thank you for the fire and coffee." She stuck out her hand.

Surprised, he took it, but the contact was brief. "What are old friends for?"

"I guess we *were* friends, weren't we?"

"Maybe we can be again."

When she didn't respond he smiled, as if the lack didn't matter, as if friendship went without saying when, of course, it was probably impossible.

More things left unsaid, their mutual talent.

"Be sure to close the doors on the fireplace before you go to bed," he said. "The chimney's just been cleaned, so it's safe enough, but that's a hot fire. You don't want any sparks popping into the room."

"Thanks, I have a fireplace in my condo."

"Then you're an expert."

She tilted her head. "At lots of things. I've been taking care of myself for a very long time." She paused. "But thank you for taking care of me tonight. I'm not sure where I would be right now if you hadn't come along."

He considered those parting words on his way home. She had been talking about tonight and where she would have been without his help. But Jo was a survivor. She would have found a way to keep from freezing even if she'd been forced to dig out the whole driveway to get back on the road.

Now he wondered where she would be if he had never come along at all, if he had never met her the summer she turned sixteen, if they hadn't made a thousand plans together, all canceled summarily four years later. Had she stopped trusting men after that? Was that why she'd never married? Had she stopped coming to Hollymeade because she had been afraid of running into him? How many choices had she made that stemmed from their past?

How many had *he* made?

He found himself at the Grants' house instead of his own. It was more than six miles from Ryan Vineyards, so he hadn't simply made a wrong turn. No, the wrong turn had come a long time ago. Now there was no telling where *this* one might lead.

He jumped down and went through his ring of keys on the way to the front door. Inside he took the steps upstairs and then those to the attic two at a time. The Grant house wasn't as large or lovely as Hollymeade, but it was a pretty Colonial with banks of windows looking over the water and decks all around, well cared for and loved.

Unlike Hollymeade this house wasn't heated in the winter, and right now the inside temperature was as cold as the outside. He kept his gloves on until he had reached his destination, a pile of boxes in the front. He knew right where they were because he had helped Eric's father move them to this spot. He'd been impressed at how carefully each one had been labeled, in case the contents were ever needed again.

He spotted the one he was looking for and began to stack the rest along the side until he could get to it.

"Eric's baby things." He grimaced at the label and shook his head, but not at the words, at himself for thinking this was a good idea.

He almost left it where it was, but in the end, he carried it across the attic to a pile of boxes that hadn't yet been sorted, a pile Lydia Grant was probably making her way through each summer.

When he left the house, the box with Eric's baby things was stored in the very back of the Grants' attic, six down on an unmarked pile, the label turned toward the wall. It was the least likely place anyone would look for it.

It might buy him the time he needed to get to know Jo again.

CHAPTER THREE

HOLLYMEADE STILL LOOKED much the same. After a breakfast of cold cereal Jo wandered the rooms, a cup of tea from the only tea bag in the house warming her hands. Some things *had* changed, though. The walls in the living area were a different color now, a silvery sage, and the sofas were new. The armchairs, though? Those she remembered from afternoons curled up with Shel Silverstein's *The Giving Tree* or Madeleine L'Engle's *A Wrinkle in Time,* even if the chairs now wore slipcovers.

The kitchen had newer appliances, and someone must have decided that updated laminate countertops were a worthwhile investment. But the pot rack with its copper-bottomed saucepans still hung near the stove. And while the curtains had to be new, they mimicked the ones she remembered, gauzy white and tied back to let in the light.

She was home.

Outside the snow continued, and now it was nearly as high as the windows. Of course there must have been snow on the ground already. Western New York was famous for the stuff. Jo couldn't believe she had gambled on reaching the grocery store today. But there would be no road trip, not until the skies cleared. While she was still in bed she'd heard a plow on the main road, but she doubted it was easy to travel.

Before breakfast she had inventoried the pantry

shelves, hoping Brody had exaggerated, but embellishing wasn't his style. She could heat a can of chicken noodle soup for lunch, snack on a candy bar midafternoon and eat the remaining hash from the can she had opened last night for dinner. If she followed that pattern, she would be okay for two more days, although she wasn't looking forward to cream-of-broccoli Tuesday. She supposed if the snow continued longer, she might be able to make pancakes without oil or eggs and eat them with sugar sprinkled on top.

She wrinkled her nose. Of course she could always call Brody to rescue her again.

When hell froze over.

Since she prepared for everything, she'd made plans in advance if she happened to run into him. A chance encounter at the grocery maybe, a few sentences of greeting and catch-up, then both of them heading off to their separate lives. Their relationship had ended a decade ago. They were hardly the people they had been. Through the years she had erased memories of him the way she routinely wiped away outdated files on her computer.

But unless a hard drive was reformatted, old files still left traces. And how did a woman reformat her heart?

As she stared outside at the winter wonderland, snow clinging to evergreen branches and icicles dripping from the roof of the boat shed, she remembered.

After her father's death, Jo's mother had resettled herself and her preteen daughter in Hollywood, using a generous life insurance payment. Sophie, darling of their town's little theater, had decided to bury her grief in an acting career. When that proved impossible, she devoted herself to making the unenthusiastic Jo into a star.

Jo, who preferred auditions to her mother's hand-wringing, found work in a few commercials, but when it became clear her daughter didn't have either drive or talent, Sophie sought work as a makeup artist. Unfortunately money dribbled through her fingers. The rental house gave way to a furnished room, and on the afternoon their landlord threatened to break down their door to collect three months of rent, Jo took over their finances.

As Sophie spiked between elation and despair, Jo covered all the other bases and kept her grades high, because by then she knew that an education and a good job would be her saving grace. Luckily her father had made sure to establish a college fund that Sophie couldn't tap, and Jo vowed that when the time came, she would use every penny to pursue a degree that promised a job at the end.

Hollymeade and her father's family faded into the background, because Sophie, fiercely possessive, refused to let her visit the lake house.

The year Jo turned sixteen, a miracle happened. As she powdered the leading man's nose on the set of a low-budget film, Sophie caught an associate producer's eye, and three weeks later they were married in Vegas. Since his next project was in Italy, Sophie and her new husband headed for Milan to spend the summer, and Jo was packed off to Hollymeade.

Jo had been thrilled to fly back to New York and settle into a room in the old house to reconnect with her father's family and disconnect from her mother. Her grandmother had been thrilled, too, and their quilting lessons had resumed. Unfortunately her cousins, whom

Jo hadn't seen in years, couldn't join them. Rachel was living in Australia, Ella in Seattle, and Olivia was enrolled in a special summer language program in Salzburg. Members of the larger Miller family came and went, some with children younger than she was, but after the thrill of reunion wore off, Jo began to feel lonely.

Until Brody Ryan showed up.

Brody was seventeen to her sixteen, ready to head off for Cornell in the fall, where he planned to study viticulture. He arrived one afternoon to deliver and split a cord of firewood for the coming winter. Jo was immediately drawn to the serious young man with the golden-brown hair and the fabulous smile, so she stacked as he chopped.

They talked about everything, then as the wood chips flew, and later as they found more excuses to be together.

Jo knew better than to draw attention to their budding relationship. Word might get back to Sophie, who was perfectly capable of flying home from Italy to interfere. Brody, too, was reluctant to share with his family. The Ryans were thrilled he had received a scholarship to Cornell, but finances were tight, and they knew he had to earn enough money to supplement his financial aid. A romance with a high school girl would have made no sense to them. So as Jo and Brody fell in love, they decided to keep their feelings to themselves.

Now she realized how successful they had been. Because when Jo graduated from high school at seventeen and had her pick of colleges, no one guessed that she chose M.I.T. because it would be easy to visit Brody at Cornell and rekindle their romance.

They were two private people, with little else that

they hadn't already been forced to share with their families. As love grew stronger, they nurtured the flame carefully, secretly.

Until the flame went out.

As she had stood at the window Jo's tea had grown cold. These days the house had a microwave, and now she crossed the kitchen to set the mug inside. As it heated she decided to think about something else. She had faced Brody, and both of them had survived the reunion. It was time to move on.

She was just summoning the energy to unwrap the fabrics for Olivia's quilt when she heard a familiar roar. From the window she watched as Brody jumped off his snowmobile, unhooked something from the seat behind him and started toward the door.

Before she could stop it her hand went to her hair. Then, realizing what she'd done, she straightened her shoulders and went to let him in. She was dressed. Her hair was probably combed. She had covered all the bases for polite society.

When she opened the door he was standing on the threshold clutching a picnic basket in his arms. He held it out to her but didn't relinquish it.

"It's heavy. Maybe I should set it down in the kitchen."

"I work out." She held out her arms.

He thrust it forward, and she realized he was right. It *was* heavy. She shifted so part of the weight rested against a hip.

"Come in while I put this on the counter. What is it?"

"A care package."

She couldn't help herself. "I didn't know you did."

"Did?"

"Care." She smiled to let him know she was teasing.

"I would refuse, of course, to show what an independent woman I am, but I might starve."

She started toward the kitchen, and in a moment—she guessed he was slipping off his boots—he followed her. She set down the basket and opened the lid to peek. Inside were at least a dozen cans, also rice, pasta, packaged mac and cheese, two jars of sauce, more cereal, half a carton of eggs, two sticks of butter, and half a small bottle of cooking oil.

Despite all internal warning signals, she was touched. "Brody, did you clean out your cupboards?"

"I split the contents."

"Bachelor food, huh? Beef stew, beans, tuna, fruit cocktail? What happened to the hot dogs?"

"Ate them last night."

"Darn."

He grinned, and only then did she realize he'd been worried about her reaction. "Don't tell me you cook gourmet meals for yourself every night," he said.

"Not *every* night." She closed the lid. "This was thoughtful. Thank you. Of course I'll replace everything once I can drive to a store."

"That wasn't the only reason I came. I thought you might like a ride over to the Grants'. To look for that box of baby stuff. But I warn you, it's going to be freezing in their attic. We won't last long."

She gestured to her corduroy jeans and waffle henley. "I'm not dressed for a snowmobile."

"I brought gear for you. It's on the sled, if you're game."

She considered. Wasn't this opening up a door best left closed? They had proved they could be polite, and she was in no hurry to look for Eric's things. She almost refused, but then she reconsidered. Brody was trying to help, and if she didn't say yes, she would be cooped up all day. Plus he would wonder why she'd refused, and that might be dangerous.

She kept her tone casual. "I'm not doing anything else, if you have the time."

NINETY MINUTES LATER Jo took off the snowmobile helmet and shook out her hair. She was dressed like a pro in Brody's sister's gear, all of which had fit, the bibbed pants, jacket, gloves, everything except the boots, which were a size too large. That hadn't mattered since she had worn them with three pairs of Kaye's wool socks and removed the boots before entering the Grants' house.

The ride had been glorious. Brody's snowmobile held two, and she had wondered if she would be required to put her arms around his waist. But there had been a handlebar to hang on to, and the ride had been as smooth as sailing, with no surprises.

They hadn't talked a lot, not even in the attic, which was a pack rat's dream. Brody said that Mrs. Grant had inherited the contents from her husband's mother, who had inherited them from *her* mother. Unlike her predecessors, she was trying to sort, then toss or label, but Brody thought she was having problems getting rid of much.

"Sentimental," he'd said. "That's why she kept Eric's baby things."

"My gain." Jo had given up after that day's search turned up nothing of Eric's except old school notebooks, one box of wooden blocks and another of 4-H trophies. By the time they'd started back to Hollymeade her teeth were chattering.

Once there, she swung her legs over the side and stepped down. She realized how much fun she'd had.

The ride, the attic search, the ride home. When had she ever jumped on a snowmobile or a motorcycle or a speedboat just for fun? When had she had time to simply be young?

Snow was falling again, a light dusting this time, but the landscape sparkled. Beyond the house she saw a cardinal, bright red and Christmassy in the branches of a spruce tree.

"Let me make you lunch," she volunteered, before she even knew the words would emerge. "It's the least I can do."

He didn't hesitate. "It would be nice to warm up."

She was surprised he had accepted so readily. That seemed to say a lot, although she knew better than to dissect a simple sentence.

Inside they perched on a bench in the entryway and stripped off their snowmobiling clothes. She realized that until now she hadn't seen him without at least a stocking cap, not even last night by the fire. His hair was longer than she remembered, as if he hadn't found his way to the barber in a while, but the color was still the same bronze, with just a hint of curl.

He still looked so much like the boy she had fallen in love with.

She realized she was clutching Kaye's outerwear as if it might shield her from old emotions. She thrust the clothing out for Brody to take home again, but he suggested she keep everything, just in case she wanted to tramp around outside or shovel more snow.

She wondered if he was planning more rides and just didn't want to announce them yet. And in true Jo style she attempted to analyze whether she had really loved the ride or the ride-with-Brody.

Inconclusive.

In the kitchen she emptied the basket and took a better look at what she had to work with. She settled on a menu, filled a large pot with water and set it on the back of the stove to boil. Then she set the oven to 350 degrees before she took out a smaller pan and began a béchamel sauce, flour stirred into melted butter, milk whisked in, a pinch of nutmeg from the spice drawer. When she was happy with the consistency, she drained a can of tuna and mixed it in.

Brody perched on a stool and watched. "What can I do?"

"Would you get brown sugar out of the pantry? And if I'm not mistaken, one of the smaller canisters contains what's left of a bag of coconut. Would you check to be sure it's okay and bring that, too?"

Fifteen minutes later they sat down to a lunch of creamed tuna on egg noodles, and hot baked peaches topped with brown sugar and coconut. Brody looked as if he'd been invited to dine with the Iron Chef.

"Where did you learn to do *this*?"

She tried to ignore how wonderful it was to see appreciation in his eyes. She tried to ignore the fact that his praise seemed to be about more than a good hot lunch.

Unsuccessful.

"As a teenager I learned to make meals out of next to nothing. Sophie didn't cook, so I had to learn or grow up on peanut butter sandwiches. Once I was out on my own I thought I would probably never cook again, but I discovered I missed it. So now I take lessons for fun, whenever I have the time." She paused. "Which isn't often."

"I'd love to see what you could do with real food." He looked up, as if he realized that sounded like he was asking for an invitation and wanted to hurry on to something else. "If the Millers get wind of this, you'll be asked to cook every meal whenever you visit Hollymeade."

"No telling when I'll get here again."

He took a second helping of peaches. "You must be incredibly busy, because I know you love this place."

She found herself telling him about her job, and then about the trip to Hong Kong, where she had carefully inched her way through negotiations for a whole new technology system that she still believed would have ramped up the corporation's productivity by more than ten percent.

"I missed my aunt's funeral so I could bring that deal to conclusion, and after all that, I failed," she finished.

"*You* failed, or the *deal* failed? Because those are different, right?"

She realized how relaxed she was and, despite everything, how easy it was to talk to Brody. "You're right, the deal failed. Basically they used us, mainly me, as consultants, with no intention of buying our services. I didn't give anything away, which is a victory of sorts, I guess, but I left empty-handed. I'm not used to losing, and my boss is making it personal. So I decided to come here and wait him out. When he's done ranting and raving maybe he'll see how valuable I am and apologize, or at least stop blaming me."

"If he doesn't?"

She shrugged, because getting this far had been the first hurdle. She wasn't quite ready for the next one. "Tell me about the vineyards."

"We still grow grapes for juice, but I've managed to expand into wine. Reisling first, then several others. Now I'm working on a boutique ice wine made from

Reisling and Vignoles grapes, but it's not ready for market. My Reisling won an award last year, but I can't *produce* enough to make enough money to produce *more*."

He said the last as if it was a joke, but she thought it probably wasn't. Brody had dreamed of making wine all his life. He had planned to start his career at a large California winery and learn from the wine cellars up. Then he had planned to come home and establish his own vineyard.

"Did you get a job outside New York after college, the way you'd planned?" she asked.

"I decided to come home."

She wondered why. Had there been a girl waiting, someone she hadn't known about? A local girl ready to settle down and have his children? Because he had wanted a family. She remembered that all too well.

If there *had* been someone, apparently the relationship was over.

"I'd better get back." Brody got to his feet and carried his dishes to the sink. "Thanks for lunch, Jo. It was great."

She walked him to the door and waited while he shrugged back into layers of warm padding, finally slipping on his boots.

"Once the roads are clear you can just give me the key to the Grants' house," she said once he stood. "Mrs. Grant said she would see about getting me one."

"It looks like this system's on its way out, so I'll be plowing like mad for the next couple of days. I won't get to their driveway right away, so you won't be able to drive over. Let's just plan to go again later this week on my sled, if that suits you. I don't mind. I'm keeping an eye on a possible leak in their roof, anyway."

At the Grants' house she hadn't noticed Brody looking skyward even once, but she nodded. "I'll see you then."

"Unless the snow keeps coming, I'll plow your drive tomorrow or the day after. I'm in the phone book if something comes up."

"In the meantime at least I won't be rationing candy bars. Thanks again."

He smiled. They couldn't seem to break eye contact. Jo's heartbeat quickened, and her temperature seemed to rise despite her proximity to the door.

"You never said when you're planning to leave," he said at last.

"I haven't decided."

He lifted his hand and lightly touched her cheek. "There aren't many places prettier at Christmastime." Then he turned, and in a moment he was gone.

She could manage only one intelligent thought. Hollymeade suddenly seemed much too large and rambling without him.

CHAPTER FOUR

Two DAYS AFTER the picnic-basket delivery, Jo woke to the noise of a snowplow, only this time in her driveway. By the time she threw on a bathrobe and ran to the window, Brody was chugging back down her driveway in a monster-sized pickup with a front blade that tamed the mounds of remaining snow as he made his way to the road.

She was free!

After she turned up the heat, she snuggled back under the covers. While she waited for the temperature to rise she stared at the ceiling and made a grocery list. Canned stew and beans had filled her stomach, but now she hankered for a real meal. Chicken, maybe, or a pork roast. Something she could eat right away, then enjoy leftover. Fresh vegetables, too, and fruit. Cheese.

She could hardly wait.

An hour later she was ready to roll. She wore her own jacket with jeans, but she pulled on Kaye's snowmobile boots. Her own boots were ruined. If Kanowa Lake had anything resembling a shoe store she would treat herself to winter boots. And real gloves. Maybe even a scarf, since the ones in Hollymeade's coat closet were awfully bedraggled.

Not a warmer jacket, though. A jacket meant she planned to stay long enough to need one. And, of course, that was silly.

Right before leaving she checked her smartphone, which was getting service again now that the storm had ended, scanning through the list of phone calls and texts she had received since yesterday. Her ringer had been off since she arrived, and she was checking both phone calls and email at her leisure. She skipped everything from her boss, read some emails from coworkers, and texted an acquaintance who was worried about her.

She noted one call from what she thought might be a Florida area code, but there was no message. Tossing the phone in her handbag, she headed for the door.

An hour and a half later she had groceries from the town supermarket, and boots and gloves from the Trading Post. The Trading Post was so named because it was purported to stand on a site where the Seneca people had once gathered to trade goods. The store had a bit of this and that, and today "that" had included an assortment of brightly colored scarves. But, Jo had reminded herself, she could stay warm with moth-eaten wool just as well as with the bright turquoise scarf from the Trading Post.

She was ready to drive away, when she slapped her palm on the steering wheel, went back inside and bought the scarf anyway.

Kanowa Lake had changed since her adolescence, but not a lot. There were too many For Rent signs in store windows. The shopping district was only two short blocks, and only half the stores and restaurants were still open, although some would resume business when summer arrived.

The town administration knew that tourism was their friend and somehow, even in the face of recession, had managed to keep the downtown spruced up and ready for visitors. The stone church at a prominent corner had been recently sandblasted, and a sign thanked donors to the project. The bandstand in a spacious park had been freshly painted and was now strung with Christmas lights.

Since she was standing on a ridge, she could see the lake beyond. Piles of fluffy white snow extended out toward the center, where the water hadn't completely frozen and now glinted bravely under the sunlit sky. She knew exactly what the lake looked like in summer, but this view, lovely in its own way, was new.

She compared her shopping trip with the one she might have made in San Diego. There she would have had dozens of stores to choose from, and after patiently navigating traffic to get to them, parking and waiting in lines to pay, she would have ended up spending many hours and dollars. Of course, for her effort, she would have found exactly what she was looking for, in the colors and materials she wanted, and sizes that fit perfectly.

Today she hadn't been shopping for anything special. She had needed gloves, boots and a scarf, not a wedding gown. She had finished quickly, and she was already wearing the boots. Plus she had heard all about the upcoming winter festival from the woman who had waited on her—who couldn't have been more friendly.

As she walked back to her car other shoppers smiled and nodded. Somebody exited the diner, and just before the door closed she caught a tantalizing aroma. Apple pies baking, she guessed, for the upcoming lunch crowd. She was too early for lunch, and now she was sorry she hadn't shopped later. A small town had its own pleasures, different from city pleasures, and she was falling easily into Kanowa Lake's rhythms.

She had hoped to find a quilt shop where she could find a pattern for her border, but there wasn't one here.

This was no problem, because she had remembered there were hundreds of books upstairs in one of the attic bedrooms. It was entirely possible that her grandmother or Aunt Glo had left some of their quilting books to use during their summer stays. The moment she got home she would look.

She was already behind the steering wheel ready to start home when she heard a buzzing noise and realized that while her ringer was off, the vibrating feature wasn't. She pulled out the phone and saw the call was from the same maybe-Florida number.

"Is this Jo Miller?" a woman asked when she answered. The woman sounded genuinely friendly, not like someone trying to sell something.

"Who's calling?" Jo asked.

"This is Lydia Grant, Eric's mother."

Jo settled back. "Mrs. Grant, it's so nice to hear from you." Then she had a thought. "Is everything... all right?"

"With Eric? Yes, honey, he's fine. We heard from him last night. And Olivia seems to be adjusting to this deployment, poor girl. She's keeping busy."

Jo wished she was close enough to her cousin to just pick up the phone and have a heart-to-heart, but she wasn't sure if Olivia would appreciate baring her soul to someone who was nearly a stranger.

"I was able to visit your house," Jo said. "Brody Ryan took me there. But we didn't find the right box. We'll try again when he's not so busy. Right now he's plowing driveways. We had quite a snowfall."

"Oh, good, I was going to give you Brody's number. Did you know him before this? From your summers as a girl?"

Jo gazed into the distance. "We'd met."

"Well, before I forget, there's also a key hidden in the wood bin just to the side of the house. It's in a little metal box. My husband reminded me last night. Now you can take your time and search without bothering Brody. The box of baby things is clearly marked, at the front of the first pile."

"Thank you, I'll look for the key, but we did look through the front pile when we were inside and didn't see it."

"Odd." Mrs. Grant paused. "Maybe the label fell off? Anyway, originally the box itself contained…let me think…oh, I remember, a set of pots and pans, and pictures of the pots are on the outside. I repacked it this summer, or, of course, I wouldn't remember. So look for that. The set was red cast aluminum. It's been gone for years, but the box was sturdy as a crate."

Jo thanked her and prepared to end the conversation.

"I like saving Brody any work I can," Mrs. Grant said. "He's the nicest young man. Eric and Olivia think the world of him, but all of us do worry."

Jo told herself not to pursue this. Just before she went ahead and asked, "Really? Why?"

"Well, he's had such a hard go of it. His dad was sick for such a long time, and Brody was right there through the thick of it, helping his mother with nursing care, handling everything on their property, trying to make a go of things so they didn't lose their home and livelihood as his dad declined. Of course, I don't know for sure, but I would guess no matter how good their health insurance was, the medical bills were probably a crushing burden."

Jo didn't know what to say. This was all news to her, and she felt a stab of sympathy for the Ryan family.

"I've never heard him complain, though," Mrs. Grant

added. "He's not somebody who would. But we still worry. That kind of thing marks you. He grew up way too fast. He works too hard and plays too little. Maybe you can cheer him up while you're there? Get him to do something fun? Old friends are the best."

They were—unless one of them had told the other to take a hike after years of planning a life together.

"I'll do what I can," Jo said.

"He needs to be young again. He's been old for years now."

"Years?"

"Oh, yes, *years*. His father died some time ago. Such a shame."

They said goodbye and Jo hung up, but she continued to stare into the distance without starting the car.

How long ago *had* Mr. Ryan died? He and Brody had been close. The whole family had been close, and she had looked forward to becoming part of it one day. Had Mr. Ryan already been sick when she knew him?

And exactly when had Brody discovered that his father would need him, discovered that the whole *family* would need him?

A long time ago...sick for such a long time...as his dad declined...

When he broke their engagement had Brody known about his father's illness? Had he believed that devoting himself to his family would take such a commitment that he simply couldn't make one to *her*, as well? Had he known that years of nursing a dying father was no way to begin a marriage, and so he'd told Jo goodbye?

She was probably wrong. But suddenly she knew she had to discover the truth, and that meant spending time with Brody. Because he wasn't someone she could simply ask, and *she* wasn't a person who asked those kinds of questions anyway. This was too personal, too intimate. She couldn't dig up the past, at least not in giant shovelfuls. She had to inch into it, a thimbleful at a time. If she cared enough.

The windshield was fogging inside and out, and she realized she was sitting inside an unheated car. She started the engine and pulled away from the curb, but once she got outside town, she didn't turn off at Holly-meade. She continued on, heading for the Grants' house. If she was lucky, Brody would already have plowed.

When she arrived, she saw the driveway was clear.

She parked in front and tramped through piles of snow, rounding the corner to the side where the wood bin was kept. The weather had warmed, and the snow was now heavy and wet, not powdery as it had been. She swept a foot of it off the top of the bin with the windshield scraper she'd gotten at the Trading Post and managed to pry it open. The metal box with the key was in plain sight.

Inside the house she took off her boots and climbed the steps to the second floor, then the attic. Ten minutes later she found the box covered with pictures of a long-departed set of pots and pans on the pile farthest from the door, the pile Mrs. Grant wasn't supposed to have gone through yet. She managed to unearth the box by moving many others away first. When she turned it to see the opposite side, the label was proof she had found the right one.

She was sorry Mrs. Grant hadn't remembered where she'd put it, but at least she *had* remembered the box it-self. Jo carefully peeled back several strips of duct tape and opened the flaps to a treasure of baby shirts and bibs and, under them, a layer of half a dozen baby quilts.

It didn't take her long to find what she wanted. Two

quilts at the bottom had been well used and loved. She could understand why Mrs. Grant hadn't been able to part with them, but they would never be used for their original purpose again. Both were literally hanging by a thread, although some of the fabric was still good.

She took them both; then she carefully repacked the box, hoping that one day a child of Olivia's might have a chance to wear something from it. Finally she considered what to do. If Brody made a concerted effort to find this box on their next visit, he might very well locate it if it remained where it was in a pile they hadn't yet searched.

Could she hide this box deep in the *first* pile, the pile they had already sorted through? Mistakes could be made, right? And until and *if* he happened on it again, she would buy more time with him in the attic, and more excuses to be together.

"My goodness, how did we miss it in this pile the first time?" she said out loud, practicing the words in case she actually needed to say them. "I can't believe we didn't find it. It was right where we looked at the beginning, Brody."

She laughed, a sound that was almost unfamiliar.

Did she dare?

When the boxes were piled exactly to her satisfaction, she relocked the door, put the key back where she'd found it and tossed big handfuls of snow on the top of the wood box again, just in case Brody noticed it had been swept free of snow.

Once she was in the car she didn't head for Hollymeade. To celebrate the emergence of this delightfully sneaky Jo Miller, she drove back into town for a piece of apple pie.

CHAPTER FIVE

JO WAS ON her way to a party.

When she'd left that morning she had missed a note from Brody tacked to her door. She hadn't found it until she finally got back to Hollymeade.

My neighbors and I have a potluck every year at my house on the first day the snow is perfect for snowmen. Will you come as my guest? People will start to gather around 3. Just bring yourself. You know where I live.

Of course she was bringing more than herself. She'd taken stock of her upgraded grocery supplies and settled on old-fashioned scalloped potatoes with sharp cheddar and lots of garlic. And because she loved to bake cookies—but knew better than to bake them just for herself—she'd made three dozen oatmeal cookies with raisins and a healthy dose of cinnamon.

She did know where Brody lived. While they hadn't revealed how close they really were, she had been to his house that first summer, sometimes with other teenagers and once for dinner when the midsummer grape harvest had begun and the house was so filled with people nobody had time to speculate on why she was there.

The lovely old farmhouse was set in gently rolling hills away from the lake, and even with the snow, she could see the neatly divided rows of vines fanning for acres away from the house.

As she pulled into the drive lined with cars she saw that not much had changed, although *some* changes might have been welcome. The white frame house was in need of paint. This climate was hard on houses, and she supposed Brody painted on a rotation and would probably paint it in the spring. But the porch sagged, as if the foundation needed shoring up, and she wondered why he had let it deteriorate. Was he stretched so thin he just didn't have time for upkeep?

She quickly forgot to wonder. Brody was approaching, wool cap covering his hair again, but the smile was right out front.

"I hoped you would come," he said, as she scooped up her contributions and got out. "But you didn't have to bring anything." He leaned over, and for a moment she thought he was going to kiss her and her breath caught. Then he reached for the casserole dish.

She wasn't sure if she was relieved or disappointed. "Any excuse to cook. And I'm returning your care basket, with thanks. I made it to the grocery store and replaced everything. It's in the back."

"You're so…" He hesitated.

"Predictable?"

"Responsible. But thanks, it saves me from having to hit the grocery store right away."

They started toward the house, and Jo saw groups of warmly clad people working on snowmen, maybe six groups or more, although individuals seemed to be going back and forth between them.

She heard laughter and smiled. "It looks like you have a crowd."

"Almost everybody's here. Some are friends from

high school, with their families, some are neighbors. You can see we have lots of kids. We've been doing this for a few years. We find any excuse to get together during the winter. This is my way of hosting. I'm the only single guy in the crowd, and they're always trying—" He stopped.

She knew what he'd been about to say. "To match you up with somebody?"

He didn't answer directly. "You get the same thing, I bet."

"My friends are few and far between. I work too many hours to keep them."

"Then I'm surprised you're still here in Kanowa Lake and not back in California slaving away."

They were nearly at the house, and people were beginning to peel off from their snowmen to come meet her.

"So am I," she said, before the introductions began. "But I'm not sorry."

By EIGHT O'CLOCK the last of Brody's guests had left. Except for Jo. He found her by the fireplace, sitting on the rug stirring the coals. He paused for a moment to admire the picture. Then he moved in to put another log on top.

"It will catch in a moment," he said. "The coals are still hot."

She smiled up at him. "You didn't have to do that. I really need to get home."

"Somebody waiting for you?"

She shook her head. He watched her hair swirl as the fire brought out the subtle red highlights. He had to restrain himself and not reach down to smooth it into place.

"Stay, then," he said. "For a little while. I have coffee brewing and some Irish whiskey to put in it."

"I have to drive."

"You could sleep here."

She looked surprised. "I think not."

"I have a guest room."

"I'll have the coffee, without the whiskey, then I'll go home."

He decided he wasn't in any hurry to pour her a cup. He settled himself on the rug beside her, careful not to touch her and scare her back to Hollymeade. "Did you like my friends?"

"Your friends are great. You're lucky to have them."

"It would be lonely here if I didn't. It's not so bad in the spring and summer when the place is buzzing. My mother's here then, and she's good company, plus I'm outside so much I don't have time for a social life. But in case you hadn't noticed, Kanowa Lake's not a metropolis. In the winter we make our own fun."

"Does Kaye really need your mom to babysit? Or does the cold bother her?"

He didn't want to explain that they couldn't afford enough heat to keep his mother comfortable, and when she was away he could set the thermostat at a minimum. Tonight he had warmed the house for the party, but when Jo left, he would turn the thermostat to 55 degrees and sleep under two down comforters.

"She loves her grandchildren," he said instead. "And she likes Arizona a lot." That, at least, was true. His mother loved being out west with her grandchildren, and in a perfect world, where she could afford a little condo of her own there, she would only spend summers in New York.

"In between giving my snowgirl a perm with pinecones and tinting her cheeks with red food coloring, I got a lot of questions from your friends. I passed the stranger test, since I'm one of the Millers from Hollymeade, but I got the feeling everybody wants to be sure I don't hurt you." She looked into his eyes. "I told them not to worry. We're old friends."

Her eyes were almost the color of her hair. Brody loved watching the firelight dancing in them.

"They'll keep asking," he said. "We've stirred their imaginations and given them a gift good enough to put under their Christmas tree and talk about for months to come."

"Speaking of trees…" Jo laughed a little, although he thought it sounded forced. "Yours is, how can I put this, Brody? Like the last Christmas tree in the lot on Christmas Eve. A Charlie Brown tree."

He glanced at the little tree he had set up in the corner for the party. "It's artificial."

"I do realize that. I just wondered what the manufacturer used as a model."

"I'm offended you think it's less than perfect. I got it at the Trading Post last year—after Christmas."

"If you paid more than a dollar, you paid too much. Aren't you going to decorate the poor thing?"

"It is decorated. Didn't you notice?"

"Brody, you hung three ornaments and a star. That's not decorated. Did you get those on sale, too?"

He smiled. "So what's on *your* tree?"

"Hey, I'm just visiting. Of course, I don't have a tree. I might not even be here for Christmas."

He didn't want to think about that. "So what would be on your Christmas tree back in California?"

"It varies. Last year I came home from work to a pale blue tree, kissing cousin to a toilet bowl brush, decorated with Japanese origami ornaments in gold and silver. Sophie had spent weeks folding them to surprise me. It was an homage to her ancestors."

"Your mother is Japanese?"

"Not in this life. Three lives ago, I think."

He heard a mixture of emotions in her voice. Humor. Love. Frustration. "Living with Sophie's like living with a roller coaster, isn't it?"

"These days it's like being visited by one. And she's better. I don't see nearly as much of her. As odd as it might be, she's making a life for herself."

"Does she know where you are right now?"

"Not exactly. I needed a Sophie break. So tell me about all those books under your tree."

He noted the neat change of subject. "Every year when we were growing up my sister and I got a new Christmas book. These days I get novels with Christmas in them somewhere, but I've kept every one of them. So has Kaye. We both put them out in December to remember those good years. Someday I want to do the same thing for my own children."

She briefly rested her fingertips on his knee. "Brody, your father died some time ago, didn't he?"

"His life was too short." He hoped that would do.

"You must miss him."

"Holidays are the worst." He decided to take a chance. "I'm glad you're here, Jo. You've brightened this one already."

Neither of them said anything for a long moment, then she broke eye contact and looked back at the fire. "Think the coffee's ready? I just take a little milk, if you have it."

He returned a few minutes later to find her on the

sofa looking through some of the books he'd stacked under the tree.

He set down the coffee and joined her.

"Do you have a favorite?" she asked, placing the books beside her.

"Probably *The Gift of the Magi,* by O. Henry. My mother used to read it to us every Christmas day, just in case we weren't wild about a present or two. To remind us that whatever's given in love is the best gift of all." He grinned. "Even if it sucks."

"I don't remember the story."

"It's about a young couple, not so much as an extra penny to spend, but very much in love. Her one prized possession is her beautiful hair. His is a gold pocket watch that's been passed down to him. Because she loves him so much she sells her hair to buy a watch chain for Christmas, and in turn, without knowing what she's done, he sells his watch to buy her a comb for her beautiful hair. In the end, of course both gifts are useless."

"But their love is absolutely clear."

"Like the Magi, they gave their best."

"It's hopelessly romantic, don't you think? Do you know anybody willing to give up so much for so little?"

"Love's a powerful motivator."

"I guess I haven't seen the proof up close."

She started to pick up her coffee, but he put his hand over hers, then he leaned forward and kissed her. Lightly. Sweetly. He took his time, and in a moment her lips softened under his and she sighed.

Heart pounding he finally pulled away. "If you were talking about us, we were awfully young, Jo. And we had so many strikes against us."

"Is that what it was?"

"Were you really ready to settle down? When I told you that *I* wasn't, you looked so relieved, I thought I'd made the right choice for both of us."

She searched his eyes. "We *were* young," she said at last.

"We aren't that young anymore."

"But we tried this once, and it wasn't exactly a rip-roaring success."

"We can take it a step at a time." He smiled. "Baby steps."

"I have a life and a job and a condo across the country."

"And who knows what kind of Christmas tree is waiting for you this year? Neon? Goth? Are you really in a hurry to go back and find out?"

With an audible sigh she cupped his cheek, her fingers threading into his hair. "This is so crazy. We can't just pick up where we left off, Brody. Ten years have gone by."

"And I've missed you for every one of them."

"You could have found me."

He heard the hurt, and it tore at his heart. He almost blurted out the truth, that he'd had nothing to offer except poverty and death. But he didn't want sympathy.

He wanted love.

"Can we just start over?" he asked. "Get to know each other? Have fun together? Will you stay through Christmas and spend it in Kanowa Lake?" He didn't add "With me," although that was perfectly clear.

He thought she was going to refuse, then she smiled, and her fingers burrowed deeper in his hair. "Friends, then, but just friends. On one condition."

"What's that?"

"You get a real Christmas tree, and we decorate it together."

"And if I put up a sprig of mistletoe?"

"You're doing fine without it," she said, right before she leaned forward to kiss him again.

CHAPTER SIX

From EllaT@puget.net: Sounds to me like you're having quite the adventure at Hollymeade, Jo. Rachel and I are shivering through your emails, and they make me sorry we didn't try harder to stay in touch all these years. I'm in the mood for an adventure, too, but I think I'll take mine without all that snow. I'm practicing my appliqué stitches, by the way, in preparation for my border. Aunt Glo would have encouraging words to say, I'm sure. And she would also have reminded you to slow down and have a wonderful Christmas. So even though I'm the youngest cousin, I'll do it for her.

JO WASN'T SURE how Christmas Eve had arrived so quickly. Ten days had passed since the potluck, and she and Brody had spent large chunks of each one together. While now she was working an hour each morning, she was still officially taking vacation time. She'd become skilled at cutting off her boss's telephone rants by citing in boring detail the reasons why her presence wasn't required until the New Year.

Sophie was even more of a challenge, but surprisingly her spirit guide agreed with Jo. Ocelot Lee had issued a decree that demanding attention from her daughter was not a step forward for Sophie's personal growth. Sophie needed more time with *him*. Jo just hoped her stepfather was watching how much money was flowing to the medium who channeled ol' Ocelot.

The moments with Brody were by far the best. She woke up every morning anxious to see him again. For a quiet little town in the frozen north, they had found plenty to do, especially after she bought a down jacket.

She was learning to cross-country ski, and for the first time since her childhood, she had strapped on ice skates and, with Brody's help, taken her first tentative glides along the frozen lakeshore. They'd Christmas shopped together at the Trading Post, baked Christmas cookies for his friends, and added a couple of snow people to his collection so that now they had a fleet of carolers on his lawn.

Twice more they had unsuccessfully searched the Grants' attic for the box with Eric's baby things. Since searching was the perfect excuse to see Brody earlier in the day, Jo managed that guilty little secret just fine.

Brody had taken his time getting a new Christmas tree, but the tree they had hauled into his house yesterday was a real beauty, cut from a hillside destined for vineyard expansion. As it turned out there were ornaments in the attic from his childhood, and he had promised to bring them down tonight. Jo was making a gourmet dinner, and afterward, they would decorate together.

Tomorrow morning she would join him at his house to open presents. Join him, that is, if she actually *left* tonight.

So far she and Brody had, as she had requested, just enjoyed each other's company. While they never talked about the past, they did talk about everything else. They had similar views on politics, and while he was more inclined to be a churchgoer than she was, their views on religion were similar, too. Their reading tastes were different—his tended toward thrillers, she was a fan of biographies—but they loved some of the same television shows. He was surprised she avoided trendy nightclubs, and she was surprised he never watched football but couldn't be pried away from the set when the World Series was in play.

Through all this, he had rarely touched her. He always kissed her good-night. That was a given, and she could tell he was reluctant to let her go afterward. She was reluctant to go, so she understood. But somehow they had taken the time to build trust, to push aside the powerful physical attraction between them and reforge the bond they had severed a decade before.

She was so glad they had waited. Weren't they mature? But now she was ready to toss maturity out the window.

She dressed carefully for the night's adventure. She hadn't brought X-rated lingerie, but she was fairly certain that lingerie of any kind wasn't going to be much of an issue. She washed her hair, shaved her legs, took a little extra care with her makeup and pulled out the new green sweater she had found at the Trading Post. By the time she left, she was satisfied. She had even pinned a twinkling Christmas wreath to the sweater, to make Brody smile. Luckily it had an off switch, because this was no night to give the man a headache.

She packed the ingredients for dinner and took them out to the car, then she packed a few toiletries and a change of underwear in a bag, too, and hid it under the front seat.

Just in case…

Snow was falling, a pillowy snow that was spreading softly over older drifts like icing on a cake. As she drove toward his house she thought about Olivia's wedding quilt. As hoped, she had found several helpful books upstairs. After looking carefully at every pattern, she had settled on a Friendship Star block, a four-pointed star that would, in partner with its neighbors, dance across her border. It was, as star blocks went, simple enough for her to stitch by hand, although the first two had varied wildly, and neither of them had been the exact size she needed.

The third, though, had been perfect, her stitches even and small enough to suit her. She had decided to use the royal blue background of the center block as the background for each block. Then the stars themselves could be a variety of different fabrics, and that was where she planned to incorporate some of the bride and groom's childhoods. She had also decided on smallish stars, so that none would stand out and take away from the perfect center block. That meant she had to sew even more of them to stretch around the quilt. In the past week she had made enough for two sides, and she was pleased at the way they had turned out.

Still, she hoped that quilt-making would be on hold tonight.

On the snow-sprinkled walk up to the house she smiled at the wreath on the front door. She had bought it on sale yesterday in the grocery store parking lot, a steal, since most people already had their decorations completed. Brody had hung it immediately. As she raised her hand to knock she noticed something new had been added. Little flags that looked like they had been made from Post-it notes and toothpicks were tucked in between the pinecones and plastic sprays of cranberries adorning the wreath.

She pulled one out and read the message out loud.

"The weather outside is frightful." She frowned, and pulled out another. "If you've no place to go." Now she smiled as she looked at the rest. He had carefully penned, then pinned, all the words to the familiar Christmas song, "Let It Snow." Even out of order, she recognized them.

"All the night long we'll be warm."

Oh, it was going to be a good night, she was sure of it.

Let it snow and snow some more!

By the time Brody answered the door, she was almost dancing with delight.

"It's so Christmassy!" she said, throwing her arms around him. "I love the wreath."

He kissed her soundly, until she was breathless. Then he stepped back. "I would have bought one and put it up weeks ago if I'd known the results."

"I have lots to bring in. Want to help?"

They finally got all the food into the house, despite pelting each other with snowballs.

She set the last of the bags on the counter and took a deep breath of cinnamon-scented air. "Something smells fabulous."

"I'm heating cider. I knew you'd be ready for a mug when you got here."

She threw her arms around his neck again and kissed him. "You're so thoughtful."

Brody slipped his arms around her waist and held her there. "Seems to me you're making me dinner. Little enough to do in return."

"Cooking in this wonderful old kitchen is a treat. I love it. I can almost taste all the amazing meals that have been cooked here."

"Doubtful. My mother loves her vegetable garden.

Then she boils the heck out of every harvest. My father used to sneak behind her and turn off burners."

"I know you miss him. I miss mine."

He kissed the tip of her nose, then released her. "Having you here makes all the difference."

"For the record, this is the best Christmas I remember in a long time."

"Because?"

He was clearly fishing for a compliment. "I'm not working, of course. At least not very much."

"And?"

"And I guess I love winter. The snow and the cold remind me of my childhood, before we pulled up stakes and headed for California."

"And?"

She cocked her head. "Well, being with you is nice."

"Nice?"

"Maybe that's a bit of an understatement."

"It had better be." He pulled her close again, and this time the kiss went on and on—and the man did know how to kiss. When she finally stepped away, the room was cartwheeling around her.

She shook her head. "You expect me to cook after that?"

"You promised me dinner. And I just hauled in at least a ton of groceries."

She sent him her most seductive smile, then she turned away before he could respond to the message in it. "No problem, I'll just boil the heck out of everything in these bags and you'll feel right at home."

OF COURSE SHE didn't. She had gone into debt for the rib roast, and she cooked it with potatoes, simmering them first so they would crisp up in the oven nestled against the roast. She served both with a spinach and artichoke casserole, fresh green beans, a cranberry, apple and walnut salad, and yeast rolls she had baked at Hollymeade that morning. For his part Brody opened a bottle of Merlot from a friend's vineyard on Long Island.

When she set everything on the table, decorated with a red tablecloth from Hollymeade, evergreen boughs and white candles, Brody looked like a man who had died and reawakened to his first heavenly banquet.

"I'm going to be rude and ask if there's dessert," he said.

"Doesn't this look like enough?"

"I have to know how much I can eat. If there's dessert, too, I might be able to rein myself in, just a bit, in preparation."

"Homemade gingerbread, and there's maple whipped cream to go with it."

He looked up from his plate. "Thank you. More than I can say."

She heard so much in his voice. *Thanks for the food. Thanks for cooking for me. Thanks for making a holiday special that would have been lonely and desolate.*

If there was more, she didn't want to think about it.

The food was as good as she had hoped. Clearly Brody thought so, too.

"You ought to be a pro, a chef," he said, as he reached for another helping of potatoes. "This is better than any restaurant meal I've ever had."

She was flattered. "Cooking's my only real hobby. I would hate to ruin it."

"You haven't talked much about your job."

She found herself telling him more about the man she worked for. "I know it's not just my fault when things go wrong," she said, "but it's hard to remember that when Frank crowns me scapegoat of the year."

"Do you have to stay there?"

She didn't know. She did know she would be in demand if she ever looked for another job. She had a large network of leads and a standing offer or two. That sounded like bragging, though, so she just shrugged. "I've invested a lot in this job. I would hate to walk away."

"You like what you do?"

"I love helping companies become more efficient. That's my main function. If we can get just the right system in place, their productivity soars and everybody's happy. It's a great feeling."

"You work with the big guys, I guess."

"Usually, but the right system, computers, software, et cetera, customized for small businesses, can make all the difference, too. And sometimes it's the difference between closing up shop or opening up markets." She pushed back from the table a little, because she couldn't eat another bite. "I'm sure you have a good system here, tailored to your needs, right?"

"I don't have the time to fool with anything new."

Or the money, she thought. The more time she spent with Brody, the more she suspected Ryan Vineyards was, at best, holding its own. Most of the land was planted with Concord grapes for juice, and Brody's passion for making wine was on a back burner. She had seen his equipment, and California girl that she was, she knew what he had wasn't state-of-the-art, as it should be to compete. The house needed attention inside and out, and one day, when she had dropped by unannounced, the temperature inside hadn't been much different from the one outside.

"I could fix you up." She said this as casually as she could, as if having a highly paid consultant revamp his entire business strategy wasn't any big deal. "Get the right technology in place without a lot of fuss and bother. And with my contacts, I could do it in a way that wouldn't break the bank. I could set up everything you need. Invoices, purchasing orders, follow-ups with potential clients, analysis of marketing campaigns. How's your website?"

She had asked the last question in her most innocent tone, but she already knew the answer. The Ryan Vineyards website, if it could be called that, was pathetic, one page that looked as if it had been constructed by a middle school student for his first computer class.

"I can tell you've seen it already," Brody said.

She nodded sheepishly. "I think I could do a thousand percent better with a minimum of work."

He didn't answer directly. "It's a lot to think about tonight, and we ought to be celebrating. Would you like to try some of Ryan Vineyards' own ice wine with dessert?"

Last week she'd had a glass of Ryan's best Reisling, and it had compared favorably with German Reislings she'd been served on business trips. She said an enthusiastic yes.

They cleared off the table together and stacked the dishes in the ancient dishwasher. Then, while she dished up the gingerbread with generous dollops of whipped cream, Brody opened the wine.

They took both to the small table near the fireplace and sat together on soft cushions, watching the flames and working on the gingerbread.

The wine was wonderful, with notes of peaches and honey, a wine to be proud of, and she told him so.

He looked pleased. "The grapes have to freeze before we pick them, which means we have to leave them on the vine and hope a freeze is on the way before they rot. Then, of course, there's not as much liquid after they freeze, so we make less wine. It's a risky business, but good ice wine can sell for five times what a bottle of the Reisling brings."

"That would make a great blog, updating people day by day on the state of the weather, the grapes, the work involved. Wine fanatics would hang on every word. They'd be standing in line for your wine when it was ready."

"If I could just be two or three people at once, I could manage something like that."

"I bet you like all the challenges."

"It's the darnedest thing. I do like challenges, always have. Take finding Eric's baby quilts, for instance."

Surprised at the nimble change of subject, she took another sip of her wine and waited.

"It's the strangest thing, Jo, but I think I may have found them."

"Really? You were in the Grants' attic without me?"

"I'm still monitoring their roof for a possible leak."

That surprised her, but she didn't let on.

"Anyway, I went upstairs, and you won't believe what I found."

She raised a brow. "Won't I?"

"The right box was there in front. Exactly where we looked that first day. Are you surprised?"

She set her plate on the table. "Not so much."

"Well, I was. Really, really surprised. Stunned, in fact. Because..." He paused dramatically. "I had *moved* that box to the back row before you ever went up there in the first place."

"Brody!"

He set his glass on the table. "Here's the thing. I needed an excuse to be with you, or at least I thought I did. But a miracle happened. After we went through that first stack of boxes together, somebody moved that box right back to the front where we'd already looked."

He had confessed. Now *she* had to, although he obviously knew the truth. "All right, after our first trip to the attic, Mrs. Grant told me where to find a house key and gave me a description of the box I was looking for. So I took out a couple of quilts and moved the box back to the front, so we wouldn't find it when we were together. Of course I didn't know that you—"

He put his arm around her and pulled her close. "Jo, do we still need excuses to be together? Do we need more time talking about our views on art or literature, about your job or mine, more snowballs and ice skating? Because it's all been great. We could be best friends, I guess, if we really worked at it."

She went into his arms without hesitation, shifting so her face was close to his. "But we were never destined just to be friends, were we?"

"I don't think so."

"Brody, just tell me this isn't about the season…." Her voice caught. "And it's not just nostalgia for lost youth."

"It's about never being able to forget you," he said, just before he kissed her.

He was right, there really was no more need for conversation. And there was certainly no need to invent ways to entertain each other. There was no need to move into the bedroom, either. The fire was warm, the pillows were soft, and their clothes slipped away as easily as their painful past.

Later, lying against him, skin-to-skin, heart-to-heart, Jo stirred a little. "If Santa Claus comes down this chimney tonight, he's going to get a big surprise."

Brody pulled her close again. "Not to worry. Santa knows he doesn't have to come. I already have my Christmas present."

CHAPTER SEVEN

JO LOVED THE handcrafted bracelet Brody had given her for Christmas. One of his friends made jewelry, and the bracelet was a chain of sterling silver leaves and tiny amethyst beads arranged like clusters of grapes. It was now two days after Christmas, and she had only removed the bracelet to shower. In turn she was afraid Brody might wear the cashmere hoodie she had given him until high summer.

Because he was making sales calls to three distant restaurants that he hoped to interest in his wines, she was back at Hollymeade for the day. She had turned down an offer to accompany him and was taking the day to catch up with email. Like clockwork she had monthly cramps and a headache that she knew would subside in a day, and she was just as glad to be alone.

Now she nestled into a comfortable chair and remembered the one time in her life when her period hadn't come the day it was expected. She had been a sophomore in college, and two weeks before she had visited Brody at Cornell for homecoming. He was graduating that year, and more than once the conversation had turned to their future. She was taking more than a full load at M.I.T., hoping to graduate early.

Brody was already fielding offers from vineyards in California and Washington State. With no experience, he wouldn't make much money at first, but his intention was to gain experience while Jo finished school.

At some point the discussion had turned to having children. He wanted several, he'd said, and sooner rather than later so he had the energy to enjoy them. She had to finish school, of course, and settle into her career, but wouldn't it be wonderful when they could be a real family?

Jo was less enthused. Since her father's death she had been a mother to her own mother, and now she was anxious to become financially stable and independent. Having children sounded like another obstacle to both, but she was sure she and Brody would eventually come to a compromise.

Except that a week went by, then two, and her period didn't start. Jo was never late, not by so much as a day, and suddenly she was frantic. The reality of children, their constant care, constant needs, overwhelmed her, even knowing this child would be Brody's. She was so irrational she refused to buy a test kit because she was terrified what she might learn.

During the second week of waiting, her schoolwork suffered. She was late turning in an important paper, and she failed a quiz. Then, just as she geared up to discover the truth, her period started.

Just like that, only, by then her whole life had changed. She had learned something important. Her past and overcoming it were more important than a family of her own. At least for the foreseeable future.

She had been searching for a way to tell Brody that she wasn't ready to have children—might not be for some time—when he'd made a surprise appearance in Cambridge to end their engagement. Later, when she surfaced from the deep pool of anger and regret, she had been able to focus on one bright spot. She could go forward with her life plan without interference or demands. With nobody in the way, independence and security were now in reach. Like a drowning woman she had grabbed for both and hung on tightly.

Until now.

Ten years had passed, and she was both independent and secure. She was also locked into a life with few other rewards. She wasn't sorry to have a career. She loved what she did. But these days she could see that combining a career and a family was possible. With more perspective she could also see that raising children was completely different from caring for her mother. Raising Brody's children? The thought was sweet.

Her cell phone rang, and she was so lost in thought that she answered without checking the caller's identity. The voice on the other end was unmistakable, Frank Conner having his daily snit. She sat back and listened to her boss's latest explosion, buffing her nails against her sweater as he shouted about a project she had only a small part in, until she realized her hands were shaking so hard she was now clenching her fingers. That was the moment when she interrupted him.

"Frank, you know what? I'm fed up with this, so I'm hanging up. Don't call back unless you can speak to me the way one intelligent adult speaks to another. You can stop using me as your punching bag, or you can fire me, but I won't let you abuse me another minute. And you'd better be careful, because, you know what? I might just start punching back."

The only thing she punched, of course, was "end." Then she turned off the ringer, shoved it back in her purse and for good measure covered the purse with a pillow.

Or at least she tried to. The pillow took two tries because she was still trembling so badly.

She had finally done it. Now, despite a stomach in turmoil, she couldn't figure out why she hadn't confronted Frank Conner sooner. It was quite possible she'd just lost her job, but did she care?

For the first time in years she could see how much more there was to life than financial security. Sure, it was nice to have investments and her own condo, to be able to take great vacations if she wanted them, to wear designer suits every day. But nobody visited the condo. She didn't take vacations because she didn't have time and she didn't want to go alone. The suits were boring even if they sported famous labels. And the investments? What were they for? An early, supremely dull retirement?

She loved what she did, but surely there was a better way and a better place to do it. If she was fired for standing up for herself, did she care?

The answer was surprisingly easy. No, she really didn't.

Something sweet and wonderful swept through her. She thought it might be freedom. Freedom from her spiteful boss. Freedom from a life that required all work and no play. Freedom from responsibility for Sophie, because even in the unlikely possibility that Sophie's new husband gave up on her, Jo had saved enough and then some to take care of her mother's future needs.

Freedom from loneliness.

Job security was great, but she was good at what she did, and she had contacts. If she needed another job, she could find a good one. But what if she didn't want to work for somebody else? What if she wanted to stay here, with Brody, and run her own business? What if she wanted to work for the little guys, the small businesses like his that needed her help so they could make a decent living, not so they could make millions more each year?

She could help put businesses like that on the road to financial security, a road that didn't sacrifice their employees' welfare or old-fashioned customer service. The very same road she planned to put Brody on. Because she could, and now she realized she needed to. Maybe it was too late to make updates to his system a Christmas present, but she didn't think he would mind.

She went to her laptop and brought up the Ryan Vineyards website. It was just as pathetic as she remembered. Website design wasn't her strong suit, but figuring out what was wrong and getting somebody else to make it right certainly was.

She pulled up another program and began to make notes and lists. She knew a woman, a brilliant designer who was now a stay-at-home mom, who could develop a website for a reasonable fee. And while the designer worked on that, Jo could start in on all the other things Ryan Vineyards needed. She would put together a software package and a list of hardware. The vineyards needed a brand, starting with a more sophisticated logo, and that logo needed to be prominent on everything they produced. She would find good prices for everything and vendors willing to work with her at substantial discounts.

She was so excited she could hardly sit still. Brody might look at all this as charity, a gift he hadn't asked for and couldn't afford to pay back, but when she convinced him it was the start of a new portfolio for the consulting business she hoped to inaugurate, she thought maybe he wouldn't mind.

Maybe he would even see that she needed Ryan Vineyards and Brody Ryan for *more* than a portfolio. Because *she* saw it now. Freedom was all well and good, and she was happy she had found it, but she was becoming more and more sure she didn't want to be free of Brody ever again.

As BRODY PARKED his car in front of his house he told himself that one restaurant out of three wasn't bad, particularly since he wasn't much of a salesman. He hated to twist arms. His wine should speak for itself, but unfortunately he didn't have fancy brochures to go with it or anything more than his home phone number to process orders. The generic label on the bottles didn't help, either. Even if the wine was good, and so reasonably priced that his only real profit would be loyal customers, his presentation screamed "amateur-on-the-premises."

Gargoyle, the aging collie from the neighboring farm, was waiting on his porch. Gargoyle wandered over from time to time, as if to make sure Brody wasn't too lonely, but he never stayed. Brody's house was too cold for a good nap when his own was much warmer.

"Hey, fellow." Brody reached down to ruffle the collie's neck. "Nice afternoon for a walk."

Gargoyle's tail beat time to his words. The dog rubbed against his leg, then, as if he'd done his duty, he headed for home.

Brody figured it was a sad state of affairs when he felt even more alone because someone else's dog was disappearing up the hill. Winter was never easy. Most of the time the old house felt like a deserted barn, cold and drafty and utterly empty. He closed off what he could and heated the rest of it just enough to keep the pipes from freezing.

Except when Jo was there.

Of course Jo was more than just a hedge against loneliness. He was deeply in love with her, had been since the first time they met. All the years apart hadn't changed that, although the reasons for their separation hadn't really changed, either.

He still had nothing to offer her. He was on the brink of losing Ryan Vineyards. There was only so much one man could do. Among other things, two late spring freezes had diminished their crop, and for someone already in debt the outcome looked grim, even if this year's crop was a roaring success.

And even if he could somehow salvage the family home and business, there was nothing in Kanowa Lake for Jo. She loved her work, even if she didn't love the man she worked for, but there was little industry here and nothing in her field.

How could he ask her to give up the work she loved when he faced almost certain failure anyway?

As he walked up to the house he remembered the day a decade before when he told her that marriage was out of the question. He hadn't been honest, of course. Had he told her then that he had just learned that his father was dying, a diagnosis that promised a long, slow decline, she would have told him that his father's condition made no difference. She was a woman who did what she had to. Of course she would pitch in and help with nursing care, just the way she had cared for her own mother most of her life. They could live through the dark years together.

Of course, the health issues would have been different, but Jo had sacrificed enough of her life to Sophie, and even then Brody had seen it and been unwilling to ask her to sacrifice more.

Now he knew that if he told her the true state of his finances she would offer to help, to stand beside him, no matter what.

He let himself in and took off his boots in a foyer nearly as cold as the outdoors. For a moment he let himself form a different picture. Jo, waiting to find out how his sales calls had gone. Hot soup waiting for lunch, maybe a fire in the fireplace, new curtains at the windows, pillows on the sofa. She would have done what she could with very little money to make his childhood home their own.

And just as likely, if she wasn't happy in her new life, she would go on that way forever, because it wasn't like her to hurt anybody. She not only did what she had to, but she also never complained.

There was only one way to make everything come together, of course. A real estate agent had contacted him last month. His company was looking for land to build vacation homes. Brody's wasn't ideal since he wasn't directly on the lake, but the lake *was* visible from many places on the property. The agent was fairly certain he could buy access for a private road down to the water and a portion of the shore beyond for a beach. He wanted to build twenty homes, efficient small summer cottages, with community tennis courts, a pool, a recreation area. He had talked about a price that would cover the mortgage and other obligations, but with little left over. If nothing else, they would be debt-free at last.

Brody could find a job somewhere else, maybe help his mom buy a little condo in Arizona near his sister, where she would be happy. He would be free to pursue a different life with Jo.

And Brody Ryan would be the last of the Ryan line

to live on these acres and struggle to bring them to life. The Ryan who finally gave up and gave in.

The Ryan whose only other alternative was to ask the woman he loved to give up her dreams for his.

The telephone rang, but he went upstairs without answering it to take a hot shower. There was nobody he could talk to about his life or his decisions. For years he had been forced to make them alone. As much as he longed to, he couldn't involve Jo, because she was at the center of every one of them.

CHAPTER EIGHT

New Year's had come and gone, and Jo was still at the lake cottage taking vacation time—sort of. She worked in the mornings, communicating with her colleagues on projects they shared, but since their phone call, she had only received two terse emails from Frank Conner. Apparently he had taken her warning to heart. There hadn't been any tantrums for a week.

The rest of her days were more fun. There was time with Brody, of course, magical time, particularly New Year's Eve, when another year stretched ahead of them with all its possibilities. But Brody wasn't the only person she socialized with.

She hadn't intended to make friends in Kanowa Lake, but somehow it had happened. A young woman she met at the Trading Post had told her about the county's quilt group and invited her to what she called a circle meeting for half a dozen quilters who sewed together every Wednesday night. Since Brody was busy that night doing paperwork, and she wanted advice on whether to group similar colored stars together on the border or scatter them throughout, she had attended.

Warmly welcomed, her hand stitching admired and advice given to mix the colors for a scrappier effect, she'd had a wonderful time. Since then she'd been invited shopping by one woman in the group and out to lunch by another. She was on her way into town for the lunch when her cell phone rang. She pulled over and checked the ID. Frank Conner was waiting for her to answer, most likely impatiently.

Juggling the phone from hand to hand she considered, but in the end she touched the screen and put the phone to her ear. She had demanded that Frank treat her like an adult and, even harder for him, that he act like one himself. He'd had a week to consider her ultimatum. Now she would learn his decision.

When she put the phone back in her purse a minute later, she knew.

She hadn't been fired. Lord, no, he had assured her in honey-sweet tones. It was only that the company was going in a new direction, and her talents were no longer needed. She was fortunate, though, because Frank was a generous man. There would be a hefty compensation package to help her make the transition to the world of unemployment, as well as a flattering recommendation. The phone call had been the briefest and most cordial they had ever shared.

She suspected he had taped every word, in case she sued.

Her services were no longer required.

She was free.

Now that the shock was over she examined her feelings the way she might examine her limbs and joints after a bike accident. She had one regret. She had allowed Frank Conner to make the decision. Still, just this once her former boss had done her a huge favor. Because despite feeling she'd been walloped from behind, the blow had thrust her into a whole new world where she could determine her own future.

She could decide where and how hard she worked, for whom and with whom, what she did and the rea-

sons she did it. No more of Frank's tantrums. No more
complaints when she deserved compliments. No more
month-long negotiations with recalcitrant executives
who refused to play fair. If she worked for herself she
could get up from any conference table, gather her
things and take the next plane out.

She was free.

The thrill subsided quickly. She had no regrets that
she'd been fired—because both she and Frank knew
that was what had just happened. But the timing was
definitely wrong. For the past week she had organized
information on starting a consulting firm. She'd spent
hours on research, printed or bookmarked documents,
made a dozen phone calls. When she wasn't with Brody
or thinking about him, she had worked on her future.

But now, whenever she explained this to Brody, he
would think she was only reacting to losing her job.
She could tell him she had contacts all over the world
who would help her find a better job, if she wanted one.
She could explain that Frank Conner's inability to keep
top executives was legendary and nobody would think
worse of her. She could detail all the exciting possibilities ahead.

No matter what, Brody would still believe, at least on
some level, that she planned to set up her own business
only because she no longer had a "real" job. Had she
resigned first, then put her plans into action, she was
sure he would have seen everything in a different light.

Of course even then he might still have believed
she'd left California just to keep him happy.

She crossed her arms over the steering wheel and
rested her forehead on them. Winter was seeping into
the little rental SUV and into her heart.

She and Brody had talked about everything, everything *except* marriage. Even if she didn't tell him today that she had been fired, what would he think when she told him she planned to start her own business, something she could do anywhere? What did she do if he suddenly looked trapped? Wait while his face paled and he tried to find a response that didn't make her feel like a fool?

They had been through this before. How well she remembered.

BRODY DIDN'T USUALLY cook real meals with fresh ingredients. He was most often inclined to dump several things into a pot and eat the result in one bowl. Stew with an extra can of green beans. Chili with a can of corn. He told himself that way he was getting all the vegetables he needed, but he never ate any of his concoctions with enthusiasm.

Tonight he owed Jo a real meal. In the weeks since she'd been here she had cooked a number of them for him, even packaged and refrigerated the leftovers for the nights they weren't together. With that in mind, today he had bought salmon on sale and some fancy pack of frozen vegetables that included sauce and a packet of bread crumbs to finish them off. He'd found baking potatoes in the fruit cellar from a good autumn harvest, and now they were roasting in the oven. The salmon, which would join them at the last minute, was bathing in marinade, a recipe he'd gotten from a friend's wife who had been so excited Brody was entertaining Jo that she had offered to come and cook the meal herself to make sure it was good.

But good or bad, Brody was determined to make the whole darned thing by himself.

The clock told him that Jo was due soon, and he realized that in the rush to clean the house and cook the meal he hadn't picked up the day's mail. He shrugged into his coat and gloves and pulled on his hat. As he shoved his feet into boots he decided to walk to the mailbox, even though the road was more than a football field away. But if he was lucky Jo would arrive in time to give him a lift back.

He was still agonizing over decisions and how to include Jo in his life, but he had promised himself to put that aside tonight. Maybe a solution would occur to him, and maybe it wouldn't. But they would have this night together.

The mailbox door was frozen in place, something he was used to. He banged his fist against the side until the ice binding it fractured enough for him to open it. He pulled out a handful of letters, bills most likely, and a large envelope from Arizona that probably contained drawings by Janna, his oldest niece, along with pictures of his mother, Kaye and her family, palm trees and sunshine.

While he loved palm trees and sunshine, he just couldn't shake the idea that they had nothing to do with a real life.

He was thinking about that when he reached for the final item and saw it was one of the wine magazines he subscribed to. He started to put it under his arm when words on the cover caught his eye.

Organic grapes, organic practices.

After using his teeth to strip off one glove he turned pages until he found the article, scanning it quickly. The glove dropped into the snow when he laughed, then read a sentence out loud.

"'Brody Ryan of Ryan Vineyards in Kanowa Lake, New York, is using a promising new method to control botrytis.'" Silently he read the rest of that section to himself before he picked up the glove, shook out the snow and slipped it back on.

He had been interviewed for the article several months ago; he couldn't even recall exactly when, but there'd been no promises his contribution would appear. Now here he was, on the pages of *Winemaking Today,* the most important magazine in his field, and the interview, more detailed than he remembered, was flattering. He was an outstanding young vintner, a pioneer in his field, a young man with few resources who was still making his mark.

He was glad the author hadn't added that he was also a young man likely to lose everything his ancestors had worked for.

He was halfway back to the house when his cell phone rang. Since Jo was rarely even a minute late he didn't check the number, assuming she was calling to tell him why she was held up.

"Brody Ryan of Ryan Vineyards?"

He wondered which bill collector had gotten his cell phone number. It wouldn't be hard. His cheesy little website listed it.

He admitted he was that person and waited for the worst.

"This is Pablo Fontanello, of Fontanello Vineyards in Napa. You've heard of us?"

Brody could only imagine the question was a joke. "Who hasn't?"

There was warm laughter, a pleasant rumble on the other end. "I just saw the article in *Winemaking Today* about your research into organic botrytis control. I'm intrigued."

Pablo Fontanello's wine was world-famous. The Fontanello family had won nearly every important honor. They had supplied wines to the White House and Buckingham Palace, produced award-winning wine in California and Italy, and there were rumors they were moving into the Bordeaux region of France. While other boys idolized baseball players or rock stars, Brody had idolized Pablo Fontanello.

"I'm glad to hear it," Brody said. "I think the sooner all of us hop on the organic wagon, the better for the environment and the better our wine."

"We've been doing a lot of experiments along those lines here, but you went in a completely different direction with good results. I like the way you think."

"Thank you, sir. That means a lot."

"How many acres do you have?"

They chatted and Brody answered questions, but he knew the man on the other end was too shrewd and busy to waste his time on small talk. He waited for the conversation to take a turn, and it did.

"The man who's been heading our organic division wants to retire. We're looking for new blood and enthusiasm. The job pays well and comes with full benefits. There's a house, too, a nice one for a family. Do you have a family?"

"Too busy trying to make a go of this," Brody said.

"Well, I won't say you wouldn't be busy if you got the job with us, but there would be time for other things. You could lease your vineyards in the meantime, because eventually you'll leave, all the good ones do, and go out on your own again. But in the meantime I'd like to think we would have something to teach you here."

"I'm sure you would," Brody said, his thoughts as scattered as the snowflakes drifting lazily from the sky.

"We'll be interviewing for the job in March. I hope

you'll give it some consideration. You have a good shot at it. I'll be sending you more information."

Brody thanked him and said goodbye, then he slipped the phone in his pocket.

He heard a car pulling into his driveway, but, head still reeling, he didn't even turn. He couldn't tell Jo about the conversation. She would ask why he would even consider such a thing, and then he would have to admit what a deep hole he was in. But if he got the job and moved to Napa, he and Jo would, at the least, be on the same side of the country. If they married they could figure out where to live and how to travel back and forth to do their jobs. There wouldn't be room for children in their lives, but they would have each other.

The old farmhouse was just a few yards in front of him now, icicles dripping from the eaves, snow outlining the slate shingles on the roof. A light shone through the front window. Generations of Ryans had lived in it, and he had lived in it most his life. Western New York was his home. Everything he knew, everything he was? All right here in this, the teensiest dot on the map.

Could he erase that and start a new life working for someone else? Despite what Pablo Fontanello had said, Brody knew he couldn't afford to lease Ryan Vineyards or run it from afar, and he would never have the money to go out on his own again. He could sell this property for vacation homes and pay off all the family's debts, but he wouldn't have anything left over to buy more land someday, not even with a good salary.

But he might have Jo.

He heard a playful honk behind him, and he turned and waved before he stepped back to watch her park. She opened the door and stepped out, and the picture of her scarlet jacket against the white snowdrifts was lovely, but it was her smile that took his breath.

"You look like you lost your best friend," she said, the smile melting away.

"I was lost in thought," he said, managing a smile to replace hers as she walked toward him. "Come and convince me it's time to stop thinking."

"I plan to. In fact I plan to spend the night, if I'm asked. I brought the sexiest nightgown I could find at the Trading Post."

He couldn't think of anything to say. He finally managed to say, "Oh?"

"Unfortunately it's flannel."

"You know the way to a man's heart, don't you?"

Her expression was inscrutable, but she nodded. "I certainly hope so."

"Dinner's in half an hour."

"Maybe," she said. "Or maybe not."

He wrapped his arms around her for a long winter kiss.

Maybe *not* was the first course of the evening.

CHAPTER NINE

Jo STAYED FOR breakfast. Midmorning, as snow began to fall, she held and dispensed tools as Brody fixed a pipe under the kitchen sink. Of course he could easily have fixed it without her, but neither of them pointed that out. She'd made omelets for breakfast, so he made grilled cheese sandwiches for lunch.

Since waking they had hardly been out of the same room. After lunch, though, as the snow grew heavier, Brody began to pull on his winter gear. "If I don't get to the hardware store right now I won't be able to do a permanent fix on the sink until Tuesday. They close Sundays and Mondays during the winter, and early on Saturdays if there's a bad storm."

Jo wasn't quite used to Kanowa Lake's laid-back winter hours. "Do you get tired of that? Not being able to get what you want when you want it?"

"We're a nation of people who've forgotten how to wait. Delayed gratification builds character."

She sent him a lazy smile. "You didn't seem too worried about your character last night. You wanted what you wanted and right that minute."

"I delayed dinner, didn't I?"

"Quite a while, as I recall."

He flashed her a wicked grin. "And once we were in bed I was the soul of patience."

She kissed the tip of his nose in answer.

He sent her one of his best dimple-creased smiles. "You don't mind if I run out? I have a couple other errands I need to do. You're staying for dinner?"

"If you invite me I'll make homemade pizza. But fresh mushrooms would be nice if you can get to the store before the snow's a problem. I saw some yeast packets in your cupboard. I'll make the dough while you're away."

"You're officially invited, but you already knew that." His expression turned serious. "I don't want you to go back to Hollymeade at all. I want every minute you'll give me before you head back to California."

"I haven't quite decided when that will be."

"How much vacation time do you have, anyway?"

That bit of trivia no longer mattered, because whatever days she hadn't claimed would simply show up in her final paycheck. But she wasn't ready to explain all that.

She settled on an answer that wasn't quite a lie. "Enough to keep me here a little longer."

"I'll take what I can get." He told her to make herself at home; then he kissed her again, a long promising kiss that was more hello than goodbye, before he headed out the door.

Jo waited until she heard Brody's pickup pull out to the road, then she crossed the house to his office. She had been hoping for some time here alone. The first thing she had to do to help bring Ryan Vineyards into the twenty-first century was find out exactly what software Brody already had and how well he was using it. Then she had to take stock of his equipment. Having peeked at his desk when he was in the shower that morning, she was fairly certain they would need to start from scratch.

In the office she did a quick survey, then settled down with a notepad and began to list what little was there. While she was discouraged that Brody was working with antiques, she found herself getting more and more excited.

It was going to be so much fun to put all this together. Once she finished, walking into this room would be a completely different experience. Everything Brody needed would be right at his fingertips. Every task he had to accomplish would go faster, and the time saved by using up-to-date, relevant software that she would program just for his needs meant he could use the extra hours to expand in new directions. They would have to sit down together and discuss his dreams, what he couldn't do now and wanted to, and figure out how to proceed, but the foundation would be laid right here in this room.

The list of hardware took no time at all. Then, feeling only slightly guilty, she woke his computer, which wasn't even password protected, to see what was already loaded there. Immediately she saw that his operating system and browser needed upgrades, although it was doubtful this machine was capable of handling the newest versions.

She looked briefly at his spreadsheet software and saw that it was underutilized as well as sadly out-of-date. She told herself the data was none of her business, but somehow she couldn't stop herself from clicking on a file he'd labeled debts, since knowing a bit about his financials would help her establish a budget.

She stared at the screen, not believing what she saw. Surely these figures couldn't be right? But as she scanned the page, her heart sank. Brody seemed to own very little outright. The property was heavily mort-

gaged. He didn't own most of his equipment but was
paying for it on installment. He had a first *and* a second mortgage on the house. He had a full year to go to
pay off his truck and substantial credit card debt. And
worst of all there was a category labeled *medical* with
a debt of more than $50,000.

She closed the program. She didn't have to look any
further to see how deeply in the hole he was, and this
one glimpse had probably turned up the reason. *Medical* might well be debt the family had run up while his
father was dying. Jo wondered how large the amount
had been at the beginning. Had they mortgaged the
property and the house to pay off the bulk?

Now the state of the front porch and the low setting
on the thermostat made sense.

Her heart ached for Brody and his mother. Fate and
medical science had dealt them a blow, and they were
struggling to pick themselves up again. Could they?
She had no way of knowing. A careful assessment of
expenses and profits might tell the tale, but in Brody's
business, weather, economy, the fickle tastes of the public plus a million other variables could affect even the
most educated estimate. Right now the Ryan family
needed an infusion of cash so the debts with the highest interest rates disappeared.

Ryan Vineyards also needed her to provide a plan
for its survival. She was more convinced than ever that
she could make a difference. If Brody would allow it.

With that in mind she did a quick perusal of the rest
of his software, shaking her head as she went. She finished with his mail program, which thankfully was a
good one that just needed updating.

An email was already on the screen when she clicked
on the mail icon. She had already invaded his privacy,

and there was no excuse good enough for having done so, but the logo under the signature caught her eye.

Fontanello Vineyards. The email was from Pablo Fontanello himself. Apparently Brody ran in exclusive company.

She couldn't have stopped herself from reading it if the roof had been threatening to cave in.

By the time she finished she had a knot in her stomach that felt like a cannonball. Fontanello wanted Brody to move to California to work for him. There was an attachment Jo didn't open, but it was clear the offer was good.

Brody was considering a move to California? Not to San Diego, where he believed she needed to live. Napa Valley, which was a day's drive from her home, or a shorter flight, although with airport security and a million other problems, no flight was short these days. There would also be a substantial drive to whatever airport he was flying in and out of. They would be in the same state, but always hours apart.

He was thinking about a move to California and he hadn't mentioned it?

Or maybe he hadn't considered where she lived at all.

What else hadn't he mentioned?

Fuming, she ignored the voice in her head that told her she wasn't playing fair, and she scanned the list of recent emails for more information. She stopped at one from Serenity Real Estate and Development and clicked on the message; then she closed the mail program and stared at his computer wallpaper, a photo of the vineyards with this house in the background.

A house that might not be his much longer.

Brody had an offer from a Realtor. Having seen his debts she knew the amount mentioned in the email would wipe them away, but only just. Of course it was only an offer, a negotiating point, but no matter what Brody managed to wring from Serenity, he wouldn't be left with much.

Dismay tightened the knot in her stomach, but it took her a moment to sort out her feelings. She realized how much she had set her heart on moving here, to this wonderful old house with all its potential, where they could settle in together and raise a family.

She didn't want a thoroughly modern commuter marriage where she and Brody saw each other infrequently. Between the two of them, with her business knowledge and his knowledge of viticulture, they had a chance of turning things around here. She could cash in some of her investments and buy in to Ryan Vineyards as a partner, letting him retire a large chunk of his debt while she helped him get his financial feet on the ground again. He needed more from her than money, too. He needed her talents and connections, not to mention her enthusiasm, to bring his business practices into the twenty-first century.

She was confident enough in her own abilities to know that income from her own consulting firm would help keep them steady as they set things right together. They wouldn't be rich at first or most likely ever. They would have to work hard. But they would be working together.

Now what good were her lofty plans for their future? Brody had kept everything a secret. When would that stop? If he really had broken their engagement because of his father's illness, then ten years ago he hadn't trusted her enough to believe they could find a way to manage together.

And now he was doing the same thing again.

Of course her own performance had been less than stellar. It was true she hadn't told Brody she'd been fired, but she hadn't told him because she had been searching for the right way to explain, to help him see that being fired was a good thing for *both* of them, a great thing.

Now she wondered if she should bother. For all she knew Brody's plans might not include a commuter marriage. Quite possibly none of them had anything whatsoever to do with her. Sure, he was delighted she was in Kanowa Lake spending lonely winter nights in his bed, but the man had never mentioned a word about love or marriage.

On top of everything *else* he hadn't mentioned!

By now she was so upset that she didn't want to stay in his house another minute. She needed Hollymeade and a fresh perspective. She wasn't sure how she would tell him what she had found—since she shouldn't have been reading his mail or checking his files. But for the moment that detail seemed less important than just getting out of the house.

She was shaking with anger, and she wasn't sure her hands were steady enough to write him a note. She threaded her way through the house to gather her things and find her coat and boots. Brody could stew over her absence and invent his own explanations.

"*WHERE'S MY DAUGHTER?* Is she with you?"

Brody held out his cell phone and squinted through the winter gloom at the number, which was only identified as "California." On the way into town he had pulled over to the side of the road when the phone rang and, after glimpsing the screen, assumed the call was from Pablo Fontanello.

He had not expected the caller to be Jo's mother.

"Who is this?" he asked pleasantly, to buy himself time while he figured out what to say.

"This is Sophie Glenn, Jovitienne Miller's mother. And I know who you are."

He had nearly forgotten that Jo's birth certificate read Jovitienne. Years ago she had told him that when she was born Sophie had hoped that someday her baby daughter would need a first name she could use on its own. In preparation she had given her a doozy. Madonna. Cher. Jovitienne.

"This is Brody Ryan," he said, as his windshield rapidly disappeared in a layer of snow. "Are you certain you meant to call *me?*"

"Please put Jovitienne on the line."

"Mrs. Glenn, I'm in a car by myself. There's nobody here but me."

"Then where is she?"

"Have you tried her cell phone? That seems like a better possibility than calling a stranger out of the blue."

"Well, you're no stranger to my daughter, are you? I may have been out of the country when you and Jovitienne were spending all that time together as teenagers, but I kept my ear to the ground, and I put facts together. You think I never figured out why she went all the way to Massachusetts for college when she could have stayed in California? You think we don't have great universities *here?*"

The words were combative, but the voice was merely tremulous. Brody gave Jo's mother the benefit of the doubt, even if the woman *had* snooped until she'd discovered his connection to her daughter. Ten years ago they had been so sure nobody had figured it out, now he wondered how many others had known.

"Jo's fine," he said. "We just spent the morning fixing my sink, and she's still at my house. But she won't answer my phone, so it won't make sense to call her there. I'll ask her to call you. Don't worry about her."

"Don't worry?" Now Sophie's voice rose. "She's been fired from a job she adores, and you don't think I should worry?"

"I'm sorry?"

"Fired. The human relations director left a message on her answering machine. I was there taking down the Christmas tree I decorated for her that she never even saw. I heard! He gave instructions on when she could come to clear her desk. Because she's been *fired!*"

"Today? On a Saturday?" Brody asked, because it was the only thing he could think of.

"Of course not. I heard the message yesterday."

Jo had been fired *yesterday*. They had been together all evening through to this morning, and she hadn't told him.

"I'm sure there's a perfectly good explanation," he said in the same soothing voice he had cultivated in his father's final days. "She seems fi–"

"Then she didn't tell you?"

"Jo's fine," he continued. "Believe me. She was perfectly cheerful when I left."

"She hides her feelings. She learned how a long time ago. God knows she had to, since I always had enough for both of us. That's why I never mentioned you to her, even though it wasn't easy. She needed something that was just hers and had nothing to do with me. But she can't be taking this well, and now she won't talk to me. She's not answering my phone calls."

"If all this is true, and there's no other explanation

for what you heard, then maybe Jo's just trying to take some time to consider it. She'll tell us whcn she's ready."

His words sounded reasonable, even calm, but inside he was seething. He understood why Jo hadn't wanted to talk to her mother, but why hadn't she told *him?* What were they to each other? Was he just somebody to have fun with while she kept the most important parts of her life to herself?

"I'm going to worry until I hear from her," Sophie said.

"I'll tell her that," Brody promised. "I'll make sure she gets your message. She probably didn't want you to worry."

"Are you serious about my daughter?"

Brody didn't know what to say. And when he didn't know what to say, he said nothing.

"You *are,* then," Sophie said. "She deserves a good man. Her life hasn't been easy, and I'm not so self-absorbed I don't realize that. Bow out now if you don't think you can make her happy. It's not my place to interfere, and I won't, but please take care of her, whatever that means. Don't hurt her."

And with that, the line went dead.

At the moment Brody wasn't thinking about taking care of Jo. He was thinking about all the things she hadn't said to him since their reunion. Nothing about the real possibility of losing her job. Nothing about future plans.

Nothing about *them.*

He wasn't really a part of her life, so she didn't have to tell him anything.

Okay, he certainly had things he hadn't shared with *her,* but he was keeping silent about his own problems to keep her from getting in over her head.

He might keep his feelings to himself, the same way she did, but this was it. He'd reached the point of no return.

He got back on the road and turned toward home. He was going to tell Jo about Sophie's phone call and see what she had to say for herself.

CHAPTER TEN

ON THE WAY back to Hollymeade Jo listened to the radio, spurred to turn it on by the snow accumulating on the road. The news wasn't good. This storm was going to be major. In fact, in some nearby areas it already was.

Of course she would be fine. She had stocked Hollymeade's pantry with canned soup, tuna fish and peanut butter. The refrigerator contained a little fresh fruit, a loaf of bread, half a rotisserie chicken and a pound of ground beef. Even if the power went out in the house and affected the gas furnace, there was plenty of wood beside the back door. The house had two woodstoves and a fireplace, and she would stay warm until the snow was cleared away.

She wondered, though, why she was thinking this way. Why was she planning to stay? She needed to get back to California and tie up loose ends. She hadn't spoken to her mother in two days, and Sophie would be frantic. She needed to meet with her lawyer to be sure the termination agreement was agreeable, needed to clear her desk. Luckily, because Frank had a reputation for firing employees on a whim, there was nothing important in her files that she didn't already have copies of. Good thing, too, because Frank would have somebody standing over her as she packed.

What was keeping her here? Brody had made it clear

he didn't need her help to make the important decisions facing him. So what was the point of hanging around?

She knew better than to try to make the trip to Buffalo to get the next available flight without checking with the state police. She'd had one close call on these roads, and she didn't need another. The moment she got back to Hollymeade she would phone the police; then, if the news was favorable, she would head right out.

If Brody wanted to talk to her, he could call her cell, but in the short time she had been in the car, she had made a decision. She wasn't going to talk to him at all unless he came clean about his life and future. All the hurt she'd experienced ten years ago was pouring through her again. Yes, she was overreacting. Yes, she was not behaving like the adult she was. But she was entitled to her feelings, and she wasn't going to pretend them away anymore.

The Hollymeade driveway was covered with new snow, but not enough to cause a problem. Inside the house she called the state police and punched numbers until she found the desk she needed. The latest road report was an hour old, but at that time the roads had been clear enough to make her trip. She knew an hour could make a big difference, and she should proceed with an emergency plan in place.

Should she chance it? If she could just get thirty miles up the road, she could find a motel if she had to wait out the storm. She decided to risk it.

She had brought very little, and the kitchen bulletin board held simple instructions on how to close up the house. She cleaned out the refrigerator, then she followed the rest of the instructions before she packed, putting the quilt block with its newly completed Friendship Star border in her carry-on for safety until she could mail it to Ella.

She made three trips to the car and finally locked the front door behind her, rezipping the canvas tent before she edged her way down the icy front steps and around back to deposit the key under the vase.

"Goodbye, Hollymeade." The words caught in her throat. She didn't know when or if she would come back. She would like to be a real part of the Miller family again, but having Brody in Kanowa Lake would be a barrier. Ten years had passed, yet like a fool she had fallen in love with him all over again. Where Brody Ryan was concerned, her heart won every battle with her head.

She started the car; then, as it warmed again, she carefully scraped ice and snow off the windshield. The snowfall seemed thicker, but she was committed now. Thirty miles and she would be fine.

At last she carefully maneuvered her way up the rapidly disappearing driveway. She was almost to the road when she heard a familiar rumble and Brody's pickup, complete with plow, turned in to block her escape.

She slapped her palm against the steering wheel. She wasn't ready for a confrontation, but that was exactly what was about to happen unless she lied and told him she had a family emergency and needed to go home.

No, it was too late for lies. For that matter it had always been too late. It was time to lay her cards on the table.

She turned off the engine and got out, but she didn't close the door. She used it as a shield and stood behind it as he got out, too.

He wasn't smiling. "Did you need to run home for something?"

She was tempted to tell him yes, that she would follow, then turn the other way once she got out to the road. She had never realized how hard talking about her feelings was, but the proof was standing right in front of her.

"I'm going home to California," she said. "And you're in my way."

If anything he looked puzzled. "Home?"

"That's right. It's past time."

"And you just decided? Last I heard we were having dinner together."

She took a deep breath. "Last I heard we meant something to each other, even if you've never really said as much. Then I found out a few things about you, Brody, that made me see the light."

He looked startled. "You found out things about *me*?"

"Let's just say I've figured out a lot of things. That ten years ago you broke off our engagement because your father was dying and you didn't trust me enough to think I could handle it."

He didn't bother to deny it. "That was ten years ago, Jo."

"Right. So let's fast forward. You've been keeping things from me again. Like how badly you're in debt. Like all the ways you're thinking about getting out of it. Big things. Things you would share with somebody you trusted, somebody you loved! But you've never trusted me, Brody, and I should have figured that out the minute I figured out the part about your father. I don't know what I am to you, but whatever it is, it's not what I want to be."

"Exactly what are you talking about, and how do you know things I haven't told you?"

She ignored the last part. "You're thinking about selling Ryan Vineyards and maybe taking a job in California, but not close to me, Brody. Somewhere far enough that distance will still be an issue. Maybe that's why it's so appealing."

"You don't think you're part of my decisions? That I'm trying to do what's right for us both?"

"How would you know what's right for me? Have you ever asked? Have you ever suggested you might *love* me enough to make me part of your equation?"

"Me?" He stepped forward and around the door so there was nothing between them. "What about *you,* Jo? I just talked to your mother. She tells me you've been fired. When were you going to stop pretending you've been hanging around Kanowa Lake because you wanted to and not because you didn't have any other place you needed to be right now?"

She set aside the fact he had been talking to Sophie to consider later. "I was trying to think of the right way to tell you, because I knew you would see the whole thing differently than it really is."

"Right, you were *protecting* me."

She had never heard him be sarcastic. It made her angrier. "Stupid me. You know, figuring out how to spend time and energy is one of my most valuable skills. Apparently I just don't know how to apply what I know to myself. Not ten years ago, and certainly not now."

"So while we're at it? Are you going to pretend you weren't relieved when I canceled the engagement all those years ago? I was looking at you. You looked like somebody who'd had the weight of the world lifted off your shoulders!"

"That's because…" She stopped herself. "What do you care? If that's how you read it, it probably made things easier for you. Bravo. You got rid of me with less guilt. You were happy. I was happy. And now you can make me happy one last time by getting out of my way. I need to put some miles behind me this afternoon while I still can."

"You shouldn't be driving in this storm."

"Don't tell me what to do!"

He stared at her. A long moment. Then he shrugged, turned around and went back to his truck. Once he was inside the cab she watched the pickup back up, turn, back up, turn once more into the narrow drive. When Brody was finally facing the road he roared away. And when the sound of the truck died, the only thing she could hear was the soft rustle of snow falling all around her.

CHAPTER ELEVEN

BRODY WAS NEARLY home before he began to think clearly. Somehow Jo had found out about the job with Fontanello and the possibility of selling his family's land, although how was a mystery.

Unfortunately for him, now that his fury was waning—and despite all inclination not to—he was beginning to understand her feelings. In Jo's mind, not discussing the future had been a signal that he didn't want to include her in it.

How could she know that he saw his own silence as the most important gift he could give her? That he hadn't dumped all his troubles on her because he hadn't wanted to burden her?

He had done this for *her*. He hadn't wanted her to rescue him. He hadn't wanted her to suffer under the weight of his problems or decisions.

Wasn't that what a man did for the woman he loved? He gave her whatever he could, even if the only thing he could give her was peace of mind? Sure, he would have loved Jo's help. He had given up any hope of that by keeping silent. But that, too, had been a gift. He had given up something he valued to give her something much more valuable.

That was what you did when you loved somebody. You didn't think about your own needs. You thought about theirs.

Why couldn't she see that and understand?

He would have preferred to bathe in self-congratulations, but something about his own logic nagged at him. The whole problem felt familiar. Of course he'd been through this situation ten years ago, sacrificing his own needs to keep Jo from throwing away her future.

But the feeling that this was something more still nagged at him.

He pulled into his parking spot and turned off the engine, but he didn't get out of the pickup.

Jo had kept something important from him, as well. Both times. Ten years ago she had seemed pleased to end their engagement. He could swear he was right about that. But she hadn't said why. Not then, and not today, although she had started to explain before she stopped herself.

And yesterday, just yesterday, she hadn't told him she'd been fired.

What was it she'd said out on the road? That she had been trying to figure out how to tell him, because she wanted him to truly understand? Like she was trying to protect him from something, but what?

Like she, too, was trying to give him a gift.

Then he knew why this entire scenario felt so familiar.

"Unbelievable." He folded his arms on the steering wheel and rested his head on them, but not before he'd slammed his forehead against them three times. "What were we thinking?"

He sat bolt upright. The snow was falling harder, but even though it meant the roads would soon be dangerous, he wasn't sorry. Jo wouldn't be making good time on her trip to the Buffalo airport. She wasn't used to snow, and she drove as slowly as a teenager with a learn-

er's permit to avoid going off the road. In the days they'd
spent together he'd teased her about her lack of courage.

Even though there were miles between them now,
he could still catch her.

He turned the key in the ignition and set off again
to do just that.

"SOUTHERN CALIFORNIA, HERE I come," Jo said as her
SUV slid on a slick spot on the road and for a moment
the wheels lost their grip.

She was saying goodbye to snow. Saying goodbye to
shopping at stores with few choices and fewer business
hours. Saying goodbye to zipping herself into countless
layers just to get the mail. Saying goodbye to a lack of
job opportunities and a need to create her own job. Saying goodbye to Brody's old house with its drafty rooms
in desperate need of paint and enthusiasm. Saying goodbye to Hollymeade and the Miller family.

Saying goodbye to Brody.

She swallowed hard, but tears filled her eyes anyway. What was it he'd implied? That she had been part
of all his decisions? Well, right, that was easy to say,
but what signs had she seen? He had never let her in.
He had kept her out of every important development
in his life. He had never told her how deeply in debt he
was, for starters.

And why not? As she slowed the car to a crawl, she
explored the question like a sore tooth. Of course there
was ego involved. What man wanted to admit he was
in that kind of trouble? But Brody never pretended to
be someone he wasn't. So maybe that wasn't all of it.

Maybe he hadn't shared his situation because he
didn't think she mattered enough. That was the explanation that hurt most. But to be fair, she couldn't

buy that one completely, either. Because she had seen the way he looked at her when he didn't think she was watching. Like a hungry man staring in a restaurant window. And not because he'd always been in the mood to jump into bed. The expression had been desire, yes, but a different kind.

The desire to connect? To share?

She shook her head. She had a great imagination for somebody whose job had rarely required it.

"You're a sucker, Jovitienne Miller," she said, rubbing one eye, then the other, with her palm before her hand dropped back to the steering wheel.

Of course she had to be fair, because, well, that's who she was. She hadn't leveled with Brody, either. Now, of course, there was no reason to. The chance had passed. But even if she had been able to tell him, he probably wouldn't have seen her hesitation as the gift it was. He probably wouldn't have understood that she had been trying to find a way to make him see the truth, that her silence had been the right thing for him, if not for her.

And why did that sound familiar? Brody had said that he'd kept everything from her *for* her, for both of them. And she knew that everything she had done had been for *him*.

Because she loved the guy.

And what did a woman who loved a man do?

She cut off her beautiful hair to buy him a watch chain for the watch he had pawned to buy her a comb for her hair.

In the end neither of them had anything of value, except their love.

Ten feet down the road she tapped the brakes until she was only crawling; then carefully, teeth gritted, she made a wide turn, wheels slipping as she went.

She breathed a deep sigh of relief when she was going back the way she had just come, in the direction of Kanowa Lake.

She couldn't believe it. She and Brody had been as foolish as the young couple in *The Gift of the Magi,* but unlike them, at the end of their fight they hadn't held on to what was most dear. They had given each other the gift of silence, and what a terrible price they had paid.

She just hoped it wasn't too late to change things.

AT FIRST BRODY couldn't believe the car coming his way was Jo's. Snow was falling thick and fast now, but the little SUV that looked so much like her rental was making excellent time. That meant it couldn't be Jo.

But it was. In a moment he saw her face behind the slapping of her windshield wipers. She slowed as he drew closer, and in a moment they had both stopped, ten yards from each other.

He opened his door and hopped down. Her door opened, and she got out. But this time she didn't use her door as a shield. This time she started toward him, slipping once but staying upright, as he loped awkwardly in her direction.

There was no hesitation. He threw his arms around her and held her close. She wrapped her arms around his waist.

"I found out my father was dying just days before I broke the engagement," he said, into her hair. "I knew it was going to be a terrible thing, a slow and awful way to die, and I knew you would stand right beside me the whole time, because that's the person you are. I couldn't do that to you. I'm sorry. I made a terrible mistake."

"Right before you came to tell me, I had a pregnancy scare." She looked up at him. "I thought I was having your baby, and I was so frightened. When it turned out not to be true I was so relieved. I realized I wasn't ready to be a mother, but I thought you wanted children right away. And the whole thing scared me to death."

He cupped her face in his hands. "We were kids. We weren't ready for kids. But we would have figured that out together."

"I wasn't glad you broke the engagement. I was just glad I didn't have to tell you what I'd gone through, that you would never have to know."

"I'm in terrible debt, Jo. The doctors thought experimental surgery might help Dad, but our insurance wouldn't pay for it. We mortgaged everything, even sold off some land. In the end it didn't help, and we haven't been able to dig ourselves out."

"I know. I was on your computer today. I was going to surprise you with a great new business plan, do all the work for you, for us. I saw."

"That's how you found out about Fontanello's offer?"

"I saw the email. I didn't start out intending to snoop, but I just got deeper and deeper. I—"

He kissed her. "A new business plan for *us?*"

"When I found out my boss had fired me I was so happy, Brody. It was the kick I needed. I'd begun thinking about going out on my own anyway, about helping small businesses like yours move up to the next level. I thought it would be fun, and I knew I could make it a success. I have contacts everywhere. I'm not bragging, but everybody who matters knows how good I am. I just couldn't figure out how to make you believe me. I was afraid you'd think I was settling for less when I could have more. I was trying to figure out how to make you see."

"See?"

"I want to be *here,* in Kanowa Lake, with *you.* I want to invest in the vineyards, get the business side off the ground, help you fix up the house and have your kids."

"That's a tall order." But he was grinning now, while his eyes shone. "It's not going to be easy, Jo, you know that? Even with an influx of cash, we'll still have a million miles to go uphill. It might be easier if we sell and start over together in Napa."

"Do you want to move to Napa?"

"This is my home."

"But I'm freezing out here, and it's not snowing in Napa."

"Do you care?"

"As long as we're together?" She wound her arms around his neck. "I don't care about anything except you, Brody. I love this place. My happiest memories are here. I say, let it snow!"

"Let it snow, then," he said.

"Just promise you'll keep me warm?"

"That will be the easiest part," he said, right before he kissed her.

* * * * *

YOU BETTER WATCH OUT

Janice Kay Johnson

CHAPTER ONE

"THESE ARE SPECTACULAR." The owner of the art gallery in the Pioneer Square area of Seattle surveyed the newly unpacked ceramic pieces with a keen eye. It was a moment before she added with discernible surprise, "Your work is changing."

Letting anyone else see her art always stirred a mix of feelings, but today Ella Torrence was torn between pride and more anxiety than usual. Her nervous glance took in the half-dozen ceramic pieces she had brought for display and sale.

"I don't want to get stale." As good an explanation as any for the new direction in an artistic process that remained a mystery to her. What she did know was that the evolution of her style had accelerated in the past six months. She even knew what had triggered the change: the call from her cousin Jo asking her to help finish piecing the wedding quilt for another of her cousins.

The call had made her part of her mother's family again, something she'd never anticipated. Never thought she deserved.

At the reminder of the quilt, her gaze flicked toward the plate-glass front windows. She wished she could see her car from here. She'd considered herself lucky to find a parking place only a block away from the gallery, but hated to have the Subaru out of her sight today. The precious quilt top, packaged and ready to go in the mail, currently sat on the floor of the passenger side. Ella had finished her part—a wide, appliquéd and embroidered border—and her next stop was the post office, where she would mail the quilt top to Rachel in Australia.

Looking again at her ceramic art, she was startled anew by how sinuous and sensual and feminine her pieces had become. This past year she'd left behind wheel and slab work for coil techniques, which allowed her to create elongated, graceful, impossibly narrow necks on the plump, shapely bottles, if that was the right word for something so nonfunctional. Just lately, the patterns she'd created by etching, glazing and even screen printing seemed to subtly draw on traditional textiles. Her eye rested on the most rounded— pregnant?—piece, on which an elusive pastel design, taken from a traditional quilt pattern, stretched like skin over the swell and became nearly transparent.

This turn in her artistic evolution unnerved Ella. She didn't think of herself as very feminine. She lived most often in glaze-and-clay-stained jeans or overalls, faded T-shirts and sweatshirts, and brightly colored— if battered—canvas Converse tennis shoes. Today, she had dressed up to present a professional image for the gallery owner's benefit. And maybe, too, for the momentous trip to the post office.

"You do like these?" she asked, then tried to hide her cringe. *Beg for reassurance, why don't you?*

Rebecca Stirling ran a finger over the curve of the very piece Ella had eyed most nervously. "Are you kidding? I'm coveting. I may have to buy this one myself. Honestly, I'll be shocked if these aren't gone within a couple of weeks, max. You do have more to replace them?"

Ella smiled to hide her doubt. "Yes, of course. Listen, I've got to run," she said. "I only paid for a half hour of parking." A few words about pricing, and she was out the door.

Even in early afternoon, traffic was stop-and-go on First Avenue, becoming yet more snarled when a parking place opened up and a driver had to maneuver to squeeze into it. The sidewalks were busy, too, with shoppers coming in and out of galleries and boutiques. The occasional homeless person—mostly men—clogged the sidewalk further, begging for spare change.

At the corner, Ella had to wait for the light to change, then dodged a cyclist illegally using the sidewalk.

Relieved to finally cross, she looked to where she'd left her aging red Subaru station wagon, only to notice that it seemed to be poking out into traffic.

She hadn't parked *that* badly, Ella thought indignantly. Had it been rear-ended and pushed forward into the single southbound lane? That might have happened if she'd left the wheels turned out. Oh, God—how much damage…?

At that moment, to her shock, the Subaru moved, pulling out into a gap in the line of traffic and starting forward. Already running, she frantically scanned the line of parked cars in case—please God—there was *another* red Subaru there, and it wasn't hers that she was watching drive away.

No, no, no…!

Tearing along the crowded sidewalk, she was blind to anything but her car, braking for a red light at the next corner. She could catch it…

She plowed into something—somebody—and went sprawling painfully onto the pavement.

BRETT HOLLISTER was having a crappy day. Topping off a crappy week and even a crappy month.

That morning, the jury had come back with a verdict for his client of "Guilty on all charges, Your Honor." The guy was a sleazebag, no question, but Brett had been sure he'd introduced enough doubt to get him off. He'd have sworn the jurors looked sympathetic during his closing argument.

Except maybe the middle-aged woman on the end, the one with the crimped mouth. He grimaced. And the former army major—Brett had reluctantly let him on to the jury because you had to choose your battles.

Edward Dunning, a senior partner in the firm, had reamed him out over lunch: "Why didn't you request an investigator's report at that juncture?"

"It's not my job to prove the client's innocence," Brett argued. "We gave the jury enough to chew on, and I didn't want to confuse them."

Dunning's expression didn't soften. His eyes were glacial. "You were wrong, weren't you?"

"Nobody wins 100 percent of the time."

"You came damn close when you actually cared about your job." The partner scrawled his signature on the credit card slip, pocketed his wallet and stood. "Your work is becoming increasingly shoddy, Hollister. Be aware. You're on thin ice with us." He took in Brett's shell-shocked expression, nodded and walked out.

Torn between anger and nausea, Brett followed more slowly. He wanted to protest that the judgment was unfair, but you didn't argue too hard with your boss if you knew what was good for you. You sure as hell didn't tell him your client *deserved* to serve a very long stretch behind bars.

Shocked at his own thought, he stopped in the middle of the restaurant. For God's sake, he was a defense attorney. Guilt or innocence wasn't the point; constitutional rights were.

Winning was.

Finally reaching the door, Brett asked himself whether he'd done his best on the case. He wanted to think so, but… He winced away from the memory of the party he'd attended last week when maybe he shouldn't have taken the time off.

In a cascade effect, he remembered all the people he had disappointed lately. Julia, his most recent lover, who six weeks or so ago had cut him loose, calling him "undependable." His father, voice both sharp with anger and heavy with disappointment, when he'd called three weeks ago to find out why Brett had missed his mother's sixty-fifth birthday party the previous night.

The foreman's sonorous voice from this morning played in a continuous loop in his head as he walked out of the restaurant.

Guilty on all charges.

He paused to take his keys from his pocket. Becoming aware that someone was running down the sidewalk toward him, he turned. Too late. The woman slammed into him, bounced and went down.

Even at a glance, it was obvious that she was no drunk. Thick, corn-silk hair spilled from some arrangement at her nape. She wore a formfitting, royal-blue knit dress over leggings and knee-high boots. No purse that he could see. He had the fleeting impression of a body that was slim, strong, lithe and sexy.

Even as he dropped to his knee, she was already struggling to get up.

"Are you all right?" he asked.

Scraped palms told him she wasn't. But her distraught expression went right past him as if he was invisible.

"My car!"

"What?" He stood as she did, using his body to protect her from being jostled as well as from the curious stares of passing people.

He'd swear she didn't even look at his face before her gaze dropped with the intensity of a laser to the keys still in his hand.

"Are you parked close by?" She was not only out of breath, she sounded frantic.

Brett gestured toward his pride and joy, tucked neatly at the curb right in front of them.

"Someone just stole my car," she gasped. Her desperate gaze now fastened on his face. "Please, I need to follow it."

Compared to going back to the office, chasing a stolen car sounded like just the pick-me-up he needed right now. So he pressed the remote to unlock his Corvette ZR1, loped to the driver's side and leaped in. Moving even faster, the woman was already in the passenger seat, buckling her seat belt.

Taking advantage of a probably-too-slim opening in traffic, he put the Corvette in gear and exploded out of the parking spot. Horns sounded behind him, but he didn't give a damn.

"Can you see your car?"

"We're so low to the ground… Yes!" Triumph lit her voice. "I think that's it, almost two blocks ahead. It's the red Subaru station wagon."

He seized on a hesitation in oncoming traffic to swerve illegally around a car that was pausing in hopes of finding a parking space. Half the downtown streets were one-way, but not First, wouldn't you know. "Watch in case your car turns," he said tersely, riding the bumper in front of him.

She leaned forward as far as the seat belt allowed, her nose all but pressed to the windshield. "I don't see it... Oh, no! It *is* turning."

He consulted a mental map. "Spring Street?"

"Yes. I think so."

"Did you call 911?"

"Call...? Oh." She clapped a hand to her mouth. "I left my phone on the seat."

Brett muttered a profanity and grabbed his own phone from his belt, thrusting it at her. "Here, call."

The hands that took it from him were shaking. "Don't lose it. Please don't lose it."

"This car accelerates from zero to sixty in three point four seconds. No station wagon is getting away from me."

The phone ringing against her ear, she cast him a dubious glance. "But you can't go sixty downtown. Or even twenty-five, or thirty, so what good does that do? Hello?" Her voice changed. Brett listened as she reported the theft and their current location. He heard the dispatcher, in a slightly alarmed tone, counsel her not to make any attempt to intercept the stolen vehicle. His unexpected passenger cut the dispatcher off midsentence.

"You still see it?"

"Yeah." He relaxed a little as they closed some of the distance. His first assumption had been that the thief was heading for the freeway, but no—a blinking signal dutifully gave notice that the Subaru would be turning north on Fourth. Did car thieves use turn signals?

Yeah, he decided, they did if they didn't want to get pulled over and have to produce a license and registration.

"Brett Hollister," he said to the woman, removing his hand from the gear shift and holding it out.

From his peripheral vision he saw her look at his hand for a long moment.

"Oh, um, I'm Ella. Ella Torrence." After a further, noticeable hesitation, she placed her hand in his and they shook.

For a very pretty woman she had interesting calluses.

"Your car doesn't look all that new," he commented.

Her vivid blue eyes flicked his way. "You mean, it doesn't cost anything near what *yours* does."

"You have something against Corvettes?"

"They seem to be manufactured for the sole purpose of speeding." She wriggled a little. "And it's not all that comfortable." Her rather cute nose wrinkled. "At least you didn't buy it in a look-at-me color."

His jaw set. "Like red, you mean?"

"I bought my Subaru used. For a good price. I didn't care about color."

His mouth twitched as his sense of humor returned. "I did. Cops keep a sharper eye out for brighter colors. Silver slides by unnoticed."

"So you *do* get speeding tickets."

"Uh…" Two in the last year, actually. He'd gotten a little more careful lately. "You were glad to hop in."

There was a moment of silence. "You're right," she said, chastened. "I'm sorry. I can't tell you how much I appreciate this. Not everyone would have agreed to take me on such a…" She hesitated.

"Wild-goose chase?"

"It won't be if we catch up," she said grimly.

The car turned right on Pike. Going for the freeway, after all? No, left on Eighth. Brett wove in and out of traffic, mentally converting yellow lights to green. No squad car had appeared, much less closed in on them. Less than a block separated him from the Subaru. He was beginning to wonder what he *would* do when he caught up.

"What year is it?" he asked, his eye on the square back of her Subaru.

Her tense stance didn't change. "'95."

"Good God. Why don't you let him have it?"

"It's not the car. I don't care about the car. It's..." She almost sounded on the verge of tears. "It's this package I was going to mail. I can't lose it. I can't!"

They'd dodged onto Olive Way now. They'd be coming up on a northbound freeway entrance momentarily. Interestingly, the driver kept going once they passed over I-5. Toward Capitol Hill. The Subaru took a quick left turn, then, a block later, a right one.

"He's spotted us," Ella said.

"Yeah, I think he has." Brett pressed lightly on the accelerator and the Corvette leaped forward. Only one other car separated them from hers. The tension was contagious. He couldn't take his eyes off the back of that Subaru.

"What's in the package?" he asked. Wouldn't it be his luck if this was the moment he found out he was mixed up in a stolen drug shipment.

"A quilt. Actually," she amended, "a quilt top."

"A *what?*" Then, "Oh, crap."

The light had switched to red ahead of them at Broadway, a major north-south thoroughfare. His prey had barely hesitated before turning just ahead of the oncoming southbound traffic. Unfortunately, the car in front of Brett's wasn't making a right. It had braked and sat stolidly, waiting. A parked car blocked any possibility that he could make it past.

"Oh, my God, oh, my God." She kept murmuring it, grating on his nerves.

"We'll catch up!" he snapped. "Give it a rest."

She slumped. "It's just that this is so important. It's…" She closed her eyes. "I knew I'd mess this up. I should never have agreed to help. What was I *thinking?*"

Brett wasn't sure he'd ever heard a tone of such bleak despair before and, considering that he was a criminal defense attorney, *bleak* and *despair* were emotions he witnessed frequently.

The light blinked green. His voice gentled. "Will you tell me why this matters so much?"

CHAPTER TWO

THIS MAN—BRETT HOLLISTER—had really been astonishingly nice. Without him, she wouldn't have had a chance. Her car and the quilt would have been long gone.

Ella took a covert look at him. Until this moment, she'd barely been aware of him in any way that didn't have to do with his being useful.

Well, that wasn't entirely true. She *had* realized that he was young and good-looking, although not in a way that usually attracted her. He was too stylish, too yuppie, too obviously aware of his appeal. His suit shouted *money* as much as his car did. His brown hair was midlength and styled to be a little spiky. His tie… Okay, she actually liked his tie; it had an asymmetrical geometric print in colors that clashed just enough to be eye-catching. The artist in her observed that he had a strong face, with prominent bones, a nose that was probably too big but worked anyway, a lopsided smile and eyes of a warm gray. He was clearly athletic, although she suspected a private downtown health club could be thanked for his physique. A man who worked with his hands didn't dress like that.

He seemed to be appraising her, too. Excruciatingly conscious of the ticking seconds that might keep them from catching the scumbag who'd stolen her car, Ella tried to convince herself that's why her skin prickled.

Not because those gray eyes glinted in a way she hadn't seen in a long time.

"There might be some tissues in the glove compartment," he said. "You could use spit to clean up."

"Clean up?" She looked down at her hands just as she became aware of the sting. "Oh."

As she extracted a handful of tissues, he said, "Your leggings are toast."

Her knees stung, too, come to think of it. She was spitting on the tissue—so sanitary—when the light changed. She opened her mouth to say something but the Corvette accelerated so fast it pressed her back into her seat. This guy was throwing himself heart and soul into the chase. The growl of the engine let her know how much power was under the hood. The scenery out her side window passed in a blur. Apparently, Brett didn't mind risking a ticket.

Or maybe he believed his silver Corvette could become invisible, she thought with a spurt of semi-hysterical humor.

She cleaned her hands even as she strained to see ahead.

Brett glanced at her. "He can't have gotten far. The way traffic's backed up, he probably got stuck at the next light."

Ella nodded and wadded the soiled tissues.

"Waste bag is behind the seat."

When she faced forward again, he was smiling with satisfaction. "Bastard turned off." He swerved left and shot up the cross street. Indeed, several blocks ahead, the Subaru was slowing for yet another turn, as if it was circling to go back the way it had come.

"I wonder if I dare try to cut him off," he muttered.

"Oh, God. I don't know."

"Best not."

They were going way too fast for this narrow street and in what was now a residential neighborhood. But Ella didn't protest.

"What is it about the quilt— top?—that has you so wound up?"

Ella wasn't much for talking about the past, especially such a painful part of it. He deserved an explanation, though.

"I grew up back East, until my dad got a job out here in Seattle when I was eleven and we moved. I had a lot of family on my mother's side there. I used to spend part of every summer at my grandparents' place in upstate New York, in this amazing old house. There were a bunch of cousins who were close to me in age, and we had a great time together. Toward the end, though—" She braced herself as they took a corner with another startling jerk. There was no way her Subaru could have turned that sharply. "Everything was changing. I was the youngest, you see. That last summer, I was eleven and sort of trailing behind the other girls. I felt left out when they talked about boys and middle school dances and high school, but even so…" This was way more than he could possibly want to hear. "It doesn't matter," she said with a shrug, not looking at him. "The thing is, I never saw any of them again. My family moved, then my mom got sick, and she died when I was fourteen. My grandparents and a couple of the aunts and uncles came out for the funeral, but I was all but catatonic." Not just with grief—or, at least, not straightforward, clean grief. But that was something she had never told a soul. Something only she and her father knew, and it had poisoned her already difficult relationship with him.

And probably, she thought painfully, all other relationships since. Another thing Brett Hollister didn't need to know.

"My father didn't especially like my mother's side of the family, or they him. And I—" How to explain without touching on her guilt? There was no way. "Um, I lost touch."

His brief, sidelong glance echoed her realization of how lame that conclusion was. He sensed there was more to the story.

Well, tough.

But he didn't press. He concentrated on his driving, and she focused on her surroundings. They were on a winding road, racing through a park she didn't remember ever seeing before. Tactical error on the thief's part—there were no cross streets.

"Call 911 again," Brett said urgently. "He doesn't appreciate having us on his bumper, and I'm not sure what to do next. If he keeps on at this speed, once he gets into a residential area again, I may have to drop back."

She called 911, and was told—again—that units would be notified, but pursuit wasn't recommended. She ended the call midlecture.

"Apparently they think we should just let him go," she said, frustrated.

Brett flashed her a wicked smile. "It's not in me to quit." The smile dimmed suddenly, and she couldn't help noticing the way his hands flexed on the leather-covered steering wheel. He'd disturbed himself, and she had no idea why.

"Go on," he prompted. "How does the quilt fit into this?"

She told him about the phone call from her cousin Rachel. "One of my cousins, the oldest, Olivia, is getting married at Christmas. Her mother had started a quilt for her, but died last year before she could finish more than the central panel. My grandmother taught all of us girl cousins to quilt, so two of them and I are going to finish the quilt before the wedding. We're integrating fabrics into the quilt that hold memories for Olivia and Eric—the guy she's marrying. His mother let my cousin Jo tear apart a couple of baby quilts of his, for example." She stopped herself. As if he cared what fabric they used in the quilt. "I did my part, a border—" She could see from his expression he didn't know what she was talking about, but she went on regardless. "I had it wrapped and ready to go in the mail to Rachel, who will make another border to finish the top. Then, before the wedding, we're all meeting up to hand-quilt it—to assemble the layers and stitch them together. My grandparents are gone now, but the cottage— Hollymeade—is still in the family. We were going to meet there and...I'd have been a part of the family again." This was so hard to say. "Only now..."

His hand left the gearshift to grip hers, which was lying on her lap. He hadn't even had to turn his head to find her hand. His clasp was strong and comforting.

"We'll get it back," he promised.

Recklessly, in her opinion. But she clung gratefully to the hand holding hers until he had to shift down to make another turn.

THE CHASE HAD begun to seem endless. Where *were* the cops, goddam it?

A couple of worries began to intrude in Brett's mind. The first was the debacle of a trial he'd lost and the luncheon he'd just suffered through. After a reprimand by a senior partner, a properly humble junior would be wise to have immediately returned to work, making sure he was seen to be slaving away. The way Brett had chosen to spend his afternoon instead was unlikely to impress the partners.

But do I care?

Brett shook off that disturbing thought. Of more immediate concern was the fact that his gas gauge was on the descending side of the arc. The tank hadn't been much above half full when they started.

"Was your gas tank full?" he asked abruptly.

She looked startled, then alarmed. "Not full. Half? Three quarters? I don't pay that much attention."

"Until you run out?"

"Until the light comes on. That gives me another gallon, which is thirty miles or so." She cleared her throat. "I don't suppose you dare take that risk, do you?"

"My mileage is better than you'd think. Twenty-one highway."

She pursed her lips.

"The car's worth it."

"If you can afford the gas."

Her dismissive attitude rubbed him like a careless touch on raw skin. He'd *worked* for this car. He was neither lazy nor careless.

So why was he acting like such a jerk lately? Something was going on with him, and he didn't know what. Only knew the goals that used to matter so much had lost their luster.

One-upping Dad by making partner at a younger age than he had? Shallow.

Okay, how about this one? Making his father proud.

Worthy, but… His mind stuttered to a stop, unable to finish a thought rooted in discontent, one he had a bad feeling would shake him out of all his certainties.

He was glad to be yanked back to the present chase

when the Subaru ahead made it through a light he
didn't. Ella looked anxious, but less so than she had
the last time this had happened. Was she beginning to
have faith in him?

"So why didn't your mother's family make more of
an effort to stay in touch with you?" he asked, turning
his edgy mood in a more useful direction. "You were
a kid. Why would they expect you to do all the work?"

She froze, her tapping fingers going still. It was a
long moment before she angled her head to look at him.
"What does it matter?"

"It matters to you," he pointed out. "It has something to do with why this quilt is so important to you."

"Yes, but…" She swallowed and glanced away. "I
don't like to talk about it."

Brett waited with his usual patience.

"Haven't you ever made a mistake?" she asked at
last, hostility vibrating in her voice.

As smooth as a switchblade, the question slid between his ribs. He was having trouble breathing for a
minute.

"Yeah." He cleared his throat. "I let my mom down
not that long ago." He looked away from her for a moment. "She gave me hell for it."

"What did you do?"

"She turned sixty-five. Dad had planned a special
evening. Family, good friends. It was supposed to be a
surprise." He thought about that. "I guess it was. Especially the part where her son didn't show up."

Her lips parted. "Where were you instead?"

"A couple of friends had invited me to spend the
weekend on a sailboat in the San Juan Islands." He felt
like scum, remembering his thoughtlessness. "I forgot

my mother's birthday party. Until the Sunday morning afterward, when I woke up and remembered."

"Oh, no," Ella murmured.

"You know that stupid saying, about how you don't have to say you're sorry to people who love you? I'm here to tell you, you say the damn words anyway, and they're so inadequate you're left with a taste like acid in your mouth."

She didn't immediately respond, which he appreciated. Quick platitudes were useless. What she finally did say was, "At least she was alive to hear your apology. And you have time to convince her she really does matter to you."

"Yeah," he said roughly. "You're right. Relatively speaking, my screwup doesn't hold much weight, does it?"

She looked at him in alarm. "What do you mean?"

"Compared to whatever's bothering you."

"That's not what I meant…" she replied quickly.

"The difference is, you were a fourteen-year-old kid. I'm thirty-three. Old enough to have grown out of self-centeredness, you'd think." He said it harshly.

He hadn't realized that his hand had knotted into a fist on his thigh until she covered it with hers and gave it a squeeze. He stared down at her hand, long-fingered and slender, with short, unpainted nails, and felt a completely unfamiliar clutch of pleasure/pain.

He focused ahead. "Damn. We're both at the same red light. I could run up there and drag the son of a bitch out of your car. If I'm going to do it, it has to be *now*."

CHAPTER THREE

ALMOST PARALYZED by temptation, Ella stared ahead.

"Surely he'll have the doors locked. What would we do? Hammer at the windows?"

Beside her, Brett made an impatient movement. "Dammit. We'd be left flat-footed when the light changed." The next moment he reached for the door handle. "What the hell. We'll catch up."

Ella grabbed his arm. "But…what if he has a gun?" She was prepared to do almost anything to get back the quilt, but she wouldn't be able to live with Brett getting hurt.

Right this second, though, she didn't care so much if *she* got hurt.

She fought with the seat-belt release and opened her door. Swearing, Brett grabbed for her, but he was too late.

So was she. The light turned green as she stood. The driver behind them leaned on his horn and she spun to glare at him before jumping into the Corvette again.

Without a word, Brett accelerated. When she turned her head, though, his jaw was clenched. He was mad.

"The quilt's on the floor of the passenger side. I thought, if that side wasn't locked…"

"Use your head," he snapped. "Why would it be unlocked? He'd have broken in on the driver's side."

"Don't tell me to use my head!" she flared. "You were about to charge up there, too!"

He had a few forceful things to say, the gist being that he was big and brawny—read male—and she wasn't.

They didn't speak for quite a while after that.

In the absence of conversation, Ella called 911 again and this time stayed on the line for ages, to no avail. The Subaru bolted onto the freeway, then off at Roanoke. With construction happening on Eastlake, they almost lost him altogether.

Once a visual had been regained, Ella stole a few looks at Brett. She supposed she'd impugned his masculinity—not so smart when she was depending on his sense of chivalry. It was also possible that she'd really scared him. Worse yet, she was embarrassed to realize that he was right. Of course the car thief wouldn't have unlocked the passenger-side door.

She opened her mouth and tried to make herself say, *You were right,* but absolutely could not force the words out.

"What do you do for a living?" she asked. There, open communication, she congratulated herself. This was better anyway.

It was a minute before he answered, and then it sounded reluctant. "Attorney." There was a long pause. "What about you?"

Since his voice had relaxed, she told him about her art, answered a few questions and asked her own, learning that he was a criminal defense attorney. He admitted to having lost at trial only this morning.

"My fault." His hands squeezed rhythmically on the wheel. He'd wear out the leather wrap if he kept venting his stress that way. "The partners seem sure."

"Was your client innocent?"

"Innocent?" Lines gathered on his forehead. "I can't let myself think of them that way—guilty or innocent."

"You defend them no matter what." She'd always struggled with that concept.

"Every person should be entitled to that much." He sounded stiff. "It's one of the rights that makes America what it is."

Ella considered him. "You don't sound as if you really believe that."

"I do." Furrows gathered on his forehead, and he rolled his shoulders. "I have my moments, that's all."

Moments? Ella sensed it was more than that. Nonetheless, she nodded, accepting his unwillingness to say more. He hadn't pushed that much when she'd balked earlier.

"I defend some real scum," he said, surprising her. "Mostly rich scum. Get some of them off, too." His mouth crooked up. "Most of them. I'm good at what I do."

Why was it she felt certain his renewed cocky good humor was put-on and not real?

As if anxious to leave the subject behind, he talked about his family. He had followed in his father's footsteps, although his father was now a judge. "Fortunately, not a court I would normally appear in, anyway. Unfortunately, he's good friends with a partner in my firm."

"Did he help you get the job?" she asked, then regretted the question.

Brett shot her an unreadable sidelong look. "I graduated at the top of my class and had the pick of jobs."

"I'm sorry…"

He shook his head. "I don't blame you for wondering. I did join the same firm where my father was partner until he went on the bench. Family tradition."

She tried to apologize again. He shook it off.

"Listen—I don't know where this chase is getting us. What if we drop back a little, make this guy believe he's gotten away? Then he might go home to roost."

"Or run out of gas."

"I'm the one who is in danger of that. A sports car doesn't get the mileage a Subaru does. If you had as much in the tank as you think…"

She pictured it—the Corvette slowing to a stop, her Subaru disappearing into the distance.

"Yes, all right."

After falling behind, the pursuit was trickier. They caught only occasional glimpses of red. The ruse seemed to work, though, because the route became less winding, as if the thief was no longer just fleeing, but was on his way somewhere. Eventually, she realized they were heading for Ballard or… No, they continued over the narrow strait that connected saltwater Lake Union to Puget Sound. Then the Subaru disappeared.

"Magnolia?" Sounding incredulous, Brett made the turn.

Did the thief hope he could lose them in this neighborhood of steep hills and winding streets? It was a strange choice, though, because Magnolia was essentially an island, connected to the mainland of the city by only a few roads. She called 911 again.

But the Subaru dodged a couple of times, and when Brett crested another hill, he saw absolutely no sign of their prey.

Tension built in Ella again as he cruised up and down streets, even risking his Corvette's suspension by bumping down rutted alleys. Nothing.

The marked Seattle P.D. car finally located them. Brett pulled to the curb and Ella erupted onto the sidewalk. "We've been begging for help for hours! Why couldn't we get it? Now my car is gone." For the first time, tears threatened.

"I apologize, ma'am," the officer said stiffly. "We have to prioritize. We'll probably find your car in the next few days, you know. If it was a newer one, I'd have guessed this was a professional job. But a '95... Could be a teenager." He looked apologetic. "With luck it won't have suffered much damage."

Brett came up behind Ella and wrapped an arm around her. Shaking, she let herself lean a little into his solid warmth. "It's not the car. It's what was in it."

When she explained, she saw something like pity on the officer's face. "Depends on who stole it. Unfortunately, no matter what, there's less of a chance we'll recover contents than the vehicle itself."

He took down all the information and then drove away. Ella stood, stunned, thinking, *It was all for nothing. The quilt's gone.*

Oh, dear lord, she'd have to tell Rachel and Jo about her failure. Ella moaned and bent forward, wrapping her arms around her stomach.

JUST DOWN THE block from Brett's condominium was a Thai restaurant that delivered. When the doorbell rang, he paid for the food, accepted the containers and took them to the dining table.

Ella had argued about coming to his condo for dinner, but after one look at her, white-faced and miserable, he'd refused to drop her off at her place, as she wanted. His condominium in the upscale Belltown neighborhood was closer anyway.

She hadn't even assessed it the way she had his car. He'd have liked to see disdain, a pursing of the lips that told him she was judging, *bachelor pad*. But no. All she did was plop down where he pointed her, and keep saying some variation of, "I don't believe it," before stumbling all over herself to thank him because, really, she was incredibly grateful. She knew he'd *tried*. The word made him sick to his stomach. So much for redeeming himself. *Tried* was a weak-ass word. He hadn't come through for her, any more than he'd come through for anyone else lately.

Despite his own frustration, he concentrated on Ella. Feeling sorry for himself wouldn't do her any good, and she was the one really hit by their failure.

No, he wasn't going to let himself off that easy. By *his* failure.

A glass of wine reduced the misery on her face, but initially she gazed without interest at the food he laid out. Finally, though, she served herself a spring roll and eyed the entrees he'd bought.

He tried to distract her with conversation while they ate—courtroom anecdotes he hoped would make her laugh. Her face was expressive, once he knew to watch for the subtle signs. They talked about their favorite foods, recent movies they'd watched, good books. Here and there, Brett hoped maybe she actually forgot about today's disaster for a few moments.

Or maybe not. At a pause while he refilled his plate, she said, "I locked it. I know I did."

"Windows rolled all the way up?" It had been a warm day.

He felt as if he'd hit her when he saw her expression. "No. Oh, God. I left them cracked. So the interior wouldn't be so hot. I don't—" She swallowed. "Didn't have air-conditioning."

"Hot-wiring a car doesn't take that long. Who pays

attention to someone fiddling under the hood for a minute? You think, Poor sucker, car that won't start, not, Hey, I wonder if he's trying to steal that car."

Ella moaned.

At that moment, Brett had the strangest sensation, as if an alien spirit had possessed him. Or maybe it was simpler than that. He had the flicker of a memory, the cop saying, "We have to prioritize."

And he realized that *his* priorities had undergone a tectonic shift. No conscious decision on his part. The fault line had been there for a while, but this day with Ella had set off the quake. He wanted his life to be different, and he'd start the changes with her.

"Nothing says we have to quit searching," he said, amazed that it had taken him this long to realize that a setback didn't mean they were done for.

Ella gaped at him. "What do you mean?" she finally asked, carefully.

He set down his wineglass. "We know, more or less, where he went to ground. The chances are good that he lives in the area. There were a lot of apartment houses and rentals right there."

She nodded.

"If he doesn't get rid of the car right away, we can still find it."

"You're serious."

"Yeah." He let her see on his face how serious he was. "I don't like failing."

Except that wasn't his entire motivation. It was more complicated than that. He hadn't liked being dismissed as "undependable" by his ex. Being told his star was dimming at the law firm had stung, even if he was willing to admit his heart hadn't been in his work lately. Maybe most of all, though, he hated that he'd hurt his mother and disappointed his father. He was better than that, wasn't he?

"Let me help, Ella," he said.

She gave a small, dry sob, and pressed her fingers to her mouth. "You'd do this for me."

Brett found himself smiling. He was a knight-errant who'd taken on a solemn quest. Here was a chance to redeem himself. All he had to do was fix the really important thing that had gone wrong in Ella Torrence's life.

And prove to himself that he didn't always screw up.

Not to mention that, damn, the glow on her face made him feel good.

During the stress of the earlier chase, he'd been all too aware of her emotions, but he had stopped himself from consciously acknowledging that he was attracted to her.

And yet, sometime during this bizarre day, attraction had morphed into something a lot stronger. So strong, he figured it might be smart to think at least twice before he made a move on her. Yeah, he would love to peel that dress off her and find out whether she went for practical or sexy lingerie. Then he wanted to dispose of the lingerie, too. As far as he was concerned, she had the perfect body. He liked sleek lines and curves that were feminine without being voluptuous. He liked firm mattresses, too. Sinking into something too soft wasn't his thing.

Ella Torrence was just right.

"You asked why it mattered so much." She wasn't looking at him. "After Mom died, I decided in my melodramatic way that I didn't deserve the love of people who'd loved her. So when they wrote, I didn't answer. Eventually, they mostly gave up. Now...having another chance..." Her voice shook, and she came to a stop.

Oh, man, he thought. Ella Torrence wasn't only sexy. Beneath a smart, assertive surface, she was also complicated, wounded, vulnerable. He tried never to get involved with women who could be hurt too easily. She rang every warning bell.

She also, God help him, made him want to heal her, protect her, understand her. And, man, did that freak him out.

Even so, he had to ask. "Do you want to tell me what happened?"

She shook her head. Hard. Vehemently. He accepted that.

Ella refused his offer of leftovers, and Brett put the food in the refrigerator before they left for her place. Her house turned out to be a 1920s-era bungalow in West Seattle. She didn't invite him in, hopping out of his car the minute he stopped at the curb.

"One o'clock tomorrow?" he prompted. "I'll pick you up here."

One hand on the car door, leaning down to meet his gaze, she hesitated. "I'll probably rent a car in the morning. You know, I can do this myself. You have to work."

He shook his head. "I don't want you hunting for that bastard by yourself."

Her chin jutted in automatic repudiation of his chauvinism.

"Let me do this, Ella."

Their eyes locked and held. "Okay," she said after a moment, softly. "One o'clock."

He waited until she disappeared inside, at which point he was disconcerted to discover that he was grinning like a fool.

Because if Ella Torrence had a guy in her life who meant anything to her, she'd have wanted *him* with her while she tried to recover the quilt. Brett had itched to ask today if she was single, but now he was pretty sure he didn't have to bother.

So much for thinking at least twice before he threw himself off the cliff.

CHAPTER FOUR

NOT HAVING A TELEPHONE was crippling, Ella discovered first thing in the morning. She really needed to call her insurance agent, she needed to rent a car, she needed to buy a new *phone*. For one thing, how else were the police to reach her if, miraculously, they located her car?

After knocking on several doors, she found a neighbor who was home and willing to let her make some calls. Two hours later, a rental car was delivered to her door. She checked her watch and decided she just had time to race to the Verizon store. There, she winced at the price of a new smartphone but bought it anyway. Things could be worse, she consoled herself—at least she'd had her driver's license and debit card as well as her car and house keys tucked in the velcro-closed pocket of a wristband she'd originally bought for when she jogged.

For some reason, she realized that she was nervous about Brett's arrival. She didn't understand why. After the hours they'd spent together yesterday, she couldn't exactly call him a stranger. But she wasn't sure she could trust her reactions yesterday or her perception of him. How could she, as upset as she'd been?

When she heard the Corvette pull up, she stood by the window and watched him get out and stretch. The sight was all it took to make her belly cramp. Maybe she shouldn't have discounted his physique because it was likely the product of a health club. Those were very nice muscles—much more apparent today with him wearing a gray T-shirt and faded jeans that she would swear were Levis, not some high-priced, rich-boy brand. And, oh my, did they fit well.

Only by stepping away from the window did she manage to get a grip on herself before he reached her porch. *Focus,* she told herself fiercely. *Remember what's important.*

He looked even better close up, his hair disheveled, his athletic shoes battered, his smile friendly and— heaven help her—sexy.

"You ready to go?"

"Yes, but…I did rent a car." She nodded toward the shiny white Nissan Versa that sat in her driveway. "I really could go out on my own. I promise not to try to confront the guy if I find him…"

He just looked at her. "No way you're leaving me out."

She hesitated, refusing to admit even to herself that she was relieved, then nodded. "Thank you."

Once they were on their way, she asked how it had gone at the law firm that morning.

He shook his head. "I decided the hell with it. I took a few days off."

She couldn't help gaping. "A few days?"

He flashed a grin at her. "However long it takes."

Rattled, Ella had no idea what to say. However long it takes? She'd been on her own so long, she wasn't sure how to react. Was he in this for the novelty, or the excitement, or was he genuinely committed because…? That's where she stumbled. *Why* would he be willing to give her so much of his time when he hardly knew her?

Selfishly, she couldn't help being glad his determination wasn't wavering. Unselfishly—she understood that by helping her he had to be damaging his standing at work.

"Um…thank you?"

A crease in his cheek deepened and he patted her thigh. She laughed and settled back to enjoy the ride, even though she was still confused and—yes—a little troubled by why he was so determined to help her.

When they reached Magnolia, she became tense and focused again, moving her head constantly to check both sides of the street and look down alleys.

They skipped the parts of the neighborhood that had a view of downtown Seattle or Puget Sound. Those houses were among the most expensive in the city. It didn't make sense that a car thief would live in a $2 million brick home with perfectly clipped hedges and a spectacular view. Gleaming Mercedes and BMWs and Land Rovers sat in those driveways, not twenty-year-old dented station wagons.

But the side of the hill that faced the industrial flats was lined with modest houses, duplexes and apartment complexes. Brett prowled every street, and then did it again.

At first they were both quiet. Then, to keep herself from going crazy, she asked what had gone wrong in the trial he'd lost.

"It's not the first one I've blown lately." He moved his shoulders as if suddenly aware of taut muscles. "Damn. I thought I had it locked down, even though…" He let out a sigh. "This guy is a real piece of work, but his daddy is big in the software world and is loaded. See, at the firm that makes him an important client. But the smug ass grated on me. I can't tell you how tempted I was to move down to the prosecutor's table."

"You never considered being a prosecutor?"

"Maybe in an early burst of idealism. I always wanted to walk in my father's footsteps, though, so…" The lines in his face had deepened, aging him. It was a couple of minutes before he grimaced and seemed to shake off the brood.

"I might just be having a bad streak. It happens. You get a judge with a prejudice, or miss a bad apple during jury selection. Now, *there's* an art."

His stories of the process were entertaining and illuminating. Ella had been summoned to jury duty only once, which involved phoning in every morning, only to be told she wasn't needed.

"I was kind of sorry," she admitted. "I thought it would be interesting."

"Yeah, it is. Or can be." He gave her another one of those crooked grins. "Most people are grouchy and don't want to do it, though. They're afraid of getting stuck on a long trial. That can be a big hit financially. This one went on for three weeks."

At his return to the trial he'd just lost, she probed a little and he admitted a few mistakes he thought he'd made. He went quiet for a while after that, and when they started talking again he wanted to know about her. She suspected he'd revealed more than he wanted to. Maybe in response to his own openness, Ella ended up telling him things she didn't usually reveal to people, talking about her parents and especially her current, very distant relationship with her dad, who was a Boeing executive.

"He remarried," she said, "but he didn't have more kids. I see him and Carol once in a great while. None of us are very motivated to get together." She hesitated. "When Jo emailed me about the quilt, I asked Dad's permission to go through Mom's stuff, in hopes that there'd be something that would hold memories for Olivia. And I got lucky when I went through the boxes—my grandmother had used the same fabrics to make Christmas tree skirts for all her kids. Ours ended up with a stain—I'm not sure why we kept it. But there was plenty of good fabric I could use." She knew she was babbling to avoid finishing the story, then she realized she wanted to tell him. "I hadn't seen Dad in months. I'd said what day I was coming, but...he wasn't there. I guess he couldn't be bothered. He never even mentioned it later."

"That stinks," Brett said, his voice rough.

"I'm better off than a lot of people. I had my mother, and the rest of my family until we moved."

"When you were eleven." Brett shook his head.

They continued to search, but they both got quieter as discouragement set in. Finally, she heard his stomach growl and, startled, she realized it was almost six o'clock.

"Buy you dinner?" she offered.

"Sure. You know what I'd like?"

Turned out, that was a burger and a shake. They went to Seattle's famous Dick's Drive-In. Ella was impressed that Brett was willing to allow food and drinks in the Corvette. After he'd let her off at home, she pictured him stopping somewhere on the way home to vacuum. She almost smiled. Surely no crumb was allowed to mar the impeccable interior of his precious car.

The slight lift in her mood lasted until she checked her email.

From: JoM@fleetmail.com
Being back at Kanowa Lake has made me remember

so much I hadn't thought of in years. We had good times, didn't we? For some reason the other day I thought about Olivia's HUGE crush on Johnny Randall. It was that last summer, wasn't it? He was helping his dad cut deadfall and split firewood for Grammy Mags. Shirtless on hot days, no less! We had endless excuses to be lurking in his vicinity, all for Olivia. Hmm. Too bad we don't have a piece of Johnny's shirt to add to the quilt. BTW, Brody says Johnny is a dentist, of all things. Probably doesn't take his shirt off on the job anymore.

Ella reread the email, her mood fluctuating between amusement and irrational depression.

She knew it wouldn't have occurred to either Jo or Rachel that so many of their memories of that last summer at Hollymeade didn't include her, except as the little kid they kindly let trail behind. This story was a perfect example. Rachel and Jo had been just old enough to understand Olivia's passion for skinny sixteen-year-old Johnny Randall. Her eleven-year-old self had only been confused.

Soon she was going to have to let Jo and Rachel know the quilt was gone. She probably should have done it right away, but…she kept hoping. Maybe she and Brett would find her car. Maybe the cops would. Maybe, miracle of miracles, the quilt would still be in it. He might tear the package open, but the average car thief would surely sneer when he saw the contents and toss the whole thing in the back where it would lie forgotten. Right?

Just…please don't let him throw it in the nearest Dumpster.

"WHAT?" ELLA EXCLAIMED, swiveling in her seat to stare at him. "You went out again last night?"

They were now into day three of their search. Brett shrugged, concentrating on the always-heavy downtown Seattle traffic. "It was still light. I figured, I don't know, he might decide it was safe to come out in the evening."

He hadn't exactly thought it through. He'd been restless, that's all, and not ready to give up the search.

Or maybe it was more than that. He still hardly knew what a quilt "top" was, but he did understand that the object itself was only symbolic.

His mouth twitched at the idea. "Are you laughing?" Ella sounded indignant.

"Ah…I took a few literature classes in college. I was set on law, so I was majoring in politics, but I figured a thorough grounding in literature would boost my ability to be eloquent."

"Yeah, so?"

"So I discovered I am totally literal. I got a C in my first class, Eighteenth-Century English Literature." Outrage still rose in him at the memory. He'd worked his butt off for that class. "I'm still not convinced all those old guys were really using symbolism."

A giggle escaped her. He flicked a glance her way. Her eyes were wide with astonishment at her own reaction.

"Now you're laughing at *me*." He leaned heavy on the disgruntlement.

"Maybe." This was the least shadowed smile he'd seen yet on her face. "It's just that I'm still mystified. Is there a point to your reminiscences?"

"Symbols," he explained, then explained his train of thought.

"Oh."

While he was making a left on Garfield and cross-ing the industrial flats to Magnolia atop its knoll, Ella was silent.

"I guess it is," she said finally. "Symbolic on a lot of levels. Or maybe I mean to a lot of people."

"To your aunt."

"Yes. The quilt was—"

"Is," he corrected, not letting her finish.

She glanced at him. "Okay, is. The quilt is the best way we have of making sure she's present for Olivia at her wedding. She started it with love for her daughter, and we wanted to finish it the same way." Her words became choked toward the end.

He took her hand. He'd discovered how much he liked holding Ella's hand.

"To me, the quilt means I've contributed something worthwhile to my family. It makes me feel as if *I* matter to them."

He had to clear his throat before he could speak. "Yeah. I know."

"And I'm guessing for all of us cousins there's this connection to my grandmother, too, who taught us how to quilt. She might be gone, and Olivia's mom is gone, too, but it's only because of them that the quilt can hap-pen. You see?"

"I do." He saw that *her* mother was in the mix, too. A link had been broken for Ella, and somehow this quilt could mend it.

"So you're right. If the quilt had meaning only to me, it wouldn't matter so much."

As far as he was concerned it would. He didn't know the woman who'd started the quilt for a daughter he also didn't know. He knew Ella. And he really hated it when Ella used words like *worthwhile* as if she wasn't. To him, that's what it all came down to. If she could safely send this quilt—*no, excuse me, quilt* top—on its way, some of her wounds might heal.

And that was why he wasn't going to give up until all hope was lost.

"All right," he said. "Let's start where we lost him on Tuesday. We'll work outward in circles."

"Makes sense," she agreed, and leaned forward like a setter catching a scent.

ELLA GRABBED HIS WRIST. "You can't go into that parking garage. What if you get trapped in there?"

He was more worried about somebody seeing him sneak in, but he wasn't about to say that. He only shook her off. "If there's no other exit, I just have to wait until somebody else opens the gate. You sit tight."

He already had his door open. He'd watched a car come down the quiet street and slow. Now the ponderous iron gate was creaking to the side, allowing access to the parking garage beneath a good-sized apartment complex. There were a lot of these in the area, but this was his first attempt to search one.

Ella was still protesting when he sprinted across the street, watched the Ford Focus turn in and move out of sight before he slipped in through the gap just before the gate closed.

There were two floors to this garage. Cars, he discovered, were double-parked, which meant roommates must have to juggle who had to leave first in the morning.

He tried to make his stride purposeful, in case anyone noticed him, his careful scan unobtrusive. A ramp carried him up to the second floor. He nodded pleasantly at two women who emerged from an elevator and headed straight for their car. It was a keyed elevator. He pretended to be searching his pockets for his keys until he heard the squeal of brakes as they descended the ramp.

A couple of times he got his hopes up when a red fender caught his eye, but none belonged to a Subaru. Finally he descended the ramp and crouched behind an SUV until he heard the gate rising. Last minute, he slipped out and returned to his car across the street.

"Oh, my God!" Ella sounded as if she was hyper-ventilating. "I was sure you'd been caught."

"Not a chance." He was pleased at his nonchalance, although he'd concluded that B&E was not going to be a new career path for him. Unless he got caught, of course, and, with a felony conviction, lost the right to practice law.

"It wasn't there?"

"Nope."

She insisted on taking her turn at the next big garage, which didn't sit well with Brett. But how could he argue?

"My car, my risk" were her exact words.

She emerged breathless, but also laughing. "Well," she said when she registered his disbelief, "I've never done anything like that." She sounded defensive. "It was a little exhilarating. Don't you agree?"

He groaned. "I've created a monster."

"What? I'm supposed to be girlie and pretend I was totally terrified?"

"Just don't get any ideas," he growled.

"Like stealing a CD out of an unlocked car?" She batted her eyes at him. "You know, this total idiot left the brand-new Snow Patrol CD lying right on the seat of an unlocked car. Can you believe it? I was thinking of buying that one."

Brett shook his head.

"Of course," she said after a minute, her voice small and chastened, "I guess I'm not really in a position to criticize anyone else, am I? When *I* left my windows cracked."

"Not the same thing," he said immediately. "Somebody had to work at stealing your car."

"If only there'd been a parking spot open in front of the gallery." She sounded mournful. "Then none of this would have happened."

Her words gave him a jolt that felt something like anger, and something like...Brett wasn't sure what.

"If your car hadn't been stolen, we probably never would have met," he said, an edge there he couldn't disguise.

Her gaze turned skittish, and he tightened his jaw against the temptation to say anything else that might panic her. He felt near enough to panic himself.

Brett made the mental effort to rewind. His mood had been seriously bad when he walked out of that restaurant. What if a frantic blonde hadn't catapulted into him? What would he have done, thought, felt over the next three days without her? The three days that had, instead, been devoted to his quest and to getting to know Ella Torrence in a way he wasn't sure he'd ever known any of his girlfriends?

He drew a gigantic blank. He didn't even want to imagine not meeting Ella.

And he hadn't even kissed her.

"Hey!" She leaned forward in a way that was familiar from their first day. "Is there any chance...?"

Half a dozen blocks down a hill, making a turn…
red, and it definitely had a square back. He shifted
gears, and sent the Corvette in pursuit.

CHAPTER FIVE

THEY CHASED a red Subaru station wagon for a good fifteen minutes before getting close enough to realize it was way newer than hers. The wasted pursuit set the tone for the rest of the day, spent in fruitless search.

Ella cooked for Brett that evening. Black bean quesadillas—not fancy, but she hadn't exactly had the chance to go grocery shopping. Then he wanted to see her studio, so she led him to the rear of her house, where walls had been knocked down to join what had been a third bedroom with a glassed-in porch. The space, now stretching all the way across the width of the house, was flooded with light. And it was roomy enough to accommodate two kilns, her potter's wheel, shelves to hold clays and glazing supplies as well as work in various stages of completion and, finally, a huge table where she kneaded and sculpted clay. Brett surprised her with his interest, although she didn't know why. She should already have figured out by now that he was a smart man who was way more complex than the cocky first impression he had given her.

As he studied her finished work, he kept sneaking glances at her. He was probably thinking, *Huh. She made this.* Only...did his *huh* mean he was impressed, or just the opposite?

She crossed her arms tightly and watched him.

He raised his eyebrows and said, "What?"

"You're asking *me* what? You're the one giving me the funny looks."

"It's just…" He slid his finger along the spiny back of a sculpture she'd created probably three years ago. She'd never quite decided if she liked it or not. "Some of these are contradictory."

"Aren't we all?"

He took her question seriously. They had a spirited debate about consistency of character that she enjoyed. She explained then how her artistic style continued to evolve, and admitted that sometimes she didn't understand what she was trying to do until she'd actually accomplished it. And not always even then.

The last one he touched was a recent piece she had almost taken to the gallery the other morning. It too was plump and curvaceous, a faint tracery of vines suggesting the fecundity that made her nervous. His covert appraisal of her boosted her unease.

"That's the most recent," she blurted.

"Huh."

Oh, good. Now he'd actually *said* it. She spun around and stalked back into the kitchen.

Brett trailed her. "What's wrong?"

"*Huh* may be my least favorite word in the English language."

"*Wherewith* is mine."

She rolled her eyes at his amusement but asked anyway. "Why?"

"Because it leads into a bunch of legal gobbledygook."

He was really good at making her laugh. "You're a lawyer! You *write* legal gobbledygook."

A smile played around his mouth now. "Sure, but that doesn't mean I like it."

She snorted.

"What's wrong with *huh?*"

"It's evasive."

"It's thoughtful," he argued, taking the cup of coffee she offered.

"It's a way of avoiding saying what you really want to say. As in, wow, this pot is weird, or, eww."

"I thought that pot was sexy." He grimaced. "Wasn't sure I should say that."

"Why not? Although I'm not sure ceramics can be sexy."

"All I know is, those curves," his hands traced some explicit curves in the air, "made me picture, uh…" His eyes dropped to her body.

She tingled everywhere his gaze touched. She felt like a kiln starting to heat. Ella was very much afraid her nipples were responding to the caressing look.

"Oh," she said softly, and not so brilliantly.

"Yeah, you know." With the not-so-articulate addendum, his gaze retraced the same route.

Ella felt herself swaying toward him. Alarm flared. This couldn't possibly be a good idea. She *liked* Brett Hollister. Sex would ruin that. It always did.

She said the first thing that came to her mind. "Pregnant, was what I thought."

He jerked back, his eyes meeting hers. *"What?"*

"I sort of thought that piece seemed…ripe. Pregnant."

His expression gave away how appalled he was. "You're kidding me. You were *trying* to make it pregnant?"

"No! It just happened," she explained.

He muttered something she suspected was a profanity. Or worse. "Yeah, that explains most pregnancies."

Her brow wrinkled. "What do you mean, *explains?*"

"*Just* implies an oops."

For some reason, that annoyed her. "Is that really what you believe? No one has a kid on purpose? Were *you* an oops?"

The heated gleam was definitely gone from his eyes. *Pregnant* was so not a sexy word to a single guy. "To tell you the truth, I'm not sure. I have two older sisters, maybe my parents never meant to have three kids."

"Did you *feel* like an oops?"

His face became expressionless. The silence stretched just a little too long. "It...never occurred to me. I have great parents. I'm lucky."

She didn't say a word.

After a moment his mouth twisted. "I've spent a lot of years trying to impress my father. There's some reason I never succeed, but I don't know what it is."

"That's why you're practicing a kind of law you're not sure you believe in anymore," she blurted out, going on instinct.

His eyes met hers. "I'm...starting to think so."

"Maybe we're all mixed up about our parents."

Brett grunted and shook his head. "Compared to you, I have nothing to complain about. My parents really *are* great. I'm sorry you don't have the same."

She bowed her head. "I wish I did, too."

"Listen." He stepped forward and lifted her chin. They stared at each other. After a minute a cross between a sigh and a groan escaped him and he shook his head. "Never mind. I should go. I'll see you in the morning, though, okay?"

Ella nodded and tried to smile.

His eyes searched hers, although she had no idea what he was looking for. He bent forward and kissed her lightly. His lips were incredibly soft, pressing just hard enough. She felt the contact so acutely her toes curled.

The next minute, he was gone. Hearing the front door close behind him, she touched her fingertips to her lips, wishing she could recapture that tender kiss.

BRETT WAS NOT thrilled later that evening when his phone rang and he saw that it was his father. They hadn't had a friendly talk since the birthday party debacle. Plus, he knew his father would have gotten a behind-the-scenes report on the trial and the rest of Brett's colorful week.

He grunted and picked up the phone anyway. There were some people he could dodge long term, but his father wasn't one of them.

"Hey, Dad."

"Where are you? Maui?"

The sarcasm made him tense and he rubbed the back of his neck. "I'd have let you know if I was going out of town."

"You didn't let me know you fell on your face on Monday."

Okay, now he was pissed. "You mean my client was convicted."

"That's what I said."

"Glad you're ready to give me the benefit of the doubt."

That led to a pause. Then his father asked, "Do you deserve it?"

"Are you asking if I screwed up?" Brett saw red. "No. I didn't. Could I have done better? Probably. Is the world better off because the jerk actually got convicted? Yeah. Don't tell me you've never felt the same way. Maybe wondered if you'd given your best, but couldn't help being glad you didn't."

"McGuinn called." His father sounded a little more hesitant. More like a father, and less like a surrogate partner in the firm. "He's not impressed with your taking time off now."

So, okay, he wasn't going to admit to any weakness.

Angry, Brett was in no mood to explain. "You planning to report back to him?" He pitched his voice to be flippant, very aware that it would irritate his father. "In that case, you can tell him I'm doing some serious thinking." He ended the call and tossed his phone back on the kitchen counter.

When five minutes of pacing didn't settle him, he grabbed his workout clothes and took the elevator down to the fitness center. He planned on using the elliptical or maybe running some hard miles on the treadmill, but he got lucky and ran into another resident. They played a vicious game of racquetball that left him both wrung out and a hell of a lot calmer.

He wasn't proud of his behavior. His father had always been on his side. He understood that. Dad expected the best from his son, and it wasn't his style to be gentle and encouraging. Brett knew who to thank for his drive and aggression, and their similar personalities meant they butted heads sometimes. Lately, though, he'd needed a dad, not a stand-in law-firm partner. Someone who would really listen if he expressed his doubts.

I've been angry at him, he realized. Feeling as if he had to measure up in a way he wasn't sure he wanted to anymore.

Fine moment to realize *this* was why he'd "forgotten" Mom's birthday party. He was ashamed to figure out that he had let his own internal tangle, his resentment of the man who'd loomed so large in his life, keep him away from home and family. *Yeah, I hurt Mom because I was sulking.*

He grimaced.

One thing was for sure: he had to tell Dad and Nial McGuinn that he was no longer in kindergarten. If the senior partner was going to continue reporting to Brett's daddy, then Brett would be moving to a new firm. A new city, if necessary.

Too late to call Dad back tonight, he saw with a glance at the clock when he let himself back into his condo. Maybe tomorrow he and Ella would find her car and he would be coming off a triumph when he had that conversation with his father.

A strange thought came to him, though, as he lay in bed waiting for sleep. What he'd said to his father might have been facetious, but it might also be the truth. He felt as if he were steadying himself, remembering who he was and what was really important to him. Family. The people he loved. Going to bed every night with the belief he was making the world a better place. Justice.

Huh.

It wasn't so much a word as a breath of air, but it made him grin when he remembered Ella's indignation. He was still smiling when he finally did fall asleep.

THE NEXT DAY was more of the same.

A sense of hopelessness had begun to envelop Ella. She wasn't wasting only her time, but Brett's, as well. Her police contact had sounded bored that morning when he'd told her, No, ma'am, her vehicle had not yet been located. What she ought to do was nag her insurance agent into issuing a check, start hunting for a used car to replace the Subaru and email Rachel and Jo with the bad news.

The only reason she hadn't was Brett. His determination kept her believing a happy ending was possible, even as they drove around for hours with no results.

The way they never ran out of things to talk about was their salvation. Ella had been on dates when she started sneaking peeks at her watch half an hour after joining the guy for coffee or whatever. When she mentally added up the hours she and Brett had spent together, she was shocked to realize how much she still wanted to know about him. The feeling seemed to be mutual.

And now sexual attraction had definitely been added to the mix. The first day, she had been too upset to think much about Brett beyond being grateful for his willingness to help her and for his persistence.

Now she found herself constantly sneaking glances at him. She loved his face in profile—okay, head-on, too, but she saw his profile more often. The nose she'd initially thought looked too big was really just right. Strong, that's all. It went with the prominent bone structure that would keep his face compelling even as he aged and added more flesh. There was the crooked smile, the way the skin crinkled beside his eyes that sometimes were unnervingly perceptive.

Oh, and he had great hands, big and long-fingered, with well-manicured nails. Sinews and veins stood out, but they weren't hairy the way some men's were. They were expressive, too—he vented plenty of his stress through them.

She couldn't believe a guy as sexy as he was didn't have a girlfriend, but she hadn't quite worked up the courage to confirm that he was single. He didn't have the same qualms, though. They'd stopped for deli sandwiches at a little place in the neighborhood where they were concentrating their search and were eating at a tiny table set on the sidewalk beneath a maple tree with spreading branches.

"You seeing anyone these days?" he asked, not sounding quite as casual as he'd probably been trying for.

Ella's cheeks flushed. "No. It's been a while."

"Really?" His incredulity was plain, and undeniably flattering. "Why?"

"For one thing, I'm self-employed. I mostly get out to take my work to galleries, and that's it." She tore a bit of the crust off her bread and began to crumble it. "Friends introduce me to guys sometimes, but..." She shrugged. "What about you?"

"I was dating a woman until a couple months ago. Nothing really serious."

"What happened?"

His expression was odd. "I guess I ignored her too often, or didn't return enough phone calls, or something. She said I was undependable."

Which had really stung, Ella could tell. And, oh by the way, answered the big question she'd been asking herself.

"That's why you're doing this, isn't it?" Her gesture encompassed herself and his Corvette. Why did she not like this new understanding? "Trying to prove to yourself that she was wrong."

Some moments he was boyishly open, and then there were moments, like now, when he was very much a man, skilled at guarding his thoughts and emotions.

"It might have started that way."

She waited for the rest. He resumed eating. After a few minutes he lifted his eyebrows at her.

"I'm almost done, and you've hardly started."

"Oh." Dammit, her cheeks were heating again—and she couldn't remember the last time she'd blushed before today. "Sorry." She focused on her meal, trying not to be so aware of him sitting across the table from her, seemingly totally relaxed.

"The last few days have made me realize," he said out of the blue, when she reached for her cookie, "that she wasn't very important to me. I'd feel a little irritated sometimes when she left a message. There was an imbalance. She wanted me to be a bigger part of her life than I wanted her to be of mine. I didn't handle it the best way I could have, but it's good that it came to a head."

"It's good for me."

"No." Now those gray eyes were steady on her face. "It wouldn't have made any difference. I'd have wanted to stick with this—with you—no matter what once we started."

Oh, heavens was all she could think. What could she say to that?

She gave him a shaky smile. "I'm really lucky it was you I ran into."

"No." His voice had dropped to a lower timbre. "I was the lucky one." After a moment, as if nothing significant had happened, he asked, "You ready to go?"

She nodded and dropped her napkin on her plate, but her thoughts were churning as they returned to the car. She wished she could take him at face value, but how could she? If she was so amazing, other men would have noticed.

Her own father would have noticed.

Ella frowned, because part of her knew she wasn't to blame for her father's coldness. But still… There had to be a catch, a reason Brett was helping her, and eventually she'd find out what it was.

CHAPTER SIX

ELLA HAD NOTICED that when Brett's phone rang, he mostly glanced to see who the caller was and ignored it. Late that afternoon when it rang, he glanced, frowned and answered, steering at the same moment to the curb. "Mom?"

As his mother talked, Ella saw his expression change into something she could only call stricken.

"Where? Okay, yeah. I'm on my way," he said, and set the phone down. He looked at Ella. "Dad may have had a heart attack. She's following the ambulance to the hospital. I need to go, too."

Ella's heart squeezed. "Oh, Brett." She reached out to touch his forearm, corded with tension. "Where is he?"

"Swedish Medical Center."

"Drop me anywhere and I'll take a bus home."

He didn't say anything for a moment. When he did, he sounded uncertain. "Is there any chance you'd come with me?" His shoulders moved uneasily. "If it drags on, you can take off."

"Are you sure you want me there?"

Filled with fear, his eyes met hers. "Yeah. But if you'd rather not—"

"Don't be silly. Of course I want to be there."

"Okay." He bent his head for a moment. "Thanks." He let out a long breath. "My dad. Oh, man. What am I sitting here for?"

He drove fast, but carefully. When they got stuck at red lights, his knuckles turned white on the steering wheel. Once parked at the hospital, she had to trot to keep up with him. They burst into the E.R. He scanned the waiting room then headed straight for the counter.

"Don Hollister. He came in by ambulance."

They had to wait five minutes before a nurse came out to get them.

"His room's getting crowded," she said cheerfully.

She was right. His father was propped in a near-sitting position in the bed, bare-chested and covered with electrodes. A technician was wiring him up, and Ella recognized that Brett's father was getting an EKG. An older woman hovered nearby, along with a younger woman accompanied by a man who couldn't be over forty. He stood to one side, looking anxious.

Every single gaze turned to Brett and Ella when they entered. Ella would have hung back if Brett hadn't been holding her hand as if that grip was all that sustained him.

For an instant nobody moved. Only the technician went back to his monitor. The other four people stared in obvious astonishment at Brett and Ella.

"Dad!" Brett exclaimed. "Hey, you don't look too bad."

His father gave a rueful smile that reminded Ella of Brett's. "They gave me nitroglycerin when I got here. Did wonders."

Brett's mother, an attractive, pleasantly plump woman with a short crop of curly brown hair, came around the foot of the bed to hug Brett and smile at Ella.

"Aren't you going to introduce us?"

He did. His mother's name was Helen. The young

woman was one of his sisters, Grace, and the man at her side was her husband, Tony.

Grace said hi, then shook her head in apparent bemusement. "You brought a girlfriend."

Ella tried to shrink toward the door. "It really is crowded in here. I don't have to…"

Brett hauled her to his side. "Don't let them embarrass you."

His dad's laugh sounded like Brett's, too. "Brett's right. It's just that he surprised us. I don't remember him ever bringing a girlfriend home to meet the family before."

Her eyes widened. "But I'm not…"

Brett's murmur in her ear wasn't much more than a vibration. "Yeah, you are."

She was? Unable to look at him, Ella quivered in surprise. Oh, dear God, had he actually *meant* what he'd implied at lunch? Was it possible that she wasn't alone in all the surprising, worrisome emotions she'd been feeling?

No matter what, Brett hadn't failed her yet, and if he needed her right now, she wouldn't let him down, either.

She touched her cheek to his shoulder, a silent acknowledgment, and felt the breath of relief he let out.

"So what's the scoop?" he asked his dad.

THEY ENDED UP staying at the hospital for several hours, until Brett's father was released. The emergency room physician believed he had had an attack of angina. The EKG showed no indication of a cardiac "event." Brett's dad left with an appointment to have a stress test the next day, followed by a visit with a cardiologist. Appearing drained, Brett's mother went to the pharmacy to pick up a prescription of nitroglycerin.

Brett remained at his father's side as they all walked out. Ella lagged behind, but was still close enough to hear the beginning of what they said.

"I need to say I'm sorry." Brett's voice was thick. "When you called—"

"You thinking you somehow precipitated this?" Don Hollister shook his head. "Don't be ridiculous. I'm here tonight because I've been neglecting my health, not because my son got tough with me."

Ella walked a little more slowly to give them privacy.

A minute later, Brett parted from his family with hugs. Ella and Brett were walking across the parking lot when he said, "I'm starved. How about if I order a pizza?"

Lunch had been an awfully long time ago. "As long as my half is veggie," she agreed. "Tell them to pile it on. I especially like green peppers. Oh, and pineapple."

He laughed, although she could tell he was still shaken. "My place or yours?"

Ella had to think. She heard again that almost soundless whisper: *Yeah, you are.* The subject was bound to come up. If anything came of it…she'd rather be home. "Mine," she decided.

He didn't argue, making the call. During the drive they talked only a little.

"That scared the crap out of me," Brett admitted.

"I don't blame you."

He took her hand. The clasp felt both comforting and the very opposite. "I shouldn't have put you through that. I didn't think about how many bad memories the hospital would resurrect for you. I'm sorry, Ella."

"No." She shook her head. "Don't be. I…was really glad to be there if it helped you. And it was nothing like Mom. She was home at the end, with hospice care.

So..." She shrugged awkwardly. "Well, I guess I don't like hospitals, because we did spend quite a bit of time in one, but that's not where she died."

"Okay." Briefly braking at a stop sign, he leaned over to kiss her cheek, giving her what felt like a nuzzle. His breath was warm on her face. Then he sat up straight to shift.

She'd learned something about him. She now understood that her story had tapped into his own powerful need for family connections. The possibility of loss he'd been hit with tonight would likely reinforce his desire to help her.

The fact that he was a loving son and brother filled her with apprehension, though. He would notice eventually how different they were. He'd missed his mother's birthday party; he hadn't missed her *death*. Take tonight—he'd raced to his father's side, no hesitation. Eventually, he was bound to notice what a loner she was, and wonder if there wasn't some lack in her that made her incapable of keeping a commitment to people.

Thanks to his planning, the pizza arrived only a few minutes after they did. Brett was obviously still wired, because while they ate he kept talking about how he hoped his father would start exercising regularly.

"He works too hard. He took more time off when us kids were home. I played sports and Dad almost never missed a game. I think he's become a workaholic since then. Mom looked shell-shocked tonight, didn't she? She never expected anything like this."

Ella let him go on until he started to wind down. "You know, your dad may just have a blockage that can be cleared up with a simple angioplasty. In which case, he'll be fine."

He offered her a crooked smile that betrayed his vulnerability. "My head knows that. But for a little while there, I was a panicked kid. The thought of losing him so soon hollowed me out. Man. I've lived to make him proud of me, but the last time he called, we argued."

"Do you want to talk about it?" she asked tentatively.

"It's all mixed up in the job. I don't want to let him down."

"Do you mean by losing?"

"It's not that. Or, not exactly." He ran his fingers through his hair. "I've kind of lost my focus lately."

"You don't want to practice law anymore."

His head shot up. "Of course I do!"

"But not as a criminal defense attorney," she said slowly.

Brett stared at her, but didn't say anything.

"Do you really think he expects you to make all the same choices he did?" she asked.

He seemed to be looking inward. "No," he said hoarsely, after a minute. This smile was even more wry, pained. "I really needed you tonight, Ella."

"I'm glad I was there," she heard herself say huskily.

His eyes searched hers. "This wasn't only you feeling like you owe me?"

She shook her head.

"Ella." It came out hoarse. He pushed back his chair and rose to his feet, circling the table to come to her.

She wanted to kiss him. She did. But she was scared, too, and not in such a different way from what he'd felt at confronting the possibility of loss. She was so bad at relationships, so incapable of trusting. She'd never gotten to the point with a guy where she cared fiercely enough to dream about possibilities and mourn in advance for what she might lose. This time she had.

Even so, she couldn't stop herself from standing, too,

trembling a little as she saw the heat and tenderness on his face. Stepping close to him felt…right.

"Brett," she whispered, and rose on tiptoe to meet his mouth.

KISSING ELLA FELT better than anything he'd ever experienced. Brett hadn't a clue whether that was because of the way his emotions had boomeranged today, or whether it was far simpler—because this was Ella, beautiful, smart, sad, argumentative and exhilarating.

Her body was supple and strong against his, instead of soft and melting. He liked that. His hands stroked the long line of her back, the swell of her hip, the inward curve of her waist. She was gripping his shoulders, learning the contours of his muscles and kneading in pleasure at the same time. Brett groaned and lifted his head just so he could look at her face. A few hours ago, at the hospital, he'd noticed how tired she was and had felt guilty. Now she blinked at him with dazed, dreamy blue eyes. Her lips were a little swollen and damp from his mouth. The tired lines had been erased. She examined his face with the same intensity he felt, as if this mattered.

An unfamiliar tenderness went along with his lust, and he gathered her close again and plunged into another kiss. Somewhere in the middle of this one, her hands found their way under the hem of his shirt while one of his cupped and gently squeezed her breast.

"Your bedroom?" he managed to ask, voice ragged.

"Oh. Um…" Her head turned as if she'd forgotten where she was. Major ego boost. "Yes. Upstairs."

They stopped for hungry, mesmerizing kisses several more times before they reached her bedroom, which he saw vaguely was colorful and filled with textures. He had to grab half a dozen throw pillows and toss them aside before he laid Ella on the bed and planted a knee between her thighs.

She kept trying to speed him up, but he slowed her down, though it took a measure of self-restraint he didn't know he had. "Easy," he whispered once, and later, "Gently." Way past coherent thought, he couldn't consciously grasp why it was so important for him to make their lovemaking extraordinary. Maybe her slight clumsiness, suggesting a lack of experience. Or maybe it was because, more than ever in his life, this was as much for her as it was for him.

Everything about her was beautiful. The way she explored him with eagerness and something like wonder really got to him, too. It was as if she'd never studied a man's body before. And she had this way of touching him that made him imagine her molding and shaping clay. She unknotted muscles and knotted other ones. He heard himself making involuntary sounds of sheer pleasure. Someday, they'd have to spend hours doing just this—exploring.

But not right now. He was too close to desperation.

He got a condom on and finally pushed inside her, one arm hooking her leg to pull it high on his hip. She tried to come off the bed to meet him. He pulled out almost languidly, then drove in hard, feeling a jolt of pleasure that threatened his control. She threw an arm around his neck and tugged his head down so their mouths met.

Brett was seriously doubting he could hold on when she flung back her head and let out a keening cry as she spasmed around him, pulling him over the edge with her. Rapture turned him inside out, left him hanging over her on arms that shook. Ella tried to pull him down onto her, but he managed to half roll so that his shoulder took most of his weight when he collapsed.

He gathered her in, refusing to even imagine a moment when he'd have to let her go.

CHAPTER SEVEN

ON MONDAY, BRETT had to go to work. Ella went alone in her rental car to check out a quilt top advertised on Craig's List. A Christmas quilt—"I piece, you quilt," according to the seller. The address was near Green Lake, not that far to the northeast from where she and Brett had lost sight of her car. But the older woman who came to the door didn't fit Ella's image of a car thief, or even his girlfriend or mother. Although everyone had a mother, right?

And the moment the woman unrolled the fabric, what little remaining hope Ella had managed to hold on to deflated. It was a folk-style quilt, but not all that skillfully made. She chatted with the woman, one quilter to another, said it wasn't quite what she was looking for, and escaped.

Ella drove home, considered working and went to her computer instead. With dread she found an email from Rachel.

From: Rachel@mailoze.com.au
I was so excited to get the photo of the quilt-to-date that you emailed, Ella. Now you've really got me thinking. What a challenge to measure up to the borders you and Jo have done. Let me know when to expect the quilt—I can hardly wait to start working on it. Al-

though I do wish I'd kept my skills up more. You two will help me fix any mistakes, won't you?

Oh, no, Ella thought, rereading that last sentence.

Nobody could fix the mistake *she* had made. Soon, even Brett would have to give up. Ella once again revised the dreaded email to her cousins she was carrying in her head.

A few more days, she begged herself.

There were two emails from gallery owners about sales and asking for her to restock, which should have cheered her up. They also should have sent her out to her studio. She hadn't accomplished a single thing in a week. Usually she found refuge in work when she was upset or unhappy, but not this time.

Instead, she clung to the knowledge that she would see Brett soon, counting the hours and minutes. That worried her almost as much as the looming necessity of sending that email. Any day he would gently say he'd done everything he could. How long after that would this relationship they'd started last?

Making love with him had been more than she'd ever imagined, but that was only from her perspective. She'd never especially enjoyed sex before; she figured lovemaking required letting go in a way she couldn't do.

Hadn't been able to do. Until Brett. Somehow he had sneaked under her guard and leveled it completely.

Unlike her, he no doubt had a vast wealth of comparisons to draw on. Ella was sure she wasn't much like his usual lovers. They probably went to work in sexy, designer suits and killer heels instead of saggy denim overalls and canvas sneakers. They'd know how to talk to the partners in his law firm, or help him entertain.

She made a face. *They* would probably cheerlead him

into keeping his "professional focus," too, not poke and pry and suggest that maybe there were more important things in life than following in his daddy's footsteps.

No, this thing she and Brett had going was probably just proximity on his part. He couldn't possibly be serious about her.

Her voice of reason was plunging her into a deep depression. It didn't help that part of her also wondered, *What if I'm wrong? What if he* is *serious?* Because it was an easy answer. She didn't know *how* to have a real relationship. She'd fail him, some way, somehow. The certainty was bone-deep.

The burning in her eyes embarrassed her and made her mad all at once. Since the day her mother died, the quilt project had been the first time anyone in her family had asked anything of her, and, what a surprise, she was letting them down. *Crash.* Why would she do any better with Brett, no matter how she felt about him? She'd loved her mother, after all. There had to be something else she lacked. Strength of character, perhaps?

Maybe *she* should tell *him* it was time to give up. What if he was too nice to say it, and he'd been counting on her to come to that conclusion on her own? Yet another failure....

STILL FASTENING HER seat belt, Ella glanced at Brett as he started the engine. "This must be the last thing in the world you want to do this evening."

Her attitude was starting to piss him off.

"Nothing I'd rather be doing," he said shortly, although that wasn't quite true. If only they could find the blasted quilt, they could stay in—eat, talk, make love.

He had a suspicion it was the making love part that was the problem. Ever since that night, she had been

trying to pull away. Either she hadn't felt anything like
the sensations and emotions he had—or else what she
did feel had scared her.

Or maybe she still doubted him. No, he *knew* she
doubted him. She didn't come right out and say, "You're
ready to quit, aren't you?" but she was definitely tiptoe-
ing around it—like with the remark she'd just made. He
knew what she was thinking, all right.

And maybe a reasonable man *would* have given up
by now. If so, Brett wasn't reasonable. She still hadn't
entirely opened up to him. He knew damn well he only
partly understood why the quilt mattered so much to
her, but that wasn't the point. He had a chance to prove
to Ella that she could depend on another person. Him.
If that meant spending his evenings and weekends all
summer long driving city streets hoping to spot her
Subaru, then that's what he'd do.

The upside was, he got to spend those evenings and
weekends with her.

Modern man so rarely got a chance to prove himself
like this, Brett thought. The days of demonstrating that
he'd die for a woman were mostly gone. He wasn't exactly sure what Ella *did* need from him, but he had to
believe that simply being there for her was a good start.

He frowned, mulling it over. That wasn't quite right.
Trusting him might be an issue, but trusting herself
was a bigger one. He remembered her saying early on
that she'd *known* she'd mess things up. Her belief that
she'd failed her mother had crippled her faith in herself.

His crusade had been all about rescuing the quilt so
she could fulfill the promise she'd made. Now he realized it was about more than that—it was about convincing her that he believed *she* was worth everything
he had to give.

Wow, he thought. Wanting her was one thing, but—
everything he had to give? Was he really ready for that?

Shaken, he reached out and took her hand. The expression on her face when she glanced at him was confused and hopeful.

"My poor car is probably in a chop shop by now," she said mournfully. "That's what they call them, isn't it?"

"Yes, but I seriously doubt that's what happened to it. Your Subaru isn't old enough *or* new enough for the parts to be worth much. In fact…" He hesitated.

"It's just plain not worth much," she finished. Her shoulders sagged. "I know. I even looked up the Blue Book price. So why was it stolen at all?"

"With electronic ignitions, a lot of the newer cars can't be hot-wired the same way. One that old was probably easy. If all the guy wanted was transportation, your car was perfect."

"And I left the windows rolled down."

He shrugged. "You ever seen an expert get into a locked car? With the right tool, it takes only seconds, even with the windows rolled up."

"I'll bet *you* didn't leave *your* windows cracked," she said gloomily.

"No, but, uh, given the price tag of this baby, I don't take any chances."

Her *harrumph* made him laugh, and after a minute she laughed at herself, too.

They wandered south through Magnolia, then north again, making an occasional zigzag.

"What if he doesn't live around here at all?" Ella said suddenly. "We made a big assumption."

"Yeah, we did." That worry had been in the back of his mind all along. How could it not be? "Call me stubborn," he said, "but I still think this is home territory for him. Magnolia is a dead end. Too easy to get trapped here."

She nodded, looking less convinced than he felt, but he couldn't blame her.

"I owe you a ton for gas. Please let me pay for the next fill-up."

Brett hardly heard her. Out of the corner of his eye he saw a red car pulling up to a stop sign on a cross street.

"Hot damn," he murmured. "Is that it, Ella?"

"What? Where?" She craned her neck. "Yes! Wait, that's not my license plate, but... Can you get behind it?"

He swung an illegal U-turn, brushing so close to the fender of a parked car she had to close her eyes, then he pulled right up behind the aging Subaru station wagon.

"Yes!" Ella was bouncing in her seat. "See that ding? It happened in a parking lot. And look how the license plate is bent! He's trying to make it hard to read."

"Yeah, he is." And he'd spotted them, too, and accelerated. "Call 911, and this time stay on the line. We're not letting him get away again. Tell them, no excuses, they'd better come through."

He had to concentrate. The streets here were narrow and the neighborhood residential. The bastard was driving too fast. Brett tried to be careful without letting too much space open up between them. The guy was smart. He shot down West Dravus, panicked when the light ahead switched to red and made a right instead. Thorndyke allowed greater speed and led toward another egress from the neighborhood, one that would take them immediately back to the crowded downtown city streets where sticking close was more difficult.

Brett heard Ella talking. Then she turned a shining

face on him. "We got lucky. An officer is waiting to intercept him on West Garfield. Oh, Brett!"

He grinned fiercely, even though he didn't take his eyes off the vehicle ahead or the road. "The son of a bitch made a mistake."

Brett had never been happier to see the flashing lights of a patrol car. He dropped back and let the SPD car slide neatly in behind the Subaru. It briefly shot ahead, then slowed in defeat and pulled to the shoulder. Brett came to a stop behind the patrol car.

The officer stayed in his vehicle for a good long while.

"What's he *waiting* for?" Ella jittered and bounced like a five-year-old restrained to her breaking point. "Is he finishing dinner? His latte? I can't stand this."

"Patience, patience." Although he didn't have much patience himself. "He's probably running the plates."

At last the officer got out and strolled forward. Brett had to grab Ella's arm to keep her from following. "Not yet."

"Why not?" she wailed.

"Because this could get ugly."

The officer opened the door of her Subaru and apparently invited the driver to step out. In moments the man had been positioned so that his hands were flat on the roof. The SPD officer frisked him.

Ella whimpered her restiveness and glared when Brett laughed at her. Triumph made him feel like he'd been pumped full of helium. He'd told himself they would find her car, but he hadn't admitted his secret doubt even to himself. But now...

Even as he watched the spectacle in front of them, he kept an eye on Ella. Waiting was killing her. What if the quilt was no longer in the Subaru?

No, don't think that.

The triumph, he slowly realized, wasn't for him. It was all for her. So maybe this never had been about redeeming himself. Maybe it always had been about Ella Torrence, the woman he was falling in love with.

He waited for the zing of shock, but it didn't happen. He hadn't thought the word yet—or ever before in his life, except in relation to his family—but the admission was no surprise. He'd been a goner for her since day one.

The minute the officer shut the suspect into the caged backseat of the patrol car, Ella flung open her door and flew out. Brett hurried to catch her.

She raced by the police car on the shoulder, stumbling once but keeping going. Brett felt obligated to stop when he reached the surprised police officer. He ignored passing traffic.

"She's more interested in something that was in the car than she is in the car itself," he explained.

"The driver insists he bought the vehicle from a private party three days ago. Says he was referred by a friend of a friend. Supposedly, the seller claimed not to have been able to put his hands on the title, but the Subaru was too good a deal to pass up. He figured he could straighten it out."

"Sure." Brett had never seen the thief's face, but he'd spent hours staring at the back of his head, and he was positive he was looking at the same head now. "He's the one who stole the car."

"I think so, too," the young cop agreed. "The plates were reported stolen the same day as your girlfriend called about the vehicle. They came off an old Toyota pickup. Besides, he almost ran for it. Doesn't cross a normal citizen's mind to step on it when he sees flashing lights in his rearview mirror."

The guy in the back of the car kept his face averted, but Brett studied him for a minute. He was thin, scruffy, no older than his early twenties. Brett observed the edge of a tattoo on his neck, and a ring through his eyebrow. His blond hair was lank, and he wore a couple of days' worth of stubble on his jaw. Twitchy. Scared, probably.

Then Brett focused on Ella. She'd whirled around her Subaru but come at last to a stop, where she stared into the rear storage area. With long strides, he went to her.

"Ella?"

The face she turned to him was pale and desolate, her eyes dark. "It's not here. The quilt. It's gone."

CHAPTER EIGHT

UNDER THE FORCE of Ella's pleas, the SPD officer opened
the door of his squad car and allowed her to ask the
man in custody about the package that had been in the
Subaru when it was stolen.

"Please." Her voice cracked. "If you have it at
home…"

The guy stared ahead, not even acknowledging that
she was talking to him.

After a moment, Brett gently drew her away. She
stood there, numb, listening as he and the officer talked
briefly. Apparently, her Subaru was to be towed until
her ownership was verified. She let Brett guide her back
to his car and urge her into it.

During the drive home, she didn't say a word until
he turned into her driveway.

Then she reached for the door handle. She had to
force the words out. "Well, that's that," she said, struggling for a matter-of-fact tone.

He looked at her like she was crazy. "Hell, no, it's
not."

"What?"

"I probably can't get the guy's address tonight, but I
promise I'll have it by morning. We'll go knock on the
door. Chances are good he lives with someone else. If
not, we'll find him the minute he's released from custody."

She was beginning to feel like one of those toys that was designed to bounce back up every time it got knocked down. The sensation was disorienting.

"But...how can you...?"

"I have connections."

"Oh." Hope was a thin trickle, but it was there, when a moment ago it had been nonexistent. "You mean it?"

He took her chin in his hand. "Have I let you down yet?"

Her lashes fluttered a few times. "No," she admitted, softly, stunned at how easily the answer came. "No." After a minute, she had to say it. "It's not you. It's me."

"That's bull," he snapped. "None of this is your fault. I want to hear you admit it."

His ferocity gave her a weird, full sensation in her chest. He was getting tired of her self-pity.

Well, she was getting tired of it, too. Would anybody else have gone to the lengths that she had to get the quilt back?

After a moment, she nodded. "You're right. Except that I should have gone to the post office before I stopped anywhere else. And except for leaving the car windows cracked..."

He leveled a glare at her.

"None of this is my fault," she said obediently. She squirmed a little. "I'm...not usually so pathetic," she said with difficulty. "This—the quilt—was just such an amazing chance for me. Losing it has stirred up all kinds of stuff for me."

"I know that." His voice had gone all soft. He snaked an arm around her shoulder and tugged her toward him, so it was easy to rest her forehead on his shoulder. She could feel the steady beat of his heart. "I do," he murmured, his other hand cupping the back of her head. "Have faith."

Faith. That almost made Ella laugh, so out of her experience was that word. And yet...he was teaching her.

The full sensation in her chest was now closer to pain.

"THIS IS IT?" Ella tilted her head to see better as Brett parked in front of a duplex with moss on the roof and a scruffy lawn overrun with dandelions. Had to be a rental. "We must have driven by this place a dozen times."

"Do you remember it?" he asked.

"Not really," she admitted.

The duplex was maybe half a mile from where they'd lost the Subaru that first day. Each side had a single-car garage, but neither had a window Ella would feel comfortable peeking into. Maybe there were windows looking out at the backyard, which was fenced.

It was morning now, and here they were. No way to tell if anyone was home. The front blinds were closed. Ella and Brett stepped onto the small square of concrete that served as a porch. When Brett rang the doorbell, there was only silence, so after a moment he knocked hard, too. Ella stared at the door, projecting the image of it opening as if she could make it happen.

Maybe she was on to something because a moment later they were looking at a woman—girl—she'd have sworn wasn't over seventeen. In the narrow gap between door and frame the girl was peering through, Ella saw she wore tattered jeans that hung on bony hips, flip-flops and a thin T-shirt with no bra. Her upper arms were stick-skinny. Mascara was smudged beneath her eyes as if she hadn't washed her face in days. Ella felt a pang of pity.

"What are you selling?" the girl asked flatly, with no noticeable interest. Then she looked past Ella and Brett to the Corvette. She showed the first signs of animation. "Oh, my God! That car is awesome. Is it yours?"

"Yes. Do you live here?"

"Who's asking?"

"What is your relationship to Kyle Bernard?" he asked in a hard voice.

Her expression became wary. "He's my boyfriend."

"You're aware that your boyfriend was arrested yesterday driving a stolen car?"

"It's a lie. He bought the car! How was he supposed to know—"

"He stole *my* car," Ella interrupted. "We followed him all over town. We know it was him."

The wariness morphed into alarm. "You can't know that because the car wasn't stolen. I told you, he bought it." She pressed her lips together and glared.

Ella glared back.

Brett cleared his throat. Ella kept her gaze locked with the other woman's.

He said, "We're not here to make a judgment about the car. What we're looking for is a package that was *in* the car. The contents of the package weren't valuable to anyone but Ella here. Give us that and we'll go away."

The girl's eyes were brown, too big for her face. Some emotion—or was it knowledge?—passed like a shadow across those eyes. The girl wrapped herself with her skinny arms and hugged. "Nobody who sells a car leaves stuff in it."

"If they saw it was only an unfinished quilt, they might," he argued.

Ella turned her head to stare at Brett. It took her a moment to realize that his tone was so gentle because he was trying to give the girlfriend an out. No surprise he was skilled at getting people to open up, given his profession.

The girl chewed on what he'd said, her forehead crinkled in puzzlement. Not so bright, or else just suspicious. Ella wasn't surprised when she said, "No way. You just want me to say Kyle stole that car, and he didn't."

"Please," Ella begged. "I don't care if he took the car or not. The quilt was made by my family. It's for my cousin's wedding. Her mother started it and then died. Some other cousins and I are finishing it. It's… irreplaceable."

The skinny girl only stared at her. Ella might as well have mimed. Shaking, trying to figure out what she could say that would make an impact, Ella must have given off too much intensity because the opening began to narrow as the girl started to shut the door.

"There's a reward for the quilt," Brett said quickly.

The door stopped moving. "How much?"

"A thousand bucks."

Her mouth fell open.

Ella gaped, too. A thousand dollars? Could she afford that?

Oh, who was she kidding? At this point, she'd do anything to get the quilt back. A cash advance on her credit card was nothing.

"Has to be the right quilt," he added. Quickly, while the opportunity was there, he thrust his business card at her. Her fingers fluttered, but she held on to it.

She was tempted. *Please, please, please.*

But suddenly the girl's jaw set and she went back to

glaring at them. "You think you can trick me, but you can't. If you don't go away, I'll call the cops."

Brett's foot shot forward, but he'd been too slow if he meant to stick it in the door. She slammed it in their faces, and they heard the slide of a dead bolt.

Ella let out a small cry.

"She has it," Brett said.

"She's probably slashing it to pieces right now, or burning it."

"No." He gripped her arm and turned her to face him. "She won't do that. She's thinking about that thousand dollars. She has my number."

Rage exploded in Ella like the swell of a nuclear explosion. She was momentarily blind, mute. When she finally could speak, her voice shook. "I'm not giving up. If I have to…to break in, I will!"

Brett's surprise made her realize how passive she'd been lately.

"You thought I'd want to give up."

"I thought you were still so busy blaming yourself, it wouldn't occur to you that you weren't doomed to fail."

"Well, things have changed." She whirled and stomped toward the car. "You've convinced me. If it's not my fault, it's *his.* That slime bucket. *And he's not getting away with it.*" Stopping on the sidewalk, she faced Brett, her chin jutting. "Do you hear me?"

"I hear you." He grabbed her and kissed her hard, then let her go to open the passenger door for her. "There's the fire I expected from the woman who hijacked my Corvette—and me—the first day."

He grinned as he circled the low-slung car to get in on his side. He looked delighted because she was fighting back on her own.

Didn't most guys want to be the hero, no competition from the heroine?

Well, she'd realized from the beginning how cocky he was. Only, she'd assumed it was a negative thing. Now Ella knew better. *Confident* was another word for the same quality. The fact that he'd let her see that confidence shaken a few times was a testament to...what? The depth of his fear for his father and his frustration with himself? Or the extent of his trust in her?

For a moment, Ella felt like the scrawny girl/woman they'd just left, peering through a cautiously preserved gap between door and frame. Except, in her case, it was a concept she was examining as if it was a stranger on her doorstep.

He trusts me.

Maybe, she thought, he could. *Would* she let him down, if she could possibly help it?

No.

She stared straight ahead through the windshield, even though she was aware that Brett was looking at her. Could she really take a chance, explore where their new and fragile relationship would take them?

She wanted to, so desperately she ached.

"I have to get the quilt back" was what burst out, as if by succeeding she'd be assured that she could trust herself.

But he gave her a look of disappointment. For all that he understood the symbolism, he didn't like it that she was tying so much of her self-esteem into this one thing. A part of her understood he was right, but letting go wasn't easy.

No. She wasn't ready to think about the possibility of failing, once and for all, and how she'd feel about herself afterwards.

"WHEN WILL HE get out of jail?" Ella asked.

She had brooded during the drive, aware of Brett's glances but unable to chat. Now they were back at her house. He was obviously comfortable here now, because he went straight to the kitchen, gave the cold coffee in the carafe a sniff, dumped it and started a new pot.

At her question, he paused. "Probably today sometime."

"Then I'm going back tonight."

"*We're* going back tonight." He leaned heavily on the *we*.

Ella sighed then nodded. Going by herself to face down a guy who had stolen her car might not have been a great plan, anyway.

"Are you going to work?" she asked.

"Soon as I have a cup of coffee." He leaned a hip against the counter edge. "Can't you tell?"

She could—he wore gray slacks, shiny black shoes, a pale yellow shirt and a firmly knotted tie. The tie—hmm. She'd been so tense earlier, she hadn't noticed that the little figures on it were multiples of the Road Runner. It made her want to smile despite everything.

"Do the other partners like your ties?" she asked.

Brett glanced down. "Why wouldn't they?"

At his sly tone, her smile broke free. "You look sharp."

For some reason his face clouded. "Yeah, that's me. Great wardrobe, cool car, fancy condo. All the perks."

Ulp, she thought. "Are you going to quit?"

He stared at her. This was one of those times she absolutely could not tell what he was thinking. "Would you mind if I did?"

"Me?" She gaped at him. "What does it matter what I think?"

A strange smile twisted his mouth. After a moment he shook his head, and she had the feeling she'd disappointed him. Maybe even hurt him.

"Um...if you're in a hurry, I can lend you a travel mug," she offered.

He accepted, although the perturbed lines between his eyebrows stayed in place. Even so, he paused on the porch. "No cheating. Wait for me."

Ella nodded dumbly. Not until he was gone did she let herself consider what he'd been implying with that question. That he wanted her to be part of his life. *All* of his life.

Fear and panic squeezed her rib cage. *He doesn't know me. When he finds out...*

Do not *think about this right now,* she ordered herself. *Maybe you misread him. Maybe that wasn't what he meant at all. Maybe...*

No more.

Filled with anxiety, she found waiting to be torture. She paced. She eyed her computer but decided she couldn't bear to check her email in case there was a message from Jo or Rachel. They must be wondering why they hadn't heard anything from her, especially after she'd sent that blasted photo she took with her camera phone. Maybe tonight she could type, *I'm mailing it in the morning.*

She ached to be able to type that, to be able to go back to enjoying the lively email correspondence that had felt like the beginning of real, adult friendship.

Finally, she made herself settle down to work, firing some already glazed pieces, carefully using and then distorting a stencil on another fat-bellied bottle. Frowning when she finished, she wondered how she'd come to use such pale colors. What was wrong with bold ones? What did it say about her that the patterns on her ceramic pieces faded into near invisibility where they swelled? That a woman lost something at the very moment she was most female? To heck with that. What if the color glowed deepest and richest where the porcelain was distended, as if to suggest the power of the life within?

For the first time all week, she became energized and lost herself in her vision. The sound of her doorbell actually caught her by surprise.

The Brett on her doorstep had shed the tie, unbuttoned his shirt at the throat and rolled up his shirtsleeves. She might have been offended when he said, "You're a mess," except that he looked happy to see her, even if she had hurt him this morning.

"I suppose I should go change."

He shrugged, appraising her. "Doesn't matter. I like the overalls. Easy to get you out of them." A smile in his eyes, he undid one strap with a deft flick of his hand.

"Hey!" She batted at his hand and slid the metal loop over the button again. It was stupid to feel giddy because he wanted her even in her slobbiest, everyday getup, but... How could she help it?

In the end, she changed into jeans and a T-shirt to make sure she didn't get wet clay or glaze on the sleek leather seats of the ZR1, which she had found online only so she could gape at the price he must have paid. He loved his car. Why would he want to quit a job that let him have all those perks?

As they zipped through the city streets, he talked about his day, more to distract her than because he had anything important to say, she suspected. His effort didn't succeed. She felt like a rubber band being stretched taut, one that was already brittle enough to have some cracks and might snap any minute under the strain. By the time he parked in front of the duplex, she was completely quiet, concentrating on remembering how mad she was. Not scared. Not feeling inadequate because what could she possibly say that would convince this guy to give her the quilt.

I am self-righteously mad.

Check.

She got out and marched up to the front door without waiting for Brett, although he caught up with her as she was leaning on the doorbell. It wasn't dark yet, so she couldn't be sure whether there were lights on inside or not. They both stood there listening. There wasn't even a whisper of sound.

"They don't have a car anymore," Ella said, not bothering to keep her voice down. "How could they leave?"

"Walk. Bus."

Rubber-band Ella snapped. Ella threw herself at the door and hammered with both fists. "I know you're in there!" she yelled.

Brett squeezed her shoulder but didn't say anything.

She spun on her heel. "I'm going to look in windows."

"Ella, you could get arrested…"

"I don't care," she yelled back, already bounding across the rough grass toward the corner of the duplex. The gate was closed, but she was able to reach over it to the latch. She dismissed the threat of a dog—if Kyle Bernard had one, it would have been howling by now. At a slight sound behind her, she whirled to find Brett shaking his head but following her anyway. "You don't have to do this," she said.

"Yeah, I do."

The tiny backyard was in worse shape than the front.

Nobody had ever bothered to landscape. A square concrete patio was separated from a presumably identical
one on the other side of the duplex by a ten-foot-long
board fence. Brown paint flaked off the boards. An old
kettle-style barbecue was a mass of rust.

Ella peeked in the first window to see the shadowy
interior of a garage. No car.

"He hasn't stolen another one yet," Brett murmured.

She found herself slowing down as she sneaked up
on the lighted kitchen window. Her heart pounded. She
glanced behind her at Brett, who lifted his eyebrows,
but was sticking with her.

Ella suddenly remembered that people who stole cars
sometimes carried guns. And she and Brett *were* tres-
passing. The creep might even be legally justified in
shooting them.

This *so* wasn't a good idea.

But what was she supposed to do? Give up?

Am I really prepared to break in if they're not home?

Yes. Yes, for the quilt she was. Heaven help her.

She pressed herself against the siding and edged toward the window. If Bernard and his girlfriend *were*
home, they'd know Brett and Ella hadn't left. All they
had to do was peek out the front window to see the Corvette in plain sight.

If you're going to do it, then do *it,* she ordered herself. Ella took a deep breath and rose on tiptoe.

CHAPTER NINE

SHE WAS STARING at the back of a head. At long, dirty, yellow hair. It was him. Hyperventilating, she dropped to a crouch.

Brett flattened himself against the side of the duplex a few feet away.

At that moment, she heard a man's voice from inside. "Can you tell what they're doing?"

The girl's reply to his question was audible but not clear enough for Ella to make it out.

With a grim expression, Brett grabbed Ella's hand and yanked her toward him. "We have to get out of here."

She gave a jerky nod. Bending over, for no good reason, they ran. Brett paused to close the gate behind them. Then they walked hastily straight to the car, neither of them looking back. Ella could feel eyes watching them.

Not until they were in and he'd locked the doors did they glance at each other.

"Well, that was fun," he said in a normal voice.

Ella stared at him then began to laugh. It wasn't long before she was crying, too.

ALL BRETT COULD think when Ella started to cry was that he'd let her down. Maybe he *was* the loser he'd been accused of being lately. He had convinced himself that determination was enough, but clearly it wasn't. Stunned, he wondered if all he'd done was give Ella hope when there wasn't any.

He held her as she cried but was unsurprised when she pulled herself together almost immediately. She straightened away from him and used the hem of her T-shirt to wipe her cheeks. Her eyes were red and swollen when she looked at him.

"It's okay. I know the world won't end. Really." She tried to smile. "Honestly, everybody will be disappointed, but what's going to change? It's not as if I even see any of those people."

Those people? Her cousins. Her family.

She was consoling *him*. That really stung. He'd let her down, and she was trying to make him feel better.

He started the engine with a vicious turn of his wrist, and without a word put the car in gear and pulled away from the curb.

"I'm sorry," Ella said after a minute.

He spared her an astonished glance. "*You're* sorry?"

"Sneaking around the house like that. I could have gotten you in trouble, too, and it would have been way worse for you. Getting arrested, I mean."

He swore out loud, silencing her. When he didn't say anything else, her eyes got bigger and after a moment she looked away. Brett would have sworn she somehow made herself smaller.

Did she *feel* smaller? he wondered incredulously, but he didn't need to wonder. Of course she did. One of the first things she'd said was, *I knew I'd mess this up. I should never have agreed to help.* He remembered the punch in her voice, as if it had been ridiculous for her to believe for a second that she could do anything meaningful for another person.

And Brett still had no idea why she felt that way about herself.

A rough sound escaped him, but she didn't even turn her head. *And I kidded myself believing I could make everything right for her. When I couldn't even pinpoint what was going wrong in my own life.*

Yeah, but thanks in part to Ella, he was beginning to see it now. Maybe he hadn't totally accepted what the changes he was considering would do to his relationship with his father, but at least he was thinking seriously now.

Great. How did any of that help *her?*

He reached over and covered her cold hand with his, but she didn't clasp his. In fact, her hand was so unresponsive that after a moment he let her go. He couldn't even blame her. In the end, nothing he'd done had helped.

When they reached her house, Brett walked her in. His chest felt weighted, his throat half-blocked. "All right," he said. "It's time you tell me why this mattered so much. I've earned that much. What happened to make you believe you failed your mother?"

She stared at him, her face leached of color. Guilt slammed him because he was hitting her at a low moment, but he needed to know. And she needed to tell him.

As the silence lengthened, though, he began to think she still didn't trust him enough to bare herself completely to him.

But then she seemed to sag, and he steered her to the sofa. Sitting on the coffee table, he faced her, close enough to touch.

"I told you she was dying," Ella said in a stifled voice, after a time. "She had leukemia. Not the childhood kind. They tried a bone marrow transplant, with one of her sisters as the donor. I wasn't a match, either, and I'm an only child."

He nodded, although she probably didn't notice it. Her gaze was now fixed on her hands, although he doubted she saw them, either.

"I was thirteen when she got sick, an awful age. I fought constantly with my father, and was mad at Mom because she took his side more than I thought she should." A huff of air served as a sort of laugh. "With hormonally driven irrationality, I believed Mom must not *want* to stay with me or she'd be fighting harder to live, wouldn't she? So there I was, her beloved daughter, being a brat instead of supporting her."

Brett remembered his own recent careless behavior and snorted in disbelief. "You were at an age when you were supposed to be pulling away. You had to be torn between helping your mom through her illness and living the life of a normal teenager. But you can't tell me there weren't days when you sat holding her hand or talking to her, making sure she knew you loved her."

Ella frowned as if in surprise. "I guess there were." Her mouth twisted. "Unfortunately, the day she died wasn't one of them. Dad had asked me to sit with her. We quarreled, I stomped out and hid in the park instead. I came home hours later to find my father sitting alone in the dark. Mom had died. I never even had a chance..." Her lips compressed, and she seemed to struggle for breath.

Oh, damn. "To say goodbye."

"Yes."

What could he say to help her let go of the guilt? He might be gifted with words in the courtroom, but everything was different with this woman, who was able to drag a host of emotions from him, some he hadn't let himself feel in years.

"At that age," he said gently, "if you'd known she was dying, not later but *right then,* would you have been able to sit beside her, kiss her cheek and say the right things? Or would you have sobbed and probably increased her distress?"

She lifted a startled face his way. "I...hadn't thought of that," she said finally. "Of course I'd have sobbed. I was all emotion and not much common sense or self-control then."

Brett nodded. "So how did you fail her? You had no idea it was her last day, and I doubt she did, either. Or your father, or he'd have stayed at her side, too." He glanced at her. "He didn't, did he?"

She sat silent for a minute, looking inward. And then she said, "I actually don't know. Isn't that strange? He's...a cold man. If he suspected what was coming, he might have convinced himself Mom would rather have me with her."

"Surely there was a nurse, too."

"Yes, of course. I've always been so focused on why I wasn't there when she died, it never occurred to me to wonder about Dad. He was so angry at me."

"Because he couldn't admit how angry he was at himself?"

"Oh, God." Her laugh was soft and sad. "I can see that. He isn't given to self-examination. Convincing himself someone else failed Mom, not him... Yes, it makes sense."

At last, she looked at him. Really looked, and he noted that the blue of her eyes had deepened to a color like twilight. Soft, befuddled, *relieved.*

"Where were you then?" she asked, voice husky. "I could have used you."

"I'm here now," he said. "And I'll be here tomorrow."

And that's when she visibly shut down.

ALL SHE SAID was "I know," and then began to hint that, gee, wasn't there somewhere else he should be?

As she retreated, he continued to ask himself: Had he really done everything possible to get her quilt back? He only had so many skills to offer. Was there anything left?

Wait. What was he best at? Practicing law. His eyes widened, but Ella didn't seem to notice. He wanted to shake his head.

Dumb. Why hadn't it occurred to him sooner that he had something Kyle Bernard needed? Real leverage.

"Hey," he said. "I don't suppose you took a picture of the quilt. Somehow, through all this, you never really described it."

Emotion flashed over her face. Probably misery—why would she want to look at the quilt she blamed herself for losing? But also, he thought, impatience. She wanted to be alone.

But she nodded after a moment. "I have the picture on my computer. I sent it to Rachel and Jo."

A moment later he was admiring it. He finally understood what she'd meant when she said she'd added a "border." There was a center panel—he couldn't gauge how large—that featured a snowy scene of a charming house with a turret, decorated for Christmas, and holly bushes embroidered with ornaments and lights. A silver star hung in the twilight blue sky, the color of Ella's eyes, illuminating the Christmas wonderland. Details were a little hard to make out, but there were a

couple of snowmen, and was that a wreath on the door
of the house?

The first border surrounding the panel had stars
pieced—he thought that had been Ella's word—from
fabrics she'd said were from both the bride's and
groom's childhoods. The second border—Ella's—was
made up of trees, as if the house were protected by a
forest. Every tree was different, as if she'd cut them out
of fabric and then sewn them to a backing. A few were
only the dark silhouette of branches. Others were ev-
ergreens, outlined against the sparkling night. And yet
more were topped by their own tiny silver stars. Here
and there, red and blue and gold ornaments peeked from
beneath branches.

He wasn't sure why he was so stunned. He was already in awe of Ella's talent as an artist, and logic said
others in her family must have some of the same gift.
Still... "It's beautiful." He touched the monitor, as if
he could feel the texture of fabrics that carried the history of the two people who would be getting married.

What if he were the groom, discovering from this
just what his bride's family would do for her? What she
meant to them?

No, he thought, with new resolution, he wasn't giving up. But he also didn't want to offer Ella false hope.

"Hey," he said, catching her hand. "There's something I have to say."

She tipped her face up. He saw her pain, but also the
indomitable quality that had drawn him from the beginning. He took her other hand, too.

"You've amazed me since I met you. For a lot of
reasons—you're funny, compassionate, talented." His
smile twisted. "Sexy. But what got me from the start
is that you're a fighter. I don't know a single other per-

son who would have shanghaied a complete stranger and talked him into chasing a stolen car. Most people are too afraid. Even I've been..." He had to clear his throat. "I've been coasting. Not being honest with myself. That's not how I want to live, Ella. You've inspired me to, uh, try to do better." He felt more and more awkward as her expression didn't change. Lifting one shoulder in a lopsided shrug, he concluded, "No matter how this ends, you did your damnedest. If you have to tell these cousins the quilt was lost, make sure they understand that, too."

She shook her head and then kept shaking it, as if she couldn't stop. "That's... I don't deserve it. You're the one... I still can't believe everything you've done, and you didn't even know me when we started."

"Your crashing into me was one of the best things that ever happened to me."

Ella stayed frozen for so long, he was about to step away. But then she gave a small cry and flung herself forward. He wrapped his arms around her and bent to press his cheek against the thick silk of her hair. She was shaking as she clung, but she stayed silent.

She didn't say, *It was one of the best things that ever happened to me, too.*

A funny kind of tension, even apprehension, crawled over him.

In confirmation of his fear, she straightened away from him, squaring her shoulders. "I have something to say, too." Her eyes were dry, her voice scratchy. "I'm really grateful for everything you've done. But now I think it's time you quit worrying about me and got over your own denial. You should focus on fixing *your* life. 'Trying' isn't good enough. Do it."

What? Was this code for, *Goodbye, nice knowing*

you? Did she still have all the contempt for him—
rich-boy attorney—that she'd had at the beginning?
God, he thought, had she been hiding how she really
felt about him until she'd wrung his usefulness dry?

He'd been attacked once in the courtroom by a
pissed-off client who blamed him for a conviction. That
fist to his gut hadn't hurt as much as this one did.

He had to get out of here. Otherwise, he'd say something he didn't mean. Or maybe something he did.

"Listen," he said, aware that he was being abrupt but
unable to help it, "you're right. There actually is something I need to do right now."

She pasted a smile on. "Sure. Probably just as well.
I'll get weepy if we do a postmortem."

He hesitated very briefly at the door. No matter how
shattered he was, he wasn't quitting. He wasn't going
to coast through life anymore.

He was tempted to tell her not to email her cousins
yet, but didn't. His throat seemed to have closed up. He
nodded and left.

CHAPTER TEN

IN THE SUDDEN silence of the house, Ella hugged herself. Why, oh why, had she done that? She felt sick, remembering the shock on his face. She hadn't meant it. *Please, I didn't.* She'd only been lashing out, ashamed of herself and of their disparity. But, heaven help her, she had never believed he'd go.

Cold reason said if he'd accepted his dismissal that easily, he'd been ready to go anyway. And look how quickly he'd taken her at her word! She'd said, Go fix your own life, and he'd admitted that he had to be somewhere—anywhere—else.

Because she'd hurt him.

Unless it was something worse. Did he hate failure so much that he associated *her* with that failure? Had he only wanted her in the first place because she made him feel good about himself?

But she didn't believe that. Not moving, she drank in the knowledge of what and who he was. A man who had refused to give up, no matter how unlikely it had ever been that they'd get the quilt back. A man who loved his family, who made mistakes but could be counted on when it mattered. A man who was funny, self-aware, smug and self-doubting all at once.

Maybe there really was something he had to do. Or maybe he'd retreated to nurse his hurt feelings. But… no matter what, he would be back. The glow inside her

felt like the warm coals in the big stone fireplace at
Hollymeade when they reached the perfect temperature for melting marshmallows for s'mores. She closed
her eyes for a moment and remembered herself and
the other cousins kneeling in front of the fire, accepting sticks and marshmallows and greedily noting the
pile of chocolate bars and packages of graham crack-
ers. Those s'mores tasted better than any other dessert
she'd eaten, then or since, because Grammy Mags allowed the grandchildren to make them only once during each visit.

It wasn't so much the taste she'd relished as it was
the togetherness and the laughter. It was knowing this
was special.

Very calmly, she recognized that the time had come
to email Jo and Rachel about the quilt. She'd sit down
before she went to bed and send that message. But she
wouldn't only say, *I lost the quilt.* She would tell them
everything she'd tried to do to recover it. She would tell
them about Brett. And she'd say, *I haven't totally given
up. I'll talk to the guy's attorney, and to the prosecutor,
and maybe they'll persuade him that returning the quilt
would make a good impression on the judge.*

She would not give up, not until she knew the quilt
had been destroyed.

Brett was right. No matter how this ended, she would
be sure she'd given her all. Bad things happened. She
wasn't always to blame.

"I didn't know Mom was going to die," she whispered, "or I would have stayed with her. I would have."

BRETT PARKED A block away and walked the short distance. He cut across the lawn, avoiding the front window to prevent forewarning Kyle Bernard and the

girlfriend. They wouldn't expect him back so soon. Maybe he'd get lucky and they'd be incautious enough to open the door.

Ding dong.

Sure enough, the door cracked open right away, Bernard's alarmed face appearing in it. He was quicker to try to slam it, but this time Brett was ready. His athletic shoe protected his foot nicely when he stuck it in the opening.

"I won't hurt you," he said urgently. "All I'm asking is that you listen to me for a minute. I want to make you an offer."

The pressure on his foot eased.

"What kind of offer?" the guy asked with acute suspicion.

"Will you let me come in?"

"Are you alone?"

"Yes."

The blinds in the front window fluttered. He continued to stand where he was while they conferred in low voices.

"Yeah, okay." With that grudging agreement, the door opened.

Brett stepped into a shabby but unexpectedly neat living room with furniture likely assembled from garage sales. Nobody invited him to sit down. Bernard and his girlfriend stood close together, huddling for comfort. In an effort to appear harmless, Brett thrust his hands into his trouser pockets.

"Here's the deal," he said. "I'm a criminal defense attorney. A lawyer," he translated when their stares remained blank. "In fact, I'm one of the most expensive—and successful—defense attorneys in King County." He named his firm, which obviously meant nothing to them. "I can't defend you myself, because I'm the one who chased you down. But if you give me the quilt now, tonight, I'll guarantee that one of my associates will defend you in court. With me looking over his shoulder, we'll get you off. I swear."

"How can you promise shit like that?" Bernard sneered.

"If I have to lie on the stand and swear you aren't the guy I saw driving the Subaru that first day, I'll do it."

There was a long, long pause, during which Brett withstood a scrutiny as intense as any he'd undergone from an entire jury box of doubtful citizens.

"Why would you do that?"

"Because this quilt means so much to Ella. My girlfriend." He enjoyed claiming her. And intended to keep claiming her. It hadn't taken him five minutes after leaving her house to know he'd been stupid to feel hurt at all. He'd just made her relive the most terrible thing that had ever happened to her. She could have been angry at him, or maybe she'd needed to say, *I'm not the only one with problems.* She was right, and that was okay.

Ella Torrence wasn't getting rid of him.

Bernard and the scrawny girl were still staring at him.

He cleared his throat, then described some of what Ella had said about the quilt—the bits of fabric from the groom's baby quilt, snippets from a dress the bride's grandma had made her when she was small. "The center part, with the house and the snowmen and the star, can never be replaced. It was made by the bride's mother, who died last year. This was her last gift of love to her daughter." Was that laying it on too thick? He continued, "A court-ordered attorney won't care much about you. He'll go through the motions, because that's his job. But to make Ella happy, I'll give your case my all."

"What if I show you the quilt, but I hold on to it until you *do* get me off?"

"No deal." There was nothing but steel in his voice. "You don't give it to me, I'm out of here."

The girlfriend stood on tiptoe and whispered in Kyle's ear. To Brett he said, "We need to talk."

Brett kept his posture relaxed. "I'll wait."

They disappeared down a short hallway. He could only make out scattered words of the whispered, urgent conversation. The very fact that they were talking at all convinced him they still had the quilt.

Bernard alone returned. "So, okay, we do have it, but that doesn't mean I stole the car." His chin had a pugnacious tilt.

"No, it doesn't," Brett agreed, as though he were calming a scared witness. "I've known people to sell houses with stuff left in the attic or basement."

Bernard stared sullenly at him. "That's right. You're not going to get me to say I stole that car."

The suspense was killing him, but Brett only nodded. "I won't even try." He paused. "Do we have a deal or not?"

There was one more agonizing hesitation. Then he gave an abrupt nod. "Yeah. Kayla is getting it."

It was all Brett could do not to pump his fist in the air or let a big grin split his face.

The girl came back with a slightly larger than expected box. The tape clearly having been ripped off. "There's a bunch of, like, old fabric in there. I guess she wants that, too?"

He hadn't thought about anything beyond the existing quilt, but nodded. "That's so the third cousin can use some of the same pieces, too, when she sews one more border around the outside."

"Oh." The girl—Kayla—nibbled on her lip. "It really is pretty. I guess I sort of wanted to keep it."

"I understand," he said gently, and he did. She probably didn't have much that was really pretty in her life. "But it will mean more to Olivia and—" What was the groom's name? "Eric," he said, grateful to remember.

She nodded and held out the box.

HAVING PUT IT off as long as she could, at nine-thirty Ella reluctantly sat down at the computer, opened her email program and began to type.

Rachel and Jo,

I'm sorry. I have the worst of news...

Five minutes later, she was reading over what she'd said when her doorbell rang.

Her heart gave a startled thump. "Who on earth...?"

Brett. It had to be Brett.

She flipped on the porch light and, through the small inset of leaded glass, could make out his face. Ella fumbled with the locks and flung open the door, ready to throw herself at him. "Brett! I'm so sorry for what I said! I didn't mean—"

She registered what he held under one arm. Her breath left her in a rush and she had to grip the door frame.

Triumph blazed in his grin. "You're not seeing things."

"How...?" was all she could manage to say.

"I made a deal." He explained in a few words.

Staring again at the box as if it held the crown jewels, she backed up and he followed her inside.

Suddenly speech was possible. "Did you look? You're sure it's mine?"

"I'm sure." He set the box on the sofa and opened it. "I checked before I shook hands on the deal."

"That's why you wanted to see a picture," Ella realized.

"Partly." He was careful when he lifted the now-folded fabric and laid it out, faceup, across the back of the sofa.

Through the blur of Ella's tears, the silver star shone with all the glory of the Christmas star that long-ago night, at least in her eyes.

"You did find it for me," she whispered. Her smile trembled and became a laugh of pure joy. "I can hardly wait to tell your mom and dad what you did."

He shook his head. What she mostly recognized on his face now was tenderness. "I didn't do it for them, or to prove anything to myself. What I wanted you to be sure of is that, when you need help, I'm here. And I need you to be there for me, too. Maybe you're used to being alone, but, uh, I'm hoping you'll learn to do things differently." There was a quick frown. "Not that I think I'm owed anything. I just want you to know I deliver when I make a promise. And," he seemed to take a deep breath, "I'd like to promise you a whole lot."

Ella was both laughing and crying when she went up on tiptoe to kiss him. "Nobody has ever done anything like this for me," she told him when their lips parted. She had to swipe at her wet cheeks. "You don't have to tell me, of all people, that you keep a promise."

He cupped her face and used his thumbs to capture her tears. "The question," he said, "is whether you believe *you* can keep a promise."

"Yes." In the miracle of the moment, her smile won over the tears. "Yes. I promise, I can. Earlier…"

He pressed his finger to her lips to silence her. He didn't even want an explanation. But she had to give him one anyway.

"I felt so inadequate." She knew she was flushed. "Just for a minute, I was mad and wanted to prove you weren't any more together than I am. But it isn't true—"

"It is." He smiled gently. "And you were right. I've been ignoring the fact that I was unhappy because I didn't want to disappoint Dad."

Ella shook her head. "I'm not so sure you will."

He waggled his head a little. "Maybe, maybe not. The point is, when I went to law school, I had a fire for justice. You can achieve that on both sides of the courtroom, but I realize now that what I'm doing isn't right for me. I'm going to quit and apply for a job at the prosecutor's office. That's where I belong." A wry smile broke out. "Crappy pay or no."

Ella laughed, though tears burned in her eyes, too. "I'm proud of you," she whispered.

Brett made a sound, raw and needy, just before he bent his head. But she stopped him with a hand on his chest. "Wait! I have to delete an email."

She rushed to her home office and the desktop, where the email was still open. Ella highlighted and deleted the text, leaving the subject heading: *The wedding quilt.*

And then, in the body, she typed, *Rachel, I'm mailing the quilt to you first thing in the morning. I can hardly wait to find out what you do to finish it. And better yet, to see you again—you and Jo and Olivia.* She added her name, and then moved the cursor to Send.

In an instant, the email was on its way, and she

turned to face the man who leaned in the doorway, his gaze resting on her face.

He understood exactly what she felt, sending that email instead of the one she had already written.

It only took her two steps to cross the small room and go into his arms.

* * * * *

NINE LADIES DANCING

Sarah Mayberry

CHAPTER ONE

RACHEL MACINTOSH KNEW she was in trouble the moment she opened the box and caught her first glimpse of the quilt.

She'd been expecting the delivery ever since her cousin Ella had emailed to let her know it was on the way. The instant the postman had handed it over, she'd ripped the box open, eager to see the fruits of her cousins' labors.

"Oh, boy. Wow." Her words echoed in the front hallway, filled with the awe she felt as she touched the delicately stitched ornaments hanging off one of the many trees that formed the outer border of the quilt.

She wasn't sure what she'd been expecting. Something a bit folksy, maybe. Like something you'd find at a church fete, handmade by someone with more enthusiasm than skill. But the quilt panel she unfolded from the box was nothing less than a work of art. From the central panel depicting the Miller family's lake house, Hollymeade, to the two intricately sewn borders, the quilt was simply stunning. Beautifully, intricately worked, crisply pieced together, the colors harmonizing wonderfully...

And she was supposed to put the final border on this gorgeous creation. Her mind boggled.

She carried the quilt into the living room of her small cottage and spread it over the edge of the sofa. Taking a step back, she surveyed the quilt in its entirety, shaking her head in wonder and growing trepidation.

She hadn't even sewed on a button in more than ten years. As for quilting… The last time she'd quilted had been that final summer she'd spent with her cousins Jo, Olivia and Ella at Hollymeade. She'd been fifteen then, and she was thirty-three now. To say her quilting skills were a little rusty was the understatement of the century.

"This is officially not good," she said.

Her first instinct, born of panic, was to email Ella and Jo and tell them that there was no way she was capable of matching their skill, and that they needed to work out another way to finish the quilt. The last thing Rachel wanted to do was tarnish everyone else's amazing contributions with a substandard offering. This quilt was far too important for that: a message of love from beyond the grave from Aunt Gloria to her daughter Olivia, a lovingly crafted reminder that although Olivia had lost her mother, she would always have her love.

But that was just her first instinct. Instead of rushing to her computer and firing off that email, Rachel sat and contemplated the quilt some more, taking in all the small, delicate details, absorbing all the love and care and creativity and attention that had gone into these few square feet of fabric and thread.

She wanted to be a part of this, even though it was daunting in the extreme. She wanted to do her bit to celebrate Olivia's upcoming Christmas wedding, and she dearly wanted to help make her aunt Gloria's final wish come true.

Which meant wimping out was not an option.

She slapped her hands against her thighs, the sound decisive and bracing at the same time. Okay. If she was going to do this, she would do it right. She would go in all guns blazing. And she would need help.

Carefully she folded the quilt and packed it back into its box. If she had the choice, she normally walked into town, as her house was located only a few blocks from the busy main street of the seaside town of Sorrento, Australia. Today she didn't have the time to walk, though, so she reversed her bright red Mini Cooper—vintage, not new—onto the street and zipped into town.

She spotted Gabby's gray head the moment she entered the other woman's wool and fabric store. Rachel's shoulders immediately relaxed. The older woman was a regular at the library where Rachel worked, and she and Rachel had had a number of friendly chats about the various quilting and other craft books Gabby borrowed. That was the thing about working at the library in a small town—Rachel knew everyone's preoccupations and peccadilloes. Their public ones, anyway.

If anyone could help her with the quilt, it was Gabby. Maybe she even offered a quilting course Rachel could take. Or some other miraculous solution to her dilemma.

Rachel studied Gabby while she waited for the other woman to finish serving someone else. In her mid- to late-fifties, Gabby wore her hair in a short bob, a style that suited her fine-boned face. Her blue eyes were warm with interest and good humor, one of the many reasons she'd become one of Rachel's favorite patrons at the library.

Finally Gabby turned to Rachel with a friendly smile.

"Rachel. Looks like it's my chance to help you for a change. What can I do for you?"

"I need your advice. And maybe a reality check."

Very aware of the other customers waiting behind her, Rachel explained the situation as succinctly as possible before unfolding a portion of the quilt to show Gabby.

"Oh, yes. This is beautiful. I can see why you're nervous."

"I'm not nervous. I'm petrified. Am I also insane to even consider taking this on?"

"Well, as long as you go slowly, I'm sure you can create something just as beautiful. How much time did you say you have?"

"Until Christmas. So, four months, give or take."

Gabby reached out and patted her arm. "Relax. We can do this."

Never in her entire life had Rachel been so pleased to hear the word *we*.

"Oh. Thank God."

"We close at one on Saturdays. Can you hang around for fifteen minutes? Then we can go over things in more detail without being rushed."

"Absolutely."

Rachel moved off to one side, extraordinarily grateful for Gabby's generosity. Twenty minutes later, the last customer was gone and Gabby leaned a hip against the counter. "I've been mulling things over while I was serving those last few people, and I think the first step is for you to decide what you'd like to do for your border. Can I suggest you do a bit of reading and looking around on the internet to see what tickles your fancy before we reconvene?"

"That makes sense. Should I keep anything in mind while I'm researching?"

"Let's take a look at the quilt properly."

Between them, they spread the quilt across the cutting counter.

"My gut instinct is that you need to keep the color

palette pretty simple," Gabby said after considering it for a few minutes. "There are so many wonderful things happening on this quilt, you don't want to introduce a new color or element and risk making it appear messy."

"So I should maybe pick one or two of the dominant colors in the piece?" Rachel said thoughtfully.

"Perhaps. But work out what appeals to you first, then we can discuss ways and means and colors. I've got a few books at home that you might find helpful— coffee-table books on quilting and a few beginners' guides."

"They sound perfect."

Gabby pulled her handbag from beneath the counter. "I'll drop them by the library for you on Monday, if you like."

"I would like. I would like very much."

Very aware that Gabby's working day was over, Rachel thanked her once again before heading home, immeasurably relieved that she now had a plan. Not much of a plan, granted, but she had faith in Gabby and the power of research. After all, what librarian worth their salt wasn't awesome at research?

She could do this. She *would* do this. For Olivia, and for Aunt Gloria.

LEO BENNETT WOKE to the sound of heavy things being moved around. He frowned, then opened his eyes and blinked blearily at the clock on the bedside table. Three o'clock. Why was his mother rearranging her house at three o'clock on a Saturday afternoon?

He used his good arm to push himself into a sitting position and reached for the glass of water beside his bed. He felt fuzzy-headed and prickly and too hot. His collarbone also ached, along with his sprained wrist.

Nothing new there. They'd been paining him the exact same way since he'd injured them three weeks ago.

Three weeks. Damn.

He closed his eyes as the reality of it hit him all over again. For a moment he could almost hear Cameron's laughter, the teasing note his mate got in his voice when he was trying to goad Leo into running another kilometer or haul ass up another flight of stairs. He saw Cameron's face, big eyed and open, always on the verge of smiling.

It just didn't seem possible that all that life, all that energy, had been gone from the world for three weeks now. But it was. He was dead.

He heard another bang, and the pressure at the back of Leo's eyes increased. He swung his feet over the side of the bed and pushed himself to his feet. The worst thing about his injuries was that they gave him too much time to think. He didn't want to think—or feel, for that matter—right now. He wanted...

He wasn't sure what he wanted.

To turn back the clock.

But that wasn't possible.

He used his good hand to pull on a pair of track pants, then slipped the sling over his shoulder and slid his bad arm into it. He found his mother on her hands and knees in the study next door, pawing through stacks of books.

"What's going on?" he asked.

"Oh, hello. How are you feeling?" She smiled up at him, her eyes filled with the mix of worried pity-sympathy that had become her stock-in-trade since she'd collected him from the hospital and brought him to his childhood home on the Mornington Peninsula to recover.

That expression made him want to grind his teeth. Among other things.

"I'm fine." He could hear how brusque he sounded, how terse, but for the life of him he couldn't moderate it.

"Do you need your pain medication? You're frowning again. Do you have a headache?" His mother started to push herself to her feet.

"I can get my own tablets."

She gave him an assessing look before sinking back to her knees. "All right. But the offer is there if you want it."

He breathed in through his nose, counting to ten. She was trying to help, to make things easy for him. She didn't understand that he didn't want things to be easy.

"What's with all the books?" he asked.

"I'm sorting through them for a friend. You might know her, actually. Rachel Macintosh? You would have gone to school together. Dark hair, dark eyes?"

The name drew a blank, but his mother was waiting expectantly, so he frowned and dug deeper. His efforts yielded only a vague, out-of-focus impression of a tall, gangly girl with mousy-brown hair.

"Yeah, maybe. She's the one from America, right?"

He vaguely remembered that she'd appeared in school in the middle of year nine or ten, a transplant from the U.S.

"That's her. She still has a bit of an accent, actually. I like it a lot. Something to do with her r's and her vowels."

"Right."

"Anyway, she's inherited a quilt that she needs to complete and I said I'd help her out."

Leo tried to seem interested as his mother explained something about round-robin quilting and a wedding at Christmas and how Rachel needed a crash course to get her skills up to scratch. But it was hard to muster interest in a stranger's sewing project.

Then again, it was hard to muster interest in much at all at the moment. The counsellor he'd been forced to see as a matter of policy had told him that depression and anger were normal reactions after both an accident and the death of a close colleague. Which made it all okay, of course. Having the official seal of approval that his feelings were "normal" made them so much easier to deal with. He was practically skipping through the meadow, he was so well-adjusted.

"Let me get you something to eat," his mother said. "I bet you haven't had anything since breakfast."

He hadn't had breakfast, either, and he still wasn't hungry. He followed her into the kitchen, though, and ate the sandwich she made him because he knew he had to eat. Life went on, after all.

"I was thinking I'd offer to give Rachel a few lessons, if that wouldn't bother you too much," his mother said as she poured him a second glass of juice.

"Why would it bother me?"

"We'd probably have to use the living room to set up the sewing machine. I don't want to cramp your style."

Where did his mum get these sayings from?

"I don't exactly have a lot of style to cramp right now. In case you hadn't noticed." He indicated his sling and casual clothing.

"I just don't want you to feel crowded if you'd rather not have people around." She said it so gently, her eyes brimming with sympathy.

"Do what suits you, Mum," he said, pushing away from the table.

He dumped his plate in the sink and retreated from her unwanted pity, returning to the guest room with its single bed, dainty Queen Anne furniture and pastel prints of thatched-roof cottages. He'd managed to man it up a little with a pile of clothes and shoes in the corner, but there was no denying the essential alienness of his environment.

He was displaced and off balance. And he had no idea how to even start regaining his equilibrium.

His best friend was dead, and he should have been there to save him.

Dropping back onto the bed, he closed his eyes and willed himself back to sleep.

A WEEK LATER, Rachel parked her Mini in front of a white-painted timber home in one of Sorrento's most coveted streets. Thirty meters away, the road petered out into a sandy dead end and a foot path took over, wending its way through a narrow band of bush until it hit the beach. Gabby's house was only one story and more rambling than opulent—the neighboring properties were far grander, although most of them were of a similar vintage to Gabby's. Old Sorrento money, in other words, as opposed to the nouveau riche currently gobbling up real estate left, right and center in town.

It was the convenience factor that made it so sought after, Rachel figured. Sorrento was a mere hour-and-a-half drive south from Melbourne, making it a favorite weekend bolt-hole for the wealthy looking to shake the dust of the city off their feet. Fortunately for the locals, most of them went back to the city come Sunday evening. From the back of her car, Rachel collected the

stack of books she'd borrowed from Gabby before sling-
ing a wicker basket over her arm. It was heavy with a
bottle of wine and a loaf cake she'd baked this morning, both gifts to say thank-you to Gabby for the books
and her invitation to lunch today. Lastly, she grabbed
the bag with the quilt in it, since it was the star of today's show. Feeling like an overloaded pack mule, she
made her way to the front door and used her elbow to
ring the doorbell.

Gabby appeared almost instantly, her face flushed.

"Rachel. Come in. Sorry, I got caught up at work and
I'm running a little behind."

Gabby led her down a bright hallway lined with an
eclectic selection of artwork—etchings and tiny oil
paintings of boats on the bay and a selection of modern tapestries. They passed what Rachel figured was a
formal lounge room before emerging into a more casual
area, complete with country-style kitchen, mismatched
antique dining setting and two big, lumpy-looking
feather-down couches upholstered in creamy linen.

"Wow. This is gorgeous. It's as if I've stepped into
Country Living magazine," Rachel said.

"Thank you. Most of it's purely accidental. Bits and
pieces I've picked up around the traps over the years.
Here, let me take some of that for you."

"I brought a cake. And wine," Rachel said, handing
over her offerings.

"Oh, the cake's still warm from the oven. How wonderful." Gabby smiled, but there was a faint air of dis-
traction about her that gave Rachel pause.

She looked tired, too, the fine lines around her eyes
and mouth more deeply etched than usual. If she and
Gabby had been closer, she would have simply come
right out and asked if everything was okay. But she

wasn't the type to wade in willy-nilly when she didn't know someone very well. One of the many side effects of being more comfortable with books than with people.

"Is there anything I can do to help?" she asked instead.

"I was just about to set the table."

"Let me do that, then." Rachel eased the cutlery from Gabby's hand and turned toward the table. It was only when she started setting out the knives and forks that she realized Gabby had handed her three of everything. She was about to comment on it when she registered that there were three place mats on the table, too.

Huh. She was pretty sure Gabby was divorced. But maybe there was a man on the scene that Rachel wasn't aware of. Very possible, given their conversations to date had been limited to books and now quilting.

"You're wondering about the third place setting. My son might be joining us. I'm not sure, though…" Gabby smiled uncertainly.

She seemed a little anxious. Because he might join them? Or because he might not?

Rachel had no idea. Either way, it was none of her business. She was here because Gabby was so generously holding her hand while she grappled with the quilt. End of story.

"Actually, I might go see if he's up yet. At least we'll know then if he's eating with us."

Gabby left the room. Rachel straightened the place mats, then spotted the glasses Gabby had set out on the counter, and allocated one per setting. All the while, she tried not to speculate about a grown adult son who was still asleep at two in the afternoon. Maybe he did shift work. Or maybe he was sick. Or maybe—

"I think we're on our own. Shall I open the wine?" Gabby said as she breezed back into the room.

"That would be nice."

Gabby insisted on looking at the pages Rachel had tagged in the books as they ate open ham-and-salad sandwiches, and they wound up with piles of books scattered across the table. They discussed the pros and cons of the various ideas that had appealed to Rachel, as well as possible color combinations, working their way through the bottle of wine.

By the time Gabby served the cake, Rachel was feeling a little flushed and very content. Relaxing into her chair, she glanced back and forth between the two pattern options they had narrowed it down to. She was well and truly torn. Option number one was a white border that seemed deceptively simple at first blush, but was in fact richly decorated with a white-on-white appliqué of scrolling vines. The second option was a simple repeating block pattern in varied dark tones.

"I feel as though I'm being asked to choose between the Dark Side and the Light Side," Rachel said as Gabby handed her some cake. She sucked on her teeth and did her best Darth Vader heavy-breathing impersonation.

Gabby laughed, then her gaze shifted over Rachel's shoulder and her eyebrows rose in surprise. "You're up. I wasn't sure if you were interested in lunch or not, but I saved you a sandwich and Rachel has brought us a gorgeous banana cake."

All the little hairs on the back of Rachel's arms stood on end. She glanced down at them, bemused, before twisting in her seat so she could greet Gabby's son.

And stopped breathing.

The man standing in the doorway wore nothing but a pair of raggedy old track pants, a sling and a five-o'clock shadow. His dark brown hair was mussed, and from the cut of his muscles he must have spent the last century or so working out in the gym.

Leo Bennett.

Gabby's son was *Leo Bennett.*

Instantly everything she'd just eaten turned to lead in her stomach. The aftertaste of wine was sour in her mouth, and the smell of freshly baked cake made her want to push her chair away from the table.

Her gaze went to her car keys, sitting on the kitchen counter.

She wanted out of here. Now.

But, of course, that wasn't going to be possible. Forcing her lips into what she hoped was a reasonable facsimile of a polite smile, Rachel prepared to be nice to one of the most obnoxious men she'd ever had the misfortune to know.

CHAPTER TWO

LEO SHIFTED HIS weight back on his heels, momentarily thrown to discover his mother wasn't alone. He'd forgotten about her lunch date with Rachel What's-her-name. He wasn't great at holding on to those kinds of details at the best of times—and this was definitely not the best of times.

His mother's guest was looking at him as though he'd just exited a spaceship, so he figured that gave him a free pass to check her out just as blatantly. She had long dark hair pulled into a high ponytail, pale skin and large dark eyes. She wasn't a knockout, but she wasn't ugly, either. Pretty, his mother would probably say. It was hard to confirm while she was sitting, but she looked as though she was probably tall and slim, maybe even a little on the skinny side.

And if the way she was averting her eyes from his bare chest was anything to go by, she didn't get out much.

"I didn't realize you had company, Mum. I can eat in my room," he said.

"Don't be silly. Come and meet Rachel. If you're nice, she might recommend some books for you to read while you recover."

Rachel shifted in her seat. Her smile seemed forced as she met his gaze.

"What sort of books do you like?"

"I don't really read."

"Oh." Her eyes darted toward his mother, as if she was wondering why his mum had mentioned books if he didn't read.

"You used to love it when you were young," his mother said. "Sit down, I'll be back in a tick."

His mother strode from the room, her pale purple shirt billowing. Rachel shifted in her seat again, then cleared her throat.

He waited for her to say something, but she didn't. *He* should probably say something to break the awkward silence. She was his mother's guest, after all. But for the life of him he couldn't think of a single thing to say.

Instead, he crossed to the fridge and collected the sandwich his mother had left for him. He glanced toward the table as he closed the fridge door. Rachel's back was to him, her head bowed as she leafed through one of the colorful books on the table.

She had a slim neck, long and elegant.

"Mum tells me we went to school together," he said.

She glanced over her shoulder, the movement making her ponytail swish across her back. "That's right."

"Did we have English together?" He had a vague memory of a tall, dark-haired girl sitting near the door of his English class.

"I don't remember."

His mother returned with a T-shirt in hand. "Here you go. So we don't have to sit and stare at your rack all through lunch."

He shook his head. "Where do you get this stuff?"

"I'm hip. You know that," his mum said, resting a hand on his good shoulder and giving him a light squeeze. "Would you like some wine?"

"No. Thanks."

The last thing he wanted was to hang out in the kitchen and be forced to make conversation, but somehow he found himself threading his injured arm through the armhole of the shirt and shrugging into it. His mother steered him into the seat opposite Rachel and placed his sandwich in front of him. Rachel reached for her wineglass and took a sip. It was only when she set it down again that he realized her grip was white-knuckle tight.

His gaze went to her face. Her expression was carefully neutral as she fiddled with one of the books again, peeling off a sticky note she'd stuck to the corner of one of the pages. She was clearly one of those shy, bookish women. Was that what the white-knuckle thing was about?

"So, Rachel and I have narrowed it down to two choices for the quilt border," his mother said as she resumed her seat.

"Right."

"Actually, I think I've decided on the white one," Rachel said. She was very careful to keep her eyes trained on his mother, not so much as blinking in his direction.

Definitely shy. Probably freaked because she'd seen him without his shirt on.

"Oh, good. That will be really beautiful. A snowy-white frame," his mother enthused. "Leo, remember how I told you Rachel's taken on this big quilting project?"

"Right." He took a big bite of his sandwich, eager to get this torture over and done with. Sewing wasn't exactly his thing.

"When was the last time you did any appliqué work, Rachel?" his mother asked.

"It's been a while. I'm going to need lots of practice."

"We can get you there, don't worry. What sort of sewing machine do you have?"

"It's an old one I bought secondhand years ago. I don't know what brand."

Leo ate the rest of his sandwich as the two women talked sewing, then silently accepted a piece of cake when his mother passed it to him. Rachel's cake was untouched, he noticed, while her wineglass was now empty.

He tuned back in to the conversation, guessing they'd come to some arrangement regarding the use of his mother's sewing machine, as she said, "Great, that's settled. I'm sure you'll find my machine much easier to work with. It's amazing how they've improved in the last ten or so years." His mother stood and went to the counter, slicing off another piece of cake. He was busy chasing the last crumbs across his plate with a fork, but some instinct made him look up just in time to catch Rachel watching him. She glanced away immediately, but not before he'd seen the unalloyed dislike in her eyes.

Whoa. Where had that *come from?*

He was still trying to work out if he'd really seen what he thought he'd seen when his mother slid a second slice of cake onto his plate.

"No, thanks. I'm done," he said, pushing the plate away.

"Humor me and have another slice. I don't want you getting scrawny on my watch."

He bit back a sigh. He got that his mother was trying to take care of him, but he didn't want her hovering over him, monitoring his food intake.

"I'm good. Why don't you have it later." He picked up the plate and offered it to her.

"I'll just leave it here for you and you can have it if

you feel like it," his mother said, putting the plate back on the table in front of him.

It was a small thing, a tiny tussle of wills, but it pushed him from mildly irritated to red-hot angry in no seconds flat. He'd been polite, played the game. She needed to listen to him. Stop assuming she knew better than he did. Stop being so damn nice and kind all the time when he didn't deserve it.

"I said no." His voice echoed harshly off the hard surfaces in the kitchen. Out of the corner of his eye he saw Rachel flinch.

What was she, a bloody field mouse or something?

He stood, not looking at either his mother or her guest as he made his way to the door to the garden. Then he was outside, the sun on his face as he strode across the lawn and into the cool leafiness of the miniature orchard his mother had created at the rear of her lot.

He stopped beneath an apple tree, resting his hand against the smooth bark. He lowered his head, staring unseeingly at the ground as the anger drained out of him like water from a bath.

After a minute he sighed and straightened, passing a hand over his face. He owed his mother an apology. Another one.

He walked farther into the orchard, stopping to check the budding fruit on what he thought might be an apricot tree. Maybe he should move back to his apartment, save his mother from his surliness. He could cope with most things on his own now, and his wrist would soon be at the point where he could start using it again.

Then he pictured himself sitting alone in his apartment in the city, imagined how empty and long the days would feel.

Maybe he'd stay with his mother for another few days, after all. If she'd have him.

"I'M SORRY ABOUT that. That was my fault. I shouldn't have pushed him."

Rachel watched as Gabby fussed around the table, clearing plates and tidying up.

"You don't have to apologize."

Leo the Loser was the one who should do that. What an ass. He hadn't changed one iota since they'd left school.

Small correction, if I may: he's filled out just a little.

Okay, fine, he'd clearly devoted some serious time to pumping iron, or whatever it was that men did to create the kind of manscape she'd just been subjected to. Big arms, defined pecs, flat belly. Shoulders to make Atlas proud.

But the rest of him was exactly the same. Arrogant. Boorish. Rude and crude.

As for him asking if they'd taken English together... Unbelievable. She'd sat next to him in Australian history for two years in a row. They'd even done a four-week assignment together on the Eureka Stockade.

But apparently a lowly creature such as herself had been beneath the notice of the great and popular Leo Bennett. Clearly she hadn't had a low enough IQ or large enough bra size to register in his world.

Which was more than fine with her because he was a jerk. The kind who took his foul temper out on his lovely, generous, kind mother.

"He's not himself at the moment," Gabby said, returning to the table. "Normally he's so sunny. A glass-half-full person. But this accident has really rocked him."

Rachel frowned. Gabby obviously had a mother's rose-colored view of her son.

"Ever since he told me he'd been accepted into the fire department, I've dreaded getting a 1:00 a.m. phone call." Gabby shook her head. "Don't get me wrong, what he does is courageous and honorable and absolutely necessary, but I hate imagining him out there, literally running into danger... He had his heart set on it, though, and he's clearly good at his job because he's risen up the ranks. But now poor Cameron is dead and I don't know what to do or say to help him get through this..." Gabby's voice broke and she used her fingertips to wipe away the tears that were spilling down her cheeks.

For a moment Rachel sat dumbly as Gabby's words sank in. Leo had been injured on the job, attending a fire. He was a firefighter. And his friend had died in the line of duty.

A horrible set of circumstances. For anyone.

Even a jerk.

Gabby sniffed and Rachel reached across the table to snag her basket, fumbling inside until she found the minipack of tissues she always carried in case her hay fever was playing up.

"Here."

She passed the tissues over and Gabby gave her a watery smile. "Thank you. Sorry about this."

"Please don't apologize. You've been so kind to me, I have no idea how I'll ever return the favor."

"It's nothing. I'm more than happy to help."

"When did all this happen?"

She didn't want to feel sorry for Leo. Not when he'd been so rude to his mother. Not when she knew how obnoxious he'd been in the past. But it simply wasn't in her to ignore another person's pain.

"It's been four weeks, give or take a day."

"Then it's early days yet. He's probably still coming to terms with everything. Trying to find his feet. I'm sure he'll come around once he's had a chance to process everything."

"I know. But it's hard to watch him be in so much pain and not be able to help. If only he'd talk to me."

"Maybe he's not ready to talk yet."

"Maybe." Gabby gave herself a shake. "Listen to me, moaning at you. Would you like a cup of tea? Or maybe a coffee?"

Rachel could only smile at Gabby's unstinting generosity. In the midst of her own crisis, Gabby still put others first.

"I'm fine. So fine, in fact, I'm going to help you clean up and then I'm going to get out of your hair and let you have the rest of your weekend to yourself."

"Oh, you don't have to go. Please don't feel that way," Gabby said.

Rachel fibbed and said she had other plans, then did her bit to help tidy up, one eye on the door the whole time, just in case Leo returned. She heaved a silent sigh of relief when they'd packed the last plate into the dishwasher and he still hadn't appeared.

"I'll see you next weekend, then?" Gabby said as she escorted Rachel to the front door.

For a moment Rachel considered coming up with an excuse that would allow her to neatly sidestep the possibility of ever having to be in the same room as Leo Bennett again. The thing was, she wasn't the sort of person who made friends very easily and she really liked Gabby. And—more important—she desperately needed Gabby's help with the quilt.

"Shall we say two again? And this time, I'll bring lunch," Rachel said.

They finalized arrangements and ten seconds later Rachel was in her car. The moment the door closed behind her, the smile dropped from her face.

She felt…rattled. Seeing Leo standing in the doorway had been a punch to the gut, there was no getting around it. Which was crazy. It had been more than *fifteen years* since he'd stomped so carelessly and callously on her teenage self-esteem. She'd convinced herself she'd moved on. She was a grown, adult woman now. She was buying her own home. She had a job she loved. She might be single at the moment, but that was by choice. She had her dancing, and her friends, and her garden. She liked who she was.

So why did Leo unsettle you so comprehensively?

She didn't like this. At all. She didn't want him to have that sort of power over her. She'd wasted far too many hours dreaming up ways of proving him wrong or hurting him in the way he'd hurt her when she was fifteen.

God, she'd been so miserable for those first six months in Australia.…

A car drove past and she glanced out the window to discover she was in her own driveway. She couldn't remember driving home.

Okay, that was a little scary.

Determined to shake off her weird mood, she let herself into her house and went straight to the iPod dock on her mantelpiece. Two seconds later, the lively beat of El Gran Combo filled the living room. Kicking off her flat shoes, she rose up onto the balls of her feet and started to dance the salsa. She held her arms high and loose, imagining that Greg was leading her around the dance floor. She swirled and spun and swiveled her way back and forth across the timber floor, letting the music sweep everything from her mind except an awareness of her body and the beat.

After five minutes she was breathless and smiling again.

She was endlessly, eternally grateful for the trick of fate that had made her win the raffle at the local school fair just over a year ago. First prize had been five salsa classes at Rosebud Dance Studio. Her first thought had been to give them to someone else, but her friend Lindy had volunteered to come with her. Five minutes into their first lesson, Rachel had made the extraordinary discovery that she had natural rhythm.

From that moment on she'd been hooked, to the point where she'd started dancing with a dedicated partner—Greg—and had even allowed herself to be talked into competing. They'd braved their first competition last month and had danced through it with flying colors. In fact, they'd made it to the next round, a statewide salsa competition where nine different studios would pit their best against one another.

The track on her iPod finished, switching to a slower, more soulful ballad. She started across the room to find something more peppy, only to stop in her tracks when she registered the very large, very fluffy cat sitting on the arm of her sofa.

"Claudius. Come on. We've had the you-don't-belong-in-here conversation a million times."

The cat blinked slowly, utterly unaffected by her warning. She sighed and advanced on him.

"Okay. You asked for it."

Picking him up, she took him to the back door and

set him on the doorstep, pointing him toward his own house next door.

"Off with you, go home."

She did a quick tour of the house to find where he'd gained entry and located a half-open window in her bedroom. She really needed to be better about keeping her windows shut because, clearly, Claudius was no respecter of property boundaries. If she wasn't careful, she would wind up with shredded furniture like Claudius's doting owner, Jane, next door. Not a happy prospect.

She pottered around the house for the rest of the afternoon and evening, doing chores and catching up on her favorite TV series, but nothing held her attention. Finally, she turned out the light at ten.

The next thing she knew, she was awake and it was dark and her body was clammy with sweat. Her heart was hammering in her chest, beating out a frantic tattoo. She blinked up at the ceiling, slowly coming back down to earth.

She'd had a bad dream. A running dream, the kind where no matter how fast or hard she ran she never escaped.

She frowned, trying to remember what she'd been running from. Vague images came to her—a dark, dimly lit room. The smell of cigarette smoke. The distant bass beat of dance music.

She swore under her breath as she realized where her dream had taken her. Back to high school. Back to that horrible night when she was fifteen years old and Leo Bennett had crushed her beneath the heel of his very cool biker boots.

She swung her legs over the side of the bed and walked to the kitchen. The house was dark and silent around her as she ran herself a glass of water straight from the tap. Standing at the kitchen sink, she gulped it down. Then she set the empty glass on the drainer and very deliberately forced herself to remember that night. Because the only way she knew how to defang the monsters under the bed was to shine a bright light on them.

She and her mother had been in Australia for only three months at that point. She'd been dragged halfway across the world by her mother's love for a big, quiet Australian man called Tom. A relationship that had lasted barely a year—but that was a whole other story. After three months, Rachel had literally still been finding her way around her new school, trying to understand the new culture she'd landed in, painfully homesick for people and places and things that were known and familiar and beloved. She'd made tentative friends with a couple of girls, but she'd still been mourning the friendships she'd left behind, and there'd been so many things in her new country that were just plain wrong. Football, for one, and there was cricket instead of baseball and she'd kept forgetting to look to the right when she crossed the road instead of the left...

But she'd really been looking forward to the school dance. Her mom had taken her shopping and bought her a new dress and new shoes and new dangly earrings. Standing in front of her bedroom mirror the night of the dance, she'd felt almost beautiful, despite the fact that she was almost a head taller than every other girl in her class and, worse still, flat chested. Her dress was silky, the color of caramel, and it made her look elegant and willowy and mysterious instead of gangly and skinny, and the tiny heels on her shoes made satisfying clicking noises when she walked.

Her mother dropped her at the school, one of many

parents issuing last-minute instructions. Still buoyed by those moments in front of her mirror, Rachel made her way to the school gym. She'd arranged to meet her friends near the door, but they were nowhere to be seen. She hovered, uncertain and increasingly self-conscious. After fifteen minutes, she decided to find the bathroom, just to make it look as though she had somewhere to go instead of standing around like a loser with no friends.

She got lost straight off the bat and wound up in the sporting-equipment storage area. It was as good a place to kill ten minutes as any, so she found herself a comfortable spot sitting on a pile of gym mats in the far corner. She was gazing off into space, composing a mental letter to her cousins back home, when the door opened and a group of laughing boys entered. She shrank back into the shadows, not wanting to get busted for hiding in here on her own—there'd be teasing and talk and questions if she was. She already had enough strikes against her with her height and her accent and her too-shy demeanor.

"Here, pass it over," one of the boys said.

She heard the snick of a lighter and smelled smoke.

They were sneaking a cigarette. Probably drinking, too. Sure enough, she heard the slosh of something liquid against glass.

"Don't be a hog," someone else said.

"What time is Sharon getting here, Leo?" the first guy asked.

Rachel realized who the guys were then: Leo Bennett and his faithful followers, Tim Young and Shane Waugh. They were all football players, and every girl in school followed them with hungry eyes. Especially Leo, with his dark hair and unusual blue-brown eyes and broad shoulders. Rachel might have been on the outer edge of the high school social scene, but even she knew Leo and Sharon Taylor had been circling each other for the past few weeks. Rumor had it that they would soon be a couple.

"Don't know. She'll find me when she gets here."

The guys thought that was pretty funny and the snick of the lighter sounded again as they started another cigarette.

"What about that Tina chick?" Tim asked next.

"What about her?" Leo said.

"She's hot for it."

"Then you give it to her," Leo said. "I've got better things to do with my time."

More laughter, then they launched into a casually efficient assessment of a number of other girls from Rachel's year level. Girls were dismissed for being too fat, having big noses, for not having any breasts. Other girls were lauded for being "hot" or "up for it." Hiding in the shadows, Rachel was both fascinated and repelled. So this was what boys talked about when there were no girls around.

Then she heard her name and forgot to breathe.

"What about that new chick? The Yank. Rachel or whatever," Shane said.

"Which one is she?" Leo asked.

"The tall one. Legs up to her armpits."

"The plank? Give us a break," Leo scoffed.

"She's not that bad," Shane said. "She's got a cool accent."

"Mate, if I woke up and found that lying next to me, I'd chew my own arm off to get away. That's how bad she is," Leo had said. "I'd rather cut it off than stick it in her. Next, please."

Rachel held her hand over mouth to stop herself from

reacting out loud and giving herself away. She sat like that for another ten minutes, waiting until they finished assassinating the rest of the female population of the school. Then she wiped away her tears and slunk out of the room and back to the gym. Her friends had arrived by then, but she'd lost any desire to dance or have fun. Instead, she sat alone on the sidelines and watched Leo and his gang of jerks own the world.

She stared across the gym at them, miserable and filled with rage and hurt. She wanted to storm across the room and punch Leo in the face or scream that he didn't know her, knew nothing about her.

She didn't, of course, just went home and cried herself to sleep. Over the next couple of days and for the rest of her high school years, in fact, she'd avoided Leo as much as possible, knowing him for what he was—a stupid, arrogant, egotistical meathead. She told herself his opinion shouldn't and didn't matter. And yet her avoidance of the most popular kid in school had kept her in the outer circle.

Then they'd graduated and he'd left town, and she'd released all of her anger and hurt like a balloon into the sky.

Until this afternoon, when she'd turned and found him standing there so unexpectedly, and she realized that some of that anger and hurt had stayed with her.

She let her breath out on a sigh and pushed her hair off her forehead. Such silly old stuff, it should have no power whatsoever over her now. But there was something about teenage hurts that made them resonate, even years later.

Still, once this quilt was done and Leo left his mother's place, he would go back to wherever it was he lived. She wouldn't let him dictate her life again.

In the meantime, she had work tomorrow. Silent as a ghost, she walked through the darkened house to her bedroom.

CHAPTER THREE

LEO HEARD THE voices the moment he let himself into the house. His mother's voice, full of amusement, and Rachel Macintosh's, her tone droll and dry as she finished a story that made his mother burst into laughter.

"You think that's funny, but believe me, I was not laughing at the time," Rachel said.

She was laughing now, though, a low, slightly husky sound that made him frown. She didn't look like the sort of woman who was capable of a laugh like that. She came across as uptight and pent up; that laugh was easy and relaxed and maybe even a bit sexy.

"You are so funny, Rachel. I think you missed your calling. You should be a stand-up comedian," his mother said.

"Hey, I'm not making this stuff up. We are surrounded by a bunch of very strange people in this town. Which is just as well, because it would be pretty boring—"

Rachel broke off the second he appeared in the kitchen doorway, the smile freezing on her face. His mother swiveled in her chair to look at him.

"That was a long walk. Where did you go?"

"Up to the point and back."

"I saved you some pasta salad. Rachel brought it."

"Great. Thanks."

"Do you want me to get some for you?" his mother asked.

"I'll get it. Thanks. I don't want to interrupt."

Rachel still hadn't raised her eyes to him, he couldn't help but notice. Instead, she'd taken hold of some kind of small sewing tool and was picking away at a seam.

"We're going great guns here. Rachel's a quick study," his mother said.

"So this is just a dry run, not the real thing?" he said to Rachel.

He figured he should make an effort to sound interested in their project since he hadn't exactly put his best foot forward last time.

Rachel didn't respond immediately, only lifting her gaze when the silence stretched to awkwardness.

"Sorry. I didn't realize you were talking to me." Her smile was stiff, her eyes sliding away from him as though she had to force herself to look at him. "Yes, it's a practice run."

She returned to her sewing. The first time he'd met her, he'd figured she was shy, but there was something about the way she couldn't meet his eyes and the flat note to her voice that made him wonder if something else was going on.

"How long before you attempt the real thing?" he asked.

"Not for a while," she said.

Again, her gaze was focused on something over his shoulder, not quite connecting with him. And, again, he found himself staring at her downturned head when she resumed her sewing.

Okay, fine. He'd made an effort. If she didn't want to make conversation, he wasn't going to shove it down her throat.

Taking his bowl of salad, he went out into the garden. The salad was good, full of smoky chunks of chorizo sausage and kernels of barbecued corn. The guys at the station would love it.

His fork fell into his almost empty bowl as the now-familiar thud of grief kicked him in the chest. He couldn't think about work without thinking of Cameron. From the moment they'd met during recruit training, Cameron had been by his side, through thick and thin. Leo couldn't imagine charging into a burning building without his buddy at his back.

Didn't want to, more to the point.

Which left a pretty large question mark hanging over his future. If he didn't have the stomach to go back to the station, where did that leave him?

He stared across the lawn, lost in his own messed-up thoughts. Gradually he became aware of laughter filtering through from the kitchen. He could hear the rise and fall of his mother's voice and Rachel responding. In sentences that consisted of more than a handful of words, too. He sat listening to Rachel talk and laugh and enjoy herself, shamelessly eavesdropping, both annoyed and intrigued by the contrast in her behavior when he was in the room.

She was telling his mother about her cousins in America, reminiscing about the summers they used to spend together. She was a good storyteller, her descriptions of their antics bringing a smile to his face as she described nighttime raids on the male members of the family, the frogs they found in their beds in retaliation and sewing sessions with her grandma Mags.

"The best thing about doing this quilt is that Jo and Ella and I are writing to each other again. I'm not sure why we stopped, really, but it's so good to know that they are still there and that we still have this connection between us," Rachel said. "I missed them so much when we first moved here when I was a kid. It was like losing half of myself."

His mother said something that he couldn't quite catch and he found himself straining to hear Rachel's response.

Okay, buddy, might want to reel it in.

There was something uniquely pathetic about a guy with a busted shoulder and messed-up life hanging on to every word of two women bonding over a sewing project. Pushing himself to his feet, he grabbed his bowl and headed back inside.

The moment he opened the door, Rachel broke off what she was saying and refocused on her sewing, just the way she had when he'd returned from his walk. He stared at the nape of her neck as he strode past, wondering what was going on inside her head. Remembering the way she'd stared at him the last time she'd visited— as though she wouldn't stoop to scrape him off her shoe.

Maybe he was wiggy from being on his own too much, but he was getting the definite impression Rachel was not his number-one fan. An impression that was reinforced when his mother threw him a searching look after seeing her guest out.

"Did something happen between you and Rachel in high school?" she asked as she returned to the kitchen.

"No. Why? Did she say something?" The moment the words were out of his mouth he chided himself for sounding like a thirteen-year-old girl.

"No. But she doesn't seem very comfortable around you. And I don't think it's just because she's a little on the shy side. Are you sure you didn't break her heart?"

She said it lightly, but he could tell she wasn't entirely joking.

"I think I'd remember if I broke someone's heart."

"I'm not so sure. I seem to remember a lot of girls hanging around you when you were a teenager."

"We're probably safe to say Rachel wasn't one of them."

For starters, his arrogant teenage self wouldn't have taken the time to look past her carefully composed demeanor to notice the small things that made her beautiful. Like the fact that her mouth turned up at the corners even when she wasn't smiling, and the neat perfection of her small, ski-jump nose. He definitely wouldn't have noticed her laugh, or the way her hips swayed when she walked, or the long elegance of her fingers and hands.

In those days, he'd been more interested in breasts— the bigger the better—and stealing beer from his father's stash and impressing his mates. Football, girls and fun had been his three gods.

It wasn't until he'd left home and started training for the fire department that he'd understood there was more to life. He'd fallen in love, and had his heart broken. He'd learned that being sober and sharp and ready to go at the drop of a hat could mean the difference between life and death, and was more important than any boozy night out with his mates. These days, he was more interested in acing his exams so he could make senior station officer and renovating his apartment than he was in partying or cruising for women.

At least, he had been. Until the accident.

"What a shame. Just think, you and Rachel could have been teen sweethearts and be married with a houseful of kids by now."

His mum was teasing him, trying to make him

squirm, but he simply cocked an eyebrow at her. "Calm your farm, Mum. You'll do yourself an injury."

She laughed and swatted his arm with a tea towel. "You should have seen your face. You'll get married one day, even if you don't believe it now."

"Sure I will. And you'll never forget to change the batteries in your smoke alarms again."

But the next Tuesday when he walked into the cool quiet of the Sorrento Public Library, Leo couldn't help remembering his mother's words. Not the part about him getting married, the part about him possibly having hurt Rachel.

His mother had charged him with returning a couple of books when she'd learned he was walking into town, and now he paused inside the doorway of the library to get the lay of the land—also unfortunately giving Rachel the opportunity to spot him before he spotted her. He knew she'd spied him because when he finally located the service desk, Rachel was leaning toward her colleague, talking quietly, her gaze fixed on Leo. The moment he made eye contact with her, Rachel swiveled on her heel and disappeared through the doorway behind the desk.

Avoiding him. He narrowed his eyes. He didn't enjoy feeling like the stinky kid. He definitely didn't enjoy the idea that someone he barely knew disliked him so much that she refused to even exchange a few civil words with him while checking in some library books. And he had no idea why.

He was aware of the other librarian giving him a curious head to toe as he slid the books into the return chute. He offered her a friendly smile. Then, as if he didn't have a care in the world, he wandered over to the nonfiction section. He watched through a gap in the shelves, keeping an eye on the door behind the counter. Rachel gave him a good couple of minutes to clear the building before she left her bolt-hole. He waited until her colleague was busy helping an elderly patron before making his move.

A couple of random books in hand, he made his way to the desk. Rachel's welcoming smile became stiffly polite when she realized who her next customer was.

"Good morning. How can I help you?" she asked, the consummate professional.

"I'd like to get a library card," he said.

"Oh. Okay. There are a couple of forms you need to fill out. Do you have any photo ID on you? If not, you can always come back another time…"

He pulled out his wallet and the hopeful light died in her eyes.

Wow. She really didn't want to spend a second longer with him than she had to, did she?

"Let's go over here to do the paperwork," she said, indicating a small desk set to one side of the counter.

He skirted the counter and sat in the guest chair. She slid into the chair behind the desk. She was wearing a dark red T-shirt with a scarf tied in a jaunty knot at her neck. Her hair was down, too, the first time he'd seen it that way. It was longer than he'd thought it would be. If she was naked, it would almost cover her breasts.

Okay. Where had that *come from?*

"I'll get you to fill your name and address details in here, and here. And we'll need that photo ID, preferably something with your address on it." Rachel slid a form across the desk toward him and indicated a pen that had been fixed to the desk via a chain. Even though they were separated by the width of the desk, it was the closest he'd ever been to her. He could smell something light and sweet—her perfume? Or maybe it was simply her shampoo.

He picked up the pen and started filling out the form. She clasped her hands on the desk, her fingers gripping each other tightly. He could see them in his peripheral vision, a tight little ball of reproach.

He set the pen down. "Do we have a problem?" he asked boldly.

She blinked, sliding her hands off the desk and into her lap. "Why on earth would we have a problem?"

"You tell me. Every time I walk into a room you act like you want to be somewhere else. And just now you disappeared so you wouldn't have to deal with me."

She stared at him, her expression utterly unreadable. He had the feeling she was sorting through possible excuses, trying to decide which lie he'd believe. Then she took a deep breath.

"Okay. Fine. You want the truth? I don't like the way you speak to your mother. I know you're going through a difficult time right now, but Gabby is a really nice person and the way you spoke to her the other day... I wouldn't speak to a dog that way."

Whoa.

He sat back in his seat. Well, he'd asked for it, hadn't he?

His first impulse was to defend himself, to tell her his relationship with his mother was none of her business. But he *was* embarrassed about the way he'd overreacted to the slice of banana cake. He'd been a dick, and even though he'd made his peace with his mother, he deserved to be called on it.

"You're right. I was out of line. And I apologized to my mum after you'd gone." He forced the words out of his mouth. He wasn't used to accounting for his behavior to anyone except his commander.

"Well. Good."

She pursed her lips, clearly surprised by his response. He'd never noticed before how full her mouth was, the lower lip verging on voluptuous. For a moment he was so fascinated by its plumpness that he almost allowed her to get away with fobbing him off.

Almost.

"But that's not the only reason you don't like me, is it? You gave me the death stare well before I said a word to my mother."

"Death stare? I have no idea what you're talking about."

She crossed her arms over her chest and proceeded to give him the death stare, mark II.

"My mother believes I broke your heart in high school."

That got her attention.

"You have got to be kidding. As if I would have been interested in a—"

She caught herself just as it was about to get good. A tide of color rose up her neck and into her face.

"You were saying?"

She glanced toward the counter. "I need to get back to work. Did you want a card or was that just an excuse?"

"I want a card," he lied.

"All right, then." She stared pointedly at the half-filled-out form.

"Maybe if you tell me what I did wrong, I can fix it," he said. "Whatever it was."

He began to wonder if he should persist with this. It wasn't as though he was ever going to see her again once his wrist was healed and he'd moved home. There was absolutely no reason for the two of them to cross paths. She could go home and stick pins in a voodoo-doll effigy of him every night if she wanted to and it wouldn't affect him or his life.

"Don't forget to create a password so you can manage your loans online," she said blandly.

"Whatever I did, it's obviously still playing on your mind. Why don't you go ahead and get it off your chest."

"I can assure you, Mr. Bennett, I have better things to worry about than an incident that happened eighteen years ago."

He did some mental math. "What are we talking here, year nine?"

She rolled her eyes. "Can you please just fill out the forms and leave?"

"I'm not going anywhere until we've sorted this out. Tell me what I did wrong so I can fix it."

"You can't. So this whole conversation is pointless."

"Tell me."

"No."

"Tell me, Rachel."

She glared at him, her color high. "There's no way I'm talking about this in public."

"Okay." He glanced around. "What's through that door?" He indicated the door she'd slipped through when he first arrived.

"The storage room."

He stood and waited expectantly. She made a frustrated sound in the back of her throat before springing out of her chair.

"This is completely pointless. Why do you care what I think of you? It's not as though Western civilization is going to crumble or anything."

He gestured for her to lead the way, and she made another harrumphing noise before walking behind the counter.

"I'll just be a minute, Jill," she said to the other librarian.

"Sure thing. I've got things covered out here," Jill said, a smile tugging at her mouth as she glanced at Leo.

Rachel shut the door once he'd followed her into the small storage room. Shelves stacked with books lined one wall, while a couple of book trolleys were pushed into the far corner.

"Let's get this over with," she said briskly.

"This is your story."

"Okay. Fine." She lifted her chin and flicked her hair over her shoulder nervously. Then she smoothed her hands down the sides of her pants. "It was year nine. The school dance. I'd only been in Australia for about three months."

He frowned, trying to remember. There had been so many school dances over the years, they'd all mushed into one memory of flashing lights and loud music and frustrated making out in dark corners.

"You and a couple of your mates went into the storage room in the gym to smoke, but I was in there already, killing time until my friends got there."

A memory tickled at the back of his brain—Tim revealing he'd stolen an inch of alcohol from every bottle in his parents' liquor cabinet and combined it all into one foul, deeply potent brew. Rocket fuel, they'd called it. They'd all been half cut by the time they'd made it to school and sneaked off for an illicit smoke to go with their illicit drink.

"You were talking about the girls in our year level.

Sharon and Tina and some of the others. Rating them. Then you—" She broke off and swallowed noisily.

Suddenly he felt a little queasy. He realized he wasn't going to like what he was about to hear.

"Turn around," she said abruptly.

"What?"

"I need you to turn around. I can't say this to your face."

He stared at her. She raised her eyebrows. He spun so she was facing his back.

This was definitely not going to be good.

"One of the guys asked what you thought of me. You didn't remember who I was until they told you I was the American girl. You called me 'the plank.' Someone said I wasn't 'that bad,' and you said if you woke up next to me you'd want to chew your own arm off. Then you said you'd rather cut your you-know-what off than put it in me. That's how bad I was."

He closed his eyes for a long beat. *Bloody hell.* Worse than he'd imagined.

"Happy now?" she said.

Oh, yeah. He was real happy that he'd once been an insensitive, brash, hormone-driven little turd. And he was immensely happy that Rachel had been the victim of said turdness. And the best thing was, he had absolutely no defense for his behavior. At all.

He faced her. She'd crossed her arms over her chest again. Her cheeks were flushed. She held his eye, though, even though he could tell it cost her.

She wasn't the one who should be embarrassed about any of this. He was the one who'd been a jerk. She'd simply been an innocent bystander.

"I guess you pretty much hated my guts all through high school after that," he said quietly.

"For a while. But in the end I realized you were just one boy. Even if you thought you were pretty special."

He winced. He'd had that coming. His fifteen-year-old self had, anyway.

He lowered his head for a moment, thinking of a suitable apology. There were no words that could undo what he'd done, but he had to try.

"For what it's worth, I'm sorry. If I could go back in time and kick my own ass, I would, believe me. We were half-drunk that night and convinced we were the coolest thing in town. An obnoxious combination. Everything that came out of our mouths was about us trying to impress each other. None of it meant anything."

"You didn't know me."

"I didn't. I was apparently too busy sticking my head up my own backside to have that opportunity."

She eyed him steadily for a beat before glancing at the door. "I should get out there again."

She opened the door and gestured for him to precede her back into the library.

"You don't really want a card, do you?" she said once they'd returned to the desk.

"My mother gave me hers in case I wanted to borrow anything," he admitted.

She studied the two books he'd brought to the counter as props.

"Like *A Guide to Companion Planting* and *Topiary Hedges Made Easy?*"

"Exactly."

"Keen gardener, are we?"

"I like to dig holes for myself. Big ones."

She handed the two books back to him. "You can use the self-checkout service. Or Jill can help you out."

She walked away. He watched her go, feeling like a fool and a heel.

He'd never been under the illusion that he'd been a saint in his youth, but it was pretty depressing to realize he'd been an unparalleled tool.

He reshelved the gardening books, making sure he put them in their rightful spots, then headed for the door. This was Rachel's turf, after all. Leaving her to it seemed like the very least he could do.

CHAPTER FOUR

RACHEL DIDN'T RELAX until Leo had exited the library. She couldn't quite believe that she'd just laid it all out at his feet. She hadn't meant to. But he'd insisted and she'd realized the only reason she was holding back was because she'd been embarrassed *for him,* because any halfway-decent person would be deeply upset to have such ugliness put at their door. Even if it was long-gone, ancient-history teenage ugliness.

She'd had to live with the hurt his words had inflicted for years. So she figured if she made Leo embarrassed, it was small potatoes compared to that.

He *had* been embarrassed, too. When he'd turned to face her, his cheekbones had been burnished with color. He'd appeared...*appalled* was the word that leaped to mind. Yes, he'd appeared gratifyingly appalled.

And yet it said something about the man he'd become that he'd looked her in the eye and apologized without hesitation or excuse.

She gave herself a mental shake. There was a queue forming at the returns desk. Time for the past to resume its rightful place in her life.

The rest of the day whizzed by, but it wasn't lost on her that whenever someone tall and male entered the library, a part of her went on the alert until she confirmed it wasn't Leo.

She told herself he wasn't coming back to the library. Not after the conversation they'd had today.

But Leo proved her wrong the very next day, walking through the door in faded jeans, a black T-shirt and battle-scarred work boots. He spotted her immediately and headed her way, his step and gaze determined.

"Hi," he said.

She nodded, since she seemed to be having trouble finding her tongue.

"I wanted to give you this." He put a glossy gift bag on the counter between them. "It doesn't make up for anything. But I wanted you to know that I'm sorry. Incredibly sorry." His blue-brown eyes held hers and his voice was gravelly with sincerity.

"You didn't need to buy me a present." There, she'd finally found her tongue.

"I wanted to make good on my promise to go back in time and beat the snot out of myself, but they were all out of time machines at the gift shop."

"I'm no expert, but I'm pretty sure beating your past self up might transgress the laws of time travel. So it's probably just as well that they were out of stock."

"Good point."

Maybe it was her imagination, but his shoulders seemed to drop a little at her easy response. Surely he hadn't been nervous to talk to her. Worried that she'd throw his gift back in his face, perhaps?

She glanced down at the gift bag, wondering what he'd bought her. She wasn't about to open it in front of him, though. It seemed too…personal. "You really didn't have to do this. But thank you." She offered him a smile—a real one.

"I did. But I'm not going to stand here and make you play witness to my mea culpa." He turned to go, then almost immediately turned around. "I almost forgot. My mother has ordered me to find something to read. She says I'm driving her crazy watching daytime TV."

"Wow. You must be really desperate."

"You could say that." His tone was light, but there was a bleakness behind his eyes. She remembered Gabby's tears on his behalf, and the cold harshness in his voice when he'd rejected his mother's kindness.

Leo presented himself as tough and gruff, but she was beginning to realize there was a lot going on beneath the surface. And that most of it wasn't happy.

"What do you enjoy reading?" She held up a hand. "Scratch that. You don't read. But you used to, your mum said. So what did you used to read?"

He fixed his eyes on his feet, clearly trying to remember. "I thought *The Hobbit* was pretty much the best thing since sliced bread for a while there."

"Fantasy. Okay, that's a good starting point. Have you caught any of the *Game of Thrones* series on TV at all?"

"No. My schedule's too irregular to follow anything on TV."

"Let me check if we have any of the books, then."

She moved to the computer, very aware of him watching her as she typed a request into the library's catalogue. She fumbled the spelling twice and felt her cheeks heat. Whether she wanted to acknowledge it or not, this man affected her.

"We have the first book in the series. Let me grab it for you."

She expected him to wait at the counter, but he surprised her by following her into the fiction section. She'd never really registered it before, but he was a good head taller than her, something she didn't encounter very often. Also, there was something different about him today. She couldn't quite put her finger on it...

"You're not wearing your sling," she said, wishing the words back the moment they were out of her mouth. Now he'd think she'd been checking him out.

"The physiotherapist wants me to start exercising my wrist more. And my shoulder seems to be in decent shape."

"That must be a relief."

"I'm sure it is for Mum. I'll be heading home in the next few weeks."

"To the city?"

"That's right."

She concentrated on finding the familiar blue spine of the book she was searching for. If he went back to the city, she probably wouldn't see him again, since she hadn't crossed paths with him in the last fifteen years.

She pulled *A Game of Thrones* from the shelf. "Here it is." She handed the book over. "It's got a little bit of everything. Sex, death, betrayal, murder, magic, prophesy, war... Something for everyone."

He hefted the book, eyeing its many pages uncertainly. "It looks pretty heavy going."

"You can always bring it back if you don't like it. That's the great thing about a library—low commitment, high return."

"Have you read it?"

"Yes."

"Did you enjoy it?"

"I loved it."

"I'll give it a shot, then."

She checked the book out for him on his mother's card before moving on to the next patron. She knew the exact moment he walked out the door, though. And she

was also aware that almost every female in the building watched him leave.

Some things hadn't changed since high school.

She tucked his gift bag beneath the counter and pretended to forget about it, though her mind came back
to it at least half a dozen times as the day wore on. She
considered opening it when she got home, but again she
put it off. She wasn't sure why.

She had dance class that night, and as usual, all her
cares dropped away the moment she buckled on her
dance shoes and stepped into Greg's arms.

"How's your week been, sweetie?" he asked as they
started a warm-up dance before their teacher arrived.
Five years younger than her, he was openly, proudly
gay and a wonderful dance partner.

"Okay. How about yours?"

They chatted briefly, then their instructor, Jack, arrived, and it was all about focus. An hour later, Rachel
was pleasantly tired and buzzed. Jack was pleased with
their progress, but he constantly reminded them that
they were but one of nine couples in the competition
and that all of their competitors would be rehearsing
just as hard. It was eating away at Rachel's confidence.

"Ignore him," Greg told her as he walked her out to
her car. "He thinks he's motivating us. Let's just concentrate on being fabulous and let the rest take care of
itself."

It was an excellent life philosophy, and she happily
hummed along to the radio during the drive home. But
the moment she walked in the door, she saw Leo's gift
on her kitchen counter and stopped in her tracks.

Okay. It was time to open it, lest it become a thing.
Which it was in danger of doing if she left it any longer.

She put it off five more minutes by having a shower,

then she pulled on her pajamas and walked into the kitchen. The glossy gift bag was stuffed with tissue paper and she had to forage for the actual gift. She emerged with a beautifully wrapped parcel the size of a hardcover book.

Frowning, she ran her thumb under the tape and eased it away from the paper—she'd never been a tearer—to reveal a deep burgundy-colored box with an illustration of a beautifully curly feathered quill on the lid. When she opened the box, she discovered a sheaf of heavily textured linen paper inside, along with matching envelopes and a pen, the lot tied together with a shiny cream-colored bow.

Her breath eased out on an appreciative sigh as she handled the paper. She'd always had a thing for stationery, and she knew enough to realize this was the good stuff. She was also aware that no one in town sold anything close to this quality. Leo had to have gone into the city to buy this.

She lifted the pen, enjoying the balance of it in her hand. She hadn't hand-written a letter to anyone for years, thanks to the advent of email, but she'd once loved the ritual of writing a letter the old-fashioned way—pondering and composing, folding it into the envelope, then, finally, fixing a stamp and slipping it into the letter box with a little prayer to the postal gods that it would find its way across the world.

She took the box into her room and propped herself against her pillows. Using a hardcover book as her writing surface, she wrote a letter each to Ella, Jo and Olivia. To Ella and Jo she talked about the quilt and her work with Gabby and asked after their own lives, but she spent some time working out how to reconnect with Olivia after several years of silence. She didn't want to give away the secret of the quilt—not yet, anyway. Jo would be the one to do that, since the wedding was to be at Hollymeade and she would be the one to deliver the quilt to Olivia. Finally, Rachel shrugged and simply wrote what was in her heart: that it had been too long, that she had been thinking of Olivia and her other cousins lately, that she hoped Olivia was well and happy.

When she finished, she had three crisp, creamy envelopes on her bedside table. She turned out the light and lay in the dark, unable to get Leo's gift or the fact that he'd traveled into the city to buy it for her out of her mind.

It doesn't mean anything. He felt guilty. That's all.

She understood that was true, but there was something about the understated carefulness of his selection that made it impossible for her to simply dismiss it as a guilt gift. He'd clearly thought about her and what might appeal to her when he'd made his purchase. And he'd gotten it—gotten her—perfectly.

Leo was on the patio finishing up a modified workout with some rehabilitation exercises when the doorbell rang on Saturday afternoon. He set down the stress ball he'd been squeezing and made his way through the house to the front door. Rachel blinked when she saw him, her gaze dropping to his chest briefly before returning to his face.

"Hi," she said.

"Come on in."

She moved past him into the house, leaving behind the same sweet, light scent he'd noticed at the library.

"Mum rang five minutes ago to say she's been held up at the shop," he explained. "Something to do with the alarm. She said to make yourself at home and she shouldn't be long."

She blinked again. "I can come back later, if that's easier…"

"She'll only be a few minutes."

"Okay. Sure."

He gestured for her to precede him up the hallway, his eyes automatically dropping to her gently swaying backside. She was wearing jeans today—not those tight, fashionable hipster ones but well-worn straight-legged jeans that looked as though they had many stories to tell.

She had long legs, he couldn't help noting. And a rather nice bottom.

She glanced over her shoulder at him as they neared the rear living room, and her brows were drawn together in a slight frown. Almost as though she'd overheard his thoughts. He raised his eyebrows in question and she shot her head to the front again.

If it was any other woman, he'd take it as a sign of awareness. The man-woman kind. But this was Rachel.

"Can I get you a coffee while you wait?" he asked as they entered the living room.

"Thanks, that would be great."

He moved into the kitchen to put the kettle on. "Milk, no sugar, right?"

Her eyes widened. "That's right."

"Station-house trick. We live on coffee," he said.

"Oh."

He crossed to the fridge for the milk. She set her things down and shrugged out of her black cardigan, revealing a tailored white shirt made out of something that looked soft to the touch. Silk, maybe. He noticed the faint shadow of her bra underneath.

"I wanted to thank you for that book you recommended to me," he said. "Turns out *The Hobbit* wasn't a fluke. Apparently I'm a closet fantasy geek."

"You're enjoying it?"

"It's awesome. Sex and death and blood and guts. Like you said, something for everyone."

"Hey, that's great. I'm glad." She beamed at him. She clearly took pleasure in turning people on to books, which probably wasn't surprising, given her profession.

"How many books are there in the series?"

"Five. At the moment. The bad news is he hasn't finished writing the series yet."

"So I should read slowly?"

"As a librarian, I endorse reading in all its forms. Fast, slow, electronic, with your lips moving, out loud."

He laughed. She had a sense of humor. As well as a shirt that he wanted to touch and legs that went on forever.

He slid her coffee across the countertop toward her. "I managed to keep my lips still. Just."

Her eyes dropped to his mouth for a second. "Good to hear."

He heard the sound of the front door opening and closing and realized he was disappointed they'd run out of time together.

To do what, exactly?

Good question.

"Here I am. So sorry to keep you waiting," his mother said as she bustled into the room.

"Not a problem," Rachel said with an easy smile. "Leo and I were just talking books."

His mother shot him an unfathomable look. "Oh, that's nice."

She and Rachel started talking about the quilt, and even though he was sweaty and sticky from his workout, he leaned against the sink, crossed his arms over his chest and sipped his own coffee. He watched the expressions play over Rachel's face—a self-deprecating smile when she talked about her sewing efforts to date, a small frown when she described something she found frustrating, a warmth in her eyes as she listened to his mother.

She had a great chin. He wasn't sure he'd ever noticed a woman's chin before, but hers was small and delicate and determined. A perfect match for her cute little ski-jump nose. All in all, she was a baffling combination of girl-next-door pretty and leggy, statuesque model.

Okay, not so much baffling as enticing. Intriguing.

And that was before he took into account her sexy, abandoned laugh and her warm, intelligent eyes.

And there you go again. You remember who you are, right? The last man she'd ever look sideways at.

"I'm going to go shower," he said, pushing away from the sink.

Neither woman so much as glanced at him as he made his way to the door, they were so engrossed in their conversation.

Which was as it should be. Rachel was there for his mother, not for him. In fact, if she had her choice, she'd probably prefer he not be there at all.

IT WAS FIFTEEN minutes past five on Monday when Rachel shut the door on the last of the library's borrowers. A further fifteen minutes later, she and Jill had tidied up for the night, locked up and parted ways. Basket over her shoulder, Rachel headed for home, her head full of plans for the evening. She wanted to cut out more pieces for her appliqué border trial run, and then she needed to drive to Teresa the costume designer's place to have a fitting for her dress for the dance final. Her first honest-to-God costume, since she'd borrowed a dress for the heats. She was dying to see what Teresa had done with all the red satin and black trim she'd bought.

She was about to leave the last shop behind when she registered the man standing still as a statue on the other side of the road. Leo's gaze was riveted on something in the side street, and even though he was several feet away, there was something in his posture that made her stop.

He was tight. Braced for pain.

Acting on instinct, she crossed to the other side. Leo was so focused he was oblivious to her approach. It wasn't until she was almost at his side that she saw what held him transfixed.

The Sorrento Fire Department had its quarters on the side street, and all three trucks were out on the concrete apron in front of the fire station, their crews rolling hoses and attending to other maintenance issues. Some of the men were in full kit, others in their gray uniform T-shirts and yellow turnout gear. They talked as they worked, smiling and laughing and ragging on each other.

Leo watched them as though he was doing penance, as though it was both torture and pleasure for him. The longing and pain in his eyes made her chest tight.

This was what went on beneath that gruff, tough demeanor, then. A world of anguish and uncertainty.

"Leo." She spoke softly and touched his arm gently.

He started, swinging to face her. For a second his gaze remained blank, unseeing, his mind clearly somewhere else entirely. Then he blinked and was back.

"Rachel."

"Are you okay?"

He shook his head. "Yes."

She wondered if he was aware that he was sending mixed signals. She glanced at the fire crew.

"Bit smaller than what you're used to, I imagine."

"A little."

"How much longer do you have off from work?" she asked, wanting to keep him talking. Wanting to somehow ease the lost look in his eyes.

"Until the doctors give me the all-clear to return to duty. I should really get going." He gestured vaguely in the direction of Gabby's place.

She studied his face, the tension around his mouth, the stiff way he was holding himself. If he was a woman, he'd be crying right now. That's what her gut told her, anyway. But he wasn't, he was a man, the kind who thrived on adrenaline and risk and running around with an ax in his hand. Allowing himself to hurt, and to seek comfort for that hurt, was anathema to him.

"I could walk with you for a bit, if you like?" she heard herself offer. "We could go down to the beach."

He looked away, his gaze going to the twinkling blue of the sea at the bottom of the hill. The silence stretched. He was going to reject her. Of course he was. They hardly knew each other. She was probably the last person he wanted to spend time with when he was so close to the edge.

"Okay."

She blinked and hoped she didn't look as surprised as she felt. "Well...good."

He turned his back on the fire station and started down the hill. After a moment's hesitation, she followed him. A few paces in, she'd matched the rhythm of her gait to his.

He didn't say anything, and neither did she, the only sound the slap of their feet on the pavement. She glanced at him out of the corners of her eyes, not quite sure why she was even here, or why he'd agreed to let her be.

His jaw was set, his mouth grim. His eyes stayed on the ground, ignoring the beauty of the Sorrento fore-shore—the tall cypress pines and the strip of pristine yellow sand and the rustic charm of the jetty, all set against the shiny azure blue of the sea.

"Your mom is worried about you, you know," she said quietly.

He didn't take his gaze from the pavement, but he tensed. "She shouldn't be. I'm fine."

He was probably regretting saying yes, wishing her to hell.

Well, tough. She would never walk away from some-one who was clearly in pain. And it wasn't as though she had anything to lose. Like his friendship, for example.

"What happened that night?" she asked.

"I don't want to talk about it."

"But maybe you should. Since the not-talking thing doesn't seem to be working out so well for you."

He shot her a glare. "How would you know?"

"Leo, if this is you happy and well-adjusted, I don't want to meet you on a bad day." His mouth curled into a grudging almost-smile. "Think of me as the world's cheapest, most disposable therapist. You can spill your guts and walk away and not see me again for another fifteen years."

He didn't say anything as they reached the bottom of the hill and waited for a break in the traffic to cross to the beach. It was only October, so the wind coming off the water was on the bracing side, even if the sun

was warm overhead. She buttoned her jacket and wondered if this was going to be the shortest, most silent
walk in the history of humankind.

She bent down to tug off first one ballet flat, then
the other when they reached the sand. After a moment
he copied her, tugging off his boots and socks. As one
they turned and started walking along the beach, the
water on their left.

"It never should have happened."

He said it so quietly, his voice so low, she almost
didn't hear him.

"The accident, you mean?"

"All of it. Cameron. This." He indicated his shoulder. "It was a derelict building, slated for demolition.
Typically, in that scenario, we'd concentrate on contain-
ment, let it burn itself out. But we had an emergency-
call recording from someone saying they were trapped
on the second floor. We had to check it out."

His face twisted with anger and she stopped in her
tracks, stunned by the thought that occurred to her.

"It wasn't a prank?" she asked.

"There were no bodies found in that building, alive
or dead," he said grimly.

"Why would someone do that? That's just perverse."

He nodded. "Yeah. It is."

It was as though a floodgate opened then. "Cameron
and I were sent in to clear the building. Visibility was
low and we crawled to the stairway at the back of the
building." His face tightened. "I stepped onto the stair
and it just collapsed beneath me. I went down on my
arm. Tore my tendon, broke my collarbone," he said
matter-of-factly. "Cameron got me out of there before
going back in with someone else from the crew. Then
there was an explosion and all hell broke loose.

"One second we were turning the tide, gaining control, the next…" He fell silent and she knew he was remembering the horror, the helplessness. "He got trapped. We couldn't get him out."

Such a simple explanation, but she could only imagine how it must have felt for Leo and his crew to stand outside a burning building and know they were unable to save one of their own.

"Tell me about Cameron," she said.

And he did. How they'd met at training, how Leo had pegged Cameron as the guy to beat and vice versa, how they'd pushed each other harder, faster, higher. How there was no one Leo would rather have at his back, no one he trusted more. No better guy, no one he'd looked up to more.

"When you go into fire, you have to know in your bones the other guy has got you. He would have died for me, and I would have died for him."

But he hadn't had the chance. He'd been in the back of an ambulance being pumped full of painkillers when a disused oil tank had blown. Despite his injuries, he'd insisted on leaving the hospital that night and being there when Cameron's fiancée was told.

"She's four months pregnant—unplanned. They were moving up the wedding to keep her parents happy."

The bleak misery in his face brought tears to Rachel's eyes. So much wasted life. A dream that had never had a chance to bloom. A woman who would now raise her child alone.

And Leo, who would forever wonder if he could have saved his mate. Or if he would have died trying. Funny how she understood that without him articulating it.

At some point they'd gravitated to the dry sand near the seawall, sitting and leaning back against the sun-warmed stone. Now Rachel regarded Leo's set jaw and dry eyes and wished there was something she could say or do that would ease him through this sad, broken time. But there wasn't. There was no shortcut through grief.

"I'm really sorry, Leo."

He nodded, his gaze fixed on the distant horizon. He looked so self-contained, so tightly wound. As though he was afraid to let himself go in case he fell completely apart. If she'd known him better, if theirs had been an established friendship instead of a tentatively burgeoning one, she wouldn't hesitate to put her arms around him. She settled for resting her hand between his shoulder blades, her body leaning against his enough to bring his right side into contact with her left. A little human warmth, nothing more, nothing less.

They sat like that for a long while, neither of them speaking. Finally, he stirred, pulling up the cuff on his sweater to check his watch.

"It's going to get dark soon," he said.

In fact, the sun was already on its way to setting, the sky a hazy apricot over their shoulders. He stood and offered her his good hand. She let him pull her to her feet, but when she tried to slip her hand free he tightened his grip.

"Thanks, Rachel," he said, his gaze holding hers.

This close, she could see the starburst of amber-brown that surrounded his pupils, could see the exact place where that brown transformed into brilliant blue. She realized he was still holding her hand and that she'd swayed forward an inch or two toward him. Blinking, she tugged her hand free and took a step backward.

"You don't need to thank me. Talk is cheap. Walking on the beach is free." She made a throwaway gesture with her hand, trying to smooth over that little lean-forward moment. Wishing that her body hadn't so obviously betrayed her.

"And you owe me nothing. Therefore, I appreciate the gift of your time and patience."

Before she understood what he intended, he was leaning forward. Her heart gave an odd little leap as he pressed a kiss to her cheek.

"Thank you," he said again.

Then, before she could respond, he collected his shoes and started back up the beach. This time she didn't follow. She simply watched him walk away, trying to pretend she couldn't still feel the warm pressure of his lips on her skin.

CHAPTER FIVE

AFTER TALKING TO RACHEL, Leo slept the whole night through for the first time in over a month. It wasn't that she'd said anything profound, or that he'd come to any amazing realizations while they'd talked, it was simply that he felt calmer after having vented some of the thoughts and emotions that had been brewing inside him.

She was a good listener. She was also incredibly easy to be with. It felt comfortable, almost familiar. As though they'd been friends for a long time.

Lying in bed the next morning, Leo could still feel the warm, gentle weight of her hand on his back. He hadn't been able to accept comfort from anyone else, but the simple, uncomplicated empathy of the gesture had somehow sneaked past his guard. He'd allowed himself to be sad, to acknowledge that he was hurting. Without guilt. He'd been so busy chastising himself for being alive, for being injured, for not being able to take all of this in stride, that he hadn't allowed himself the small, human luxury of simply sitting with his feelings.

After a while, though, he'd been more aware of the press of her body against his. The weight of her breast against his arm. The rhythm of her breathing. The smell of her perfume.

So... Time to be honest with himself: he was developing a bit of a thing for the town librarian. Given their history, it was probably doomed to be a one-sided thing. His past actions were so beyond the pale, it was a wonder she had even stopped to give him the time of day, let alone extended the hand of friendship to him.

But she had, because she was kind and generous as well as smart and quietly funny and incredibly hot.

Okay. Maybe it was a little more than a thing. Maybe he was well and truly infatuated.

He was scheduled to touch base with the hospital that morning to arrange for follow-up X-rays to track the progress of his recovery. He made the call over breakfast, then sucked up his gumption and called the station. Another firefighter, Danny, answered, and they spent a few minutes shooting the breeze before Leo asked to be put on to the commander, Mack.

"Bennett. Was wondering when we'd be hearing from you." There was a question in Mack's voice, one Leo wasn't sure he was ready to answer.

"Yeah. Things have been going a little slower than I thought they might." It wasn't exactly a lie. His body was healing, but his head was still a mess. He still wasn't sure he wanted to continue doing the job he'd once loved without his buddy by his side.

"We've got the big fund-raiser Saturday. You should swing by and catch up with the guys."

"Sounds good," he said, carefully not committing to anything. The aim of the fund-raiser was to raise money for Cameron's fiancée, Carrie, and the baby, but he wasn't sure he could face her yet.

There was a small pause.

"We all miss him, mate," the chief said. "But you throwing in the towel isn't going to bring him back."

Leo rubbed the bridge of his nose. He had no idea how the chief knew what was on his mind, but he couldn't deny that was exactly how he felt—he had no right to just pick up the threads of his life and carry on as if nothing had changed when his best mate was dead.

"I'll try to make it to the fund-raiser," he said.

"Good man. And if you need to talk before then, my door's always open."

"Thanks."

He couldn't figure out what to do with himself after ending the call. He tidied his mother's kitchen, then thought about mowing the lawn, but wasn't sure his wrist was up to it yet.

He floated restlessly around the house for a few hours before heading out for a walk. It was well past lunchtime by the time he hit town, but he bought some muffins and dropped into his mother's shop, knowing it would make her happy to see him. It did, but his restlessness wouldn't let him stop and chat for long. He walked some more before making his way down to the beach. He was sitting with his back against the sea wall, the same spot where he and Rachel had talked yesterday, when he glanced up and saw a tall, slim figure walking along the edge of the water, shoes in her hand.

Rachel.

He watched as she drew closer, breaking away from the water's edge to cut across the dry sand. She stopped in front of him, using her free hand to tuck a strand of hair behind her ear.

She didn't say anything, and neither did he. He had no idea how she'd known he'd be here, but it was only now that he was looking into her eyes that he understood why he'd been so restless today, and why, no matter how far he'd walked, he'd kept circling back into town.

She dropped her shoes to the sand and let her bag slide down her arm. Then she sat beside him.

"Windy today," she said after a moment.

"Yeah."

"I just talked to your mum at the shop. She said you'd been in. That maybe you weren't having a great day."

Ah. That explained it, then.

"Define 'great.'"

She smiled and drew her knees up, looping her arms around them as she gazed out to sea. "I don't know. Happy? Content? Comfortable in your own skin, maybe?"

"Then, no, not a great day."

She didn't push, and he didn't volunteer. Instead, they talked about the weather, about George R.R. Martin, about their favorite holiday spots and least favorite foods.

"Where are you from, originally?" he asked after she'd finished denigrating brussels sprouts as the Worst Food Ever.

"New York. The state, not the city. Syracuse, to be exact."

"Been back recently?"

She shook her head. "Nope. Keep meaning to, but…" She shrugged. "I guess there's not much for me there now. Everyone's got their own lives. What am I going to do, drive my rental car past our old place? Mum's still here in Melbourne. There's no reason for me to want to be anywhere else."

"So you're an Aussie now?"

She glanced at him just as the wind lifted her hair and blew it out behind her like a pennant. "I wouldn't go that far. I can't stand Vegemite. I still don't understand Australian Rules Football. And it will *always* be aluminum to me, not aluminium."

"Vegemite is an acquired taste. You have to persevere. The secret is lots of butter."

"It's a cultural joke. I think it's time you guys just came right out and admitted it. You laugh yourselves silly every time you convince a foreigner to stick a teaspoonful in their mouth."

He laughed, aware of something in his chest loosening for the first time in weeks. "I guess the really important question is how do you feel about beer?"

"I like it. Quite a bit, actually."

He nodded approvingly. "Bottle or glass?"

She gave him a sideways look. "Bottle. What planet are you from?"

They talked for nearly an hour before it started getting dark. He walked her back up the beach and into town. She stopped on the corner of Main Street and gestured toward a side road.

"This is me."

"Then I guess I'll see you around."

"I guess you will."

This time he lingered ever so briefly when he ducked his head to kiss her cheek. Her skin was soft and sweet smelling, and he paused to draw her essence into his lungs before pulling back.

She gave him a small, slightly uncertain smile before turning away.

He opened his mouth to ask her if he could take her out for dinner, but the words wouldn't come. He didn't want to overstep and ruin this...whatever it was that was happening between them. It was very possible that yesterday and today had been about pity, pure and simple. She was a nice person, after all. She cared for people.

Maybe the feeling he had when he was with her was completely one-sided. Maybe she wasn't immediately happier when he was around, as though the world was a better place. Maybe he was just some messed-up sad sack she was being kind to.

She glanced back over her shoulder as she headed down the road, raising her hand in farewell.

He waved. Not so long ago, he wouldn't have hesitated to go after what he wanted. But he wasn't sure he had the right to inflict himself on anyone at the moment. Rachel deserved better. Hands in his pockets, he headed for home.

HE WAS WAITING for her outside the library the next day. And the next. By the time her Friday-evening dance class rolled around, Rachel's head was full of him.

Things he'd said, the way he moved. The smell of him—clean clothes and soap and man. The way his five-o'clock shadow only accentuated the clean lines of his jaw, the low rasp of his laughter.

She knew without asking that she was not the sort of woman Leo typically dated. She'd seen his girlfriends in high school.

Then again, he wasn't her typical type, either. She tended to go for men who wore suits and glasses, men who worked behind desks for a living.

Yet there was no denying the excited thud she felt in the pit of her belly every time she exited the library and found Leo waiting for her. No surprises there—he was a good-looking man with an amazing body, and she'd discovered he'd successfully shaken off the jerkishness of his teen years to become a thoughtful, funny, insightful man.

She was only human. She wasn't proof against such a deadly combination.

But she also wasn't silly enough to let their walks take on any significance in her mind. He was a man in crisis. Injured and heartsore, he was in Sorrento on a time-out, staying in his childhood home, taking a step back from his real life. Their walks and conversations were part of that time-out, and she would be a very foolish woman indeed if she started to read anything more into their relationship than there was.

The thing was—

"Ow. Got me good there, Rach," Greg said.

They stopped spinning across the floor as she registered that she'd all but impaled her dance partner's foot on the heel of her shoe.

"I'm so sorry. I lost track of where we were. Are you okay? Have I crippled you for life?"

Greg laughed. "All's well, sweetie. Do you need a break? Shall we take five?"

That was his diplomatic way of saying, "Girlfriend, get your head in the game." And he was right. This was their last class before the competition on Sunday. They were supposed to be polishing and finessing their routine now, not fumbling around because her head was in the clouds.

"Five minutes sounds good," she said, offering him a sheepish smile.

He squeezed her shoulder, then crossed the parquet floor to confer with Jack.

Rachel walked to the coffee urn in the far corner and poured herself a big cup. Hands clasped around the warm china, she did her best to clear her mind of everything except the steps she and Greg had been rehearsing.

Leo is not an option. He is a mirage. A sad, sexy mirage. Get him out of your head.

She'd done well at her studies in school, well enough to have gone into medicine or law if she'd wanted to. She was a smart cookie, as her grandma Mags used to say. Smart enough to know when to protect herself. The problem was, she wanted to throw caution to the winds whenever Leo laughed at something she said, or looked into her eyes in that slow, steady way he had. And when he kissed her cheek...

Yep. Definitely hard to keep her head when he did that. Which meant maybe it was time to curtail their little walks. Purely as a self-protective measure.

She stared down into her coffee. She would miss him. His laugh. The way he viewed the world.

But he was getting better, she could see it in his eyes, hear it in his voice. Soon, he'd be going back to his life in the city. So this little time-out of theirs would be over soon anyway.

"Okay, ready to go?" Jack called, clapping his hands together imperatively.

Rachel downed the last of her coffee in one scalding swallow, dumped her mug in the sink and took a deep breath. "Ready."

She joined Greg in the center of the floor and together they took up their starting position. Jack started the music, and she and Greg began to move.

"Much better, Rachel. But make sure you keep your hands loose, give Greg the room to lead."

They stepped and spun and flourished their way across the floor, Jack calling out encouragement and reminders.

"No looking at feet, please."

"Chin high."

"Small steps, people. Conserve your energy."

A smile started to build inside her as the dance progressed, fueled by the sense that she and Greg were getting it right this time around. It simply *felt* right, everything flowing, her body perfectly attuned to Greg's. As they headed for the finale, she couldn't stop herself from laughing with the sheer joy of it.

Then Greg whipped her out to the side, reeled her in and she let herself fall back into his arms as the music ended.

Greg was grinning like a loon as he hoisted her to her feet.

"Great, guys," Jack called.

"Let's do that again," she said. "That felt *amazing*."

Then she noticed the man standing behind Jack, his big arms crossed over his chest, a bemused smile curving his mouth.

"Leo."

LEO BLINKED AT the pink-cheeked, tousle-haired vixen standing in the center of the dance floor. Dressed in black stockings, some kind of gauzy, floaty-skirt thing and a spaghetti-strapped tank top, she looked as though she'd stepped out of a poster for a Latin dance club.

She did not look like a librarian, or the woman who came to his mother's place every Saturday to sew, or the woman who'd walked in companionable silence with him every day this week. Yet it was undeniably Rachel standing in front of him in another man's arms. He'd known it the moment he walked in and discovered her spinning and strutting her way across the dance floor.

"What are you doing here?" She was frowning, her chest rising and falling as she attempted to catch her breath.

"I was on my way back from the city and I saw your car parked out front," he explained.

It sounded dumb when he said it out loud, but a few minutes ago it had made perfect sense to pull over and go find her. Her little red car had stood out like a beacon, drawing his eye. The next thing he knew, he'd pulled over and climbed out of the car. The dance school was the only business still open at this time of night, so it had been a no-brainer to look for her in here.

"I didn't realize you danced," he said stupidly.

The understatement of the century. Because Rachel didn't just dance, she *danced.* She and her partner had burned up the dance floor, moving as one, their movements both crisp and languid at once, the whole appearing effortless and damn impressive.

"Well, I do." She was very pink, and he realized she was embarrassed.

"You're amazing," he said, just in case she wasn't aware of that fact.

"Thanks." She couldn't hide her smile at his compliment, but it was obvious she wasn't quite sure what to do with it, either. "I'm just learning, really."

"You're kidding me."

She shook her head, her smile broadening. "Greg and I are only beginners."

He forced himself to make eye contact with her partner. The guy who'd been throwing her around the dance floor and gyrating his hips against hers and manhandling her in the most intimate way possible. Greg nodded an acknowledgment, curiosity plain in his face as he followed their conversation.

"Hey," Leo said, returning the other man's nod with one of his own.

"Hey, yourself," Greg said.

Something inside Leo relaxed when he heard the lilting cadence to the other man's speech. He was gay. Thank God. Now he wouldn't have to resist the urge to flatten him for the way he still had his arm around Rachel's shoulders.

The skinny blond guy who'd been shouting instructions from the side of the dance floor checked his watch. "You know what, guys? I think we'll call it a night."

"Okay, sure," Rachel said. "As long as you're happy…?"

"Do that again on Sunday and I'll be more than happy," the blond said.

Rachel's gaze slid to Leo. Then she took a deep breath and walked toward him. He watched her hips, the sway of her body. No wonder he'd always been fascinated by her walk.

"I think this officially makes you a dark horse," he said.

"It isn't a secret."

"And yet you haven't mentioned it once."

She used the back of her hand to push a damp strand of hair off her forehead. "It's kind of a hard thing to work into a conversation."

"Is it?"

Her lips twitched a little. "Okay, maybe I'm a little shy about putting it out there. Greg and I have only been in one competition. I don't want to make a big deal out of something so small."

"Speak for yourself, sweetie," Greg said as he came up behind her. He draped Rachel's cardigan over her shoulders and handed her her gym bag. "Text me, okay?"

She smiled her assent before Greg gave Leo another nod and headed for the exit.

"We should probably go, too, so Jack can lock up," she said.

Leo followed her outside, still a little dazed. As though he'd fallen down the rabbit hole.

"What other secrets do you have?" he asked as she opened the hatch of her car and stowed her gear.

"None."

"I don't believe you."

She looked startled. "Don't you?"

"No. I'm beginning to believe you're like one of those Russian nesting dolls, always another revelation just under the surface."

She laughed. "I'm a *librarian,* Leo."

"A bloody sexy one."

Her eyes widened and her throat worked nervously. Then her gaze dropped to his mouth.

So…she was aware of him as a man. She'd thought about kissing him the way he'd thought about kissing her.

Suddenly all the reasons why he should keep his distance didn't hold water anymore. She was standing in front of him, pink and a bit flustered, her body warm from dancing, and the only thing on his mind was claiming some of that warmth for himself.

"Rachel." He reached for her, his hand sliding around her waist, palm flattening against her back as he drew her close. Her breath hitched, her eyelids fluttered. Her head fell back slightly in wordless invitation.

Desire rocketed through him like a freight train, fierce and undeniable. She rested a hand on his shoulder as he pulled her body against his. They matched perfectly, breast to chest, hip to hip. He ducked his head, but instead of finding her mouth, he pressed a kiss to the soft skin beneath her ear. He'd been wondering about that little patch of tender flesh. Wanting to taste it.

She gave a low sigh as he teased her with his tongue. He was already aroused, but that small, helpless sound pushed him over the edge. Fingers curling into her slender body, he pressed his mouth to hers.

She tasted of coffee and heat. He stroked her tongue with his, his free hand rising to cup the sweet shape of her jaw.

She tasted good, alive and real and eager. He started making calculations in his head, working out in whose car they would leave here, how long it would take to get to her place, where he could get her naked. Because he needed to do that, very badly. He needed to—

He was suddenly holding air, nothing but space where warmth had been, and she was out of reach, shaking her head, one hand reaching up to touch her lips as though she couldn't quite believe what had just happened.

"What's wrong?" he said, his body thrumming with desire.

"This is a bad idea."

"Didn't feel bad to me. Did it feel bad to you?" He took a step toward her, but she held up a hand.

"Leo. Don't, please." She took a shuddery breath. "We both know you could seduce me if you really put your mind to it. But it wouldn't end well, and I'd rather not go there."

"Who says it wouldn't end well?"

She dropped her hand to her side. "You would never have even known I existed if you hadn't had your accident. You would never have glanced twice at me."

He flinched. "You're making a lot of assumptions."

"Am I wrong? Go out with a lot of mousy librarians, do you?"

"You're not mousy."

She half turned away, drawing in a long breath. "You have no idea how much I want to just let this happen, but you're going to go back to your old life soon. So let's just be friends, okay? That way when you don't call I won't have to feel like an idiot."

There was something exquisitely fragile in the way she held herself and he understood what she was really saying—that he had the power to hurt her, if he chose to. That she already had feelings for him, and that if he pushed this, it had to be about more than curiosity and desire and a need for comfort and release.

He was silent too long. She nodded, then turned away.

"Drive carefully, Leo."

"Rachel—" A million thoughts and protests crowded his mind, stilling his tongue.

"It's okay, Leo. I understand. I really do."

She smiled sadly before opening her car and slipping inside. He took a step back from the curb as she started the engine and pulled out into the street. Then she was gone, and he was standing in the dark.

CHAPTER SIX

GOING TO GABBY'S house the next day was one of the hardest things Rachel had ever done. She wanted to cancel their sewing session with every fiber of her being, but Christmas was just over two months away and the quilt wasn't going to finish itself.

So, she put on her big-girl panties and she went. And when Leo answered the door, she gave him her brightest, friendliest smile and did her damnedest to act as though nothing had happened last night.

"Great day. You can really feel summer in the air, can't you?" she said as she brushed past him.

His hand shot out, catching her arm above the elbow. "Rachel." He lowered his voice, took a step toward her.

Dear God. He's going to kiss me again. And I am terrified that I will not stop him.

"Can we talk about last night?" he said, his voice low.

He smelled minty, as though he'd just brushed his teeth. Something he might have done at her place this morning—if she hadn't backed off at a million miles an hour last night.

"There's not really much to say, is there?"

He was standing so close. If she leaned forward an inch or two she could press her lips to the triangle of skin exposed by the V-neck of his T-shirt.

"I wasn't looking for a one-night stand, if that's what you thought."

"Oh, I figured it would be more than one. Maybe a week or two. Until you were ready to go back to the city."

He frowned, his fingers tightening on her arm. "Rachel—"

"Oh. I beg your pardon. I didn't mean to interrupt." It was Gabby, wide-eyed and embarrassed as she reversed up the hallway.

"We were just talking," Rachel said quickly. "You weren't interrupting anything."

She tugged on her arm and Leo let her go. She didn't look at him as she followed Gabby into the rear living room. Her face was warm, and she noticed Gabby was embarrassed, too.

"I'm sorry. I didn't realize…" Gabby said, her gaze bouncing from Rachel to Leo and back again.

"There's nothing to realize. Honestly. We were just talking about a book."

It sounded lame, even to her own ears.

"Well. Would you like a cup of tea?" Gabby asked.

"Yes, thanks."

Gabby glanced at her son. "I won't ask you if you want some, because you've got your fund-raiser thing to get to. Unless you've decided not to go?"

"I'm going."

There was a grating, determined quality to Leo's voice, as though he was girding his loins for the task ahead. She studied him, took in his set jaw and the closed-off expression on his face. She remembered then that he'd mentioned a family-day fund-raiser being held by his old crew, the proceeds of which would go toward Cameron's fiancée.

She hadn't realized it was this weekend, though. He

couldn't not go, but she understood it was going to be hard for him.

"Is Carrie going to be there?" she asked quietly.

He'd spoken about Cameron's fiancée at length during one of their walks, about how hard it had been to witness her grief.

"I don't know. Probably."

"Just…take it easy, okay?" she said.

They locked eyes. More than anything she wanted to offer him the comfort of a hug. But last night's kiss had ruined any possibility of that happening.

"Okay." He turned to his mother. "I'm not sure what time I'll be home. I'll call if it's going to be late."

"Be careful on the road," Gabby said. "They're forecasting rain and it always seems to hit hardest down here on the peninsula."

"Will do."

Leo threw one last glance Rachel's way before he left. Rachel fussed with her sewing things as she waited to hear the front door close. Only then did she let her shoulders relax.

"Earl Grey or English breakfast?" Gabby asked.

Rachel's head came up. "Um, Earl Grey, thanks."

She watched Gabby set out cups and saucers, aware of the tension in the room. She was tempted to reiterate what she'd said before—that nothing was going on—but Gabby beat her to it.

"This is silly. We're all adults here, after all. There's no need to pussyfoot around." Gabby set her hands palm down on the counter and fixed Rachel with a very frank look. "I like you, Rachel. And I love my son. Normally, the last thing I would want to do is get involved in his romantic life. But I'm going to make an exception because I've really enjoyed becoming friends with you over the past few weeks. You're a lovely, smart, attractive woman."

Rachel felt herself warming all over again. "Thank you. I've really enjoyed becoming friends with you, too."

"It never occurred to me that something might happen between you and Leo. Oh, in my fondest fantasies I'd love for him to fall in love with a woman like you. Someone with a big heart. But the sad fact is that Leo has always been a bad bet in that area, Rachel." Gabby stared down at the counter. "I'm not sure what it is. Maybe he's had it too easy with women all his life. Maybe there really is such a thing as being too handsome for your own good. I don't know. But I do know that I would feel horrible and responsible if I let you embark on something with him without giving you fair warning. So here it is, my fair warning—my son sucks at commitment, so please don't fall in love with him."

Rachel blinked, suddenly aware she was a hairbreadth from crying. "Okay. Thank you. Warning noted." She hated the way her voice was thick with emotion.

Gabby's face crinkled with concern. "Don't tell me it's too late?"

"No. I don't think so," Rachel said, taking a deep breath. "Close, but no cigar."

"I've upset you."

"You haven't said anything I don't realize already. I might be a librarian, but I'm not a nun."

"Well…good. I feel guilty and disloyal now, but Leo would be the first to admit that just the thought of settling down makes him break out in a rash. Which doesn't bode well for my quest for grandchildren, sadly." Gabby pulled a face.

Rachel forced a smile. "Maybe he'll meet someone one day and she'll knock his socks off and everything will click for him."

The kettle clicked to announce it had boiled. Gabby crossed to collect it.

"It's a nice idea, isn't it?" Gabby said wistfully.

It *was* a nice idea. And maybe it really would happen that way for Leo. Somehow she and Gabby managed to get back on track for the rest of their sewing session. The practice border she'd been working on was her best yet. Just as well, given that she needed to ship the finished quilt panel back to Jo soon so her cousin had enough time to quilt the top to the backing before the wedding.

Still, she felt distinctly flat when she left Gabby's, and not even the prospect of collecting her finished costume from the dressmaker could lift her mood.

Teresa had done a lovely job, creating a salsa-friendly version of a flamenco dancer's dress, the hemline having been considerably lifted to allow for the movements of the dance, and she'd pared back the ruffles to just three rows. The central split was almost indecently high, but it wasn't as though she was dressing for church. This was Latin dancing, after all—showy and sparkly and flashy.

The pièce de résistance was the black fringing that formed the hem of each of the three ruffles. When she spun, the fringe would fly out, accentuating every movement of her hips and backside.

It really was a glorious thing, and by the time she'd taken the dress home, hung it on the door of the wardrobe in the spare room and stared at it for half an hour or so, she was feeling quite a bit better. Tomorrow was going to be exciting and nerve-racking and fun. She would concentrate on that and ignore the ache in her chest that had started when Gabby had issued her warning.

The storm that had been threatening all day finally broke at sunset, the last of the daylight smothered by thick gray clouds. The ominous sound of thunder made her shiver as she slipped into her pj's before padding barefoot into the living room to fire up her laptop. She'd sent an email to Jo and Ella that morning to confirm plans for the delivery of the quilt panel to Jo, and she wanted to check to see if either of them had responded. She sat back on her heels when she saw Jo's response.

I've been thinking about this, and I have a proposal for you both. How do you feel about a trip to Hollymeade for Christmas? I'd love Olivia to be a part of this quilt, so maybe all four of us could get together like old times to finish the quilt together. And maybe Olivia will take pity on us and let us stay for the wedding, too.

What do you think? Is it a crazy idea, or inspired brilliance?

Rachel didn't have to consider long to make her decision. Not so long ago, Leo had asked if she'd ever gone back home and she'd said there wasn't much there for her anymore. That wasn't true—she had three very good reasons to revisit her home. The chance to reconnect with her cousins in person, to play a part in the quilt's final journey, would be a gift. A treasure.

Inspired genius, I think you mean, she typed back. *I'm in. Tell me when and where and I'll be there. With sleigh bells on.*

She hit Send and went into the kitchen to make herself dinner with a big smile on her face. Christmas at Hollymeade. Finishing the quilt with her cousins. It seemed like the perfect way to end the quilt's journey.

Her thoughts turned to Leo as she pulled ingredients from the fridge. She wondered if he'd made it home yet, and what sort of day he'd had. She hoped it was better than he'd thought, that being with Carrie and his crew again had given him the push he'd needed to reengage with his old life.

She was about to set the wok on the stove, when the sharp sound of a knock echoed through the house. She wiped her hands on a tea towel, then went to see who it was. Greg, perhaps, freaking out over tomorrow's competition. She'd spent an hour counseling him on the phone the night before their previous heat.

She peered through the spy hole. She couldn't see anything but a set of broad shoulders covered by a sopping-wet navy shirt, but she instantly recognized who it was.

Leo.

She wrestled with the lock, then the door was open and he was standing there, hair plastered to his skull, clothes saturated, eyes dark with misery and confusion.

"Leo. Come in," she said, reaching out to draw him over the threshold.

She shut the door on the wet, wild world outside and then faced him.

"You're soaking. Let me get you a towel…" She hustled down the corridor to the bathroom, returning with a couple of towels as she said, "What happened? Did your car break down or something…?"

She stopped dead when she really saw him, the way he was staring at the ground, the hunch to his shoulders.

It had been a bad day.

She let the towels fall to the ground. She stepped forward and flung her arms around him, offering him the comfort of her body. He went very still for a moment, then returned her embrace, his arms closing around her fervently, fiercely. He lowered his head, pressing it into the crook of her shoulder, and she rested her cheek against his wet hair.

"It's okay, Leo. I've got you," she said quietly.

A shudder went through his body, and then he was holding her tighter, and his mouth had opened on her neck and she could feel the hot wetness of his tongue as he kissed her. She closed her eyes as desire rushed through her, accepting before he'd even lifted his head that this had been inevitable from the moment she'd opened the door to him.

His mouth slid across her jaw, trailing kisses, and then he was tilting her head back, his tongue in her mouth. She gave him everything he needed and more, and then she slid a hand around to the nape of his neck and stood on her toes so she could whisper in his ear.

"Come on, Leo. Let's go to bed."

SHE WOKE BY slow degrees, memories washing over her like the rising tide.

Leo on her doorstep, soaked and despairing. That first kiss in the hallway, the feel of his hard, cold body against hers. He hadn't been cold for long, though. Not once they'd stripped off his clothes and tumbled into her bed.

She smiled a cat-that-got-the-cream smile. It had been wonderful. He had been wonderful. Tender and passionate by turns, utterly bent on her pleasure. So gentle and loving.

The way he'd looked at her...

The way he'd touched her...

It had been perfect, and if last night had been the best of it, the best of them, if it was all downhill from here...well, then, so be it. She'd gone in with her eyes wide open. And she wouldn't have done it any other way, because despite what she'd told Gabby yesterday, she loved him. That much had become clear to her last night. She couldn't ignore his need. Not when it had been within her power to offer him comfort.

Not that last night had only been about comfort. It had been about healing, and it had been about understanding and connection, and it had been about lust and desire.

As she'd said, perfect.

She could feel the heat of his body along the length of her spine, could hear the steady rhythm of his breathing. If she moved her feet back, she could slide them down his long, hairy shins. Smiling to herself, feeling more than a little daring, she did so. His response was to snake a hand around her middle and pull her back against his chest.

"Tell me again how mousy you are," he murmured against the nape of her neck.

He kissed her neck, which soon led to kissing other parts of her body, and before she knew it they were making love again, their bodies dappled by the sunlight streaming through her bedroom window.

Afterward, she glanced at the clock and realized that she only had three hours until she had to be in the city for the dance competition. She bolted up, adrenaline surging through her. She'd been so absorbed in Leo that she'd forgotten how big today was.

"What's wrong?" he asked, eyebrows raised in surprise.

"The dance final is in three hours. I need to have breakfast and get moving."

"You're in a dance final? I thought you said you and Greg were beginners?"

"We are. But we made the final." She shrugged modestly.

"Impressive."

She shrugged again, even though she was privately pleased by his praise. Sliding out of bed, she grabbed her robe and pulled it on, very aware of him watching her from the bed.

"Do you want some breakfast?"

"Sounds great." He stretched his arms over his head, the action making his stomach muscles ripple.

"Okay." More than a little dazed by the display, she went into the kitchen.

He looked awfully good in her bed. Comfortable and completely at home. She could get used to waking up with all that sexiness beside her.

My son sucks at commitment, so please don't fall in love with him.

The memory of Gabby's words stole the smile from her face as the danger of what she was doing hit her. It was one thing to say her eyes were open, to decide to take what she could from her time with Leo, no matter how long or short it might be, but it was another thing entirely to allow herself to be swallowed whole by the fantasy.

Watching the bread starting to brown in the toaster, she realized she was going to have to be constantly vigilant with herself if she wanted to have a hope in hell of coming out of this whole.

Who are you kidding? You're crazy about him. No matter what happens, you're going to be a mess.

Her chest tightened painfully as she imagined how hard it would be to have Leo and then lose him. But it was too late—she'd made her decision last night.

"So, this competition. Can anyone watch?" Leo asked.

She started, caught off guard by his sudden appearance in the kitchen wearing nothing but his boxer briefs.

"Sorry. Didn't mean to sneak up on you," he said.

"It's okay. I'm not really used to having houseguests."

"We'll have to see what we can do about that."

He came up behind her, slipping his arms around her middle before dropping a kiss onto her shoulder. The smallest of affectionate gestures, but it made her chest even tighter. Words filled her head, words she desperately wanted to say.

I love you.

You're a good man.

Please allow yourself to be happy, Leo. Please let me help you be happy.

But she couldn't say any of those things to him. Leo had enough on his plate without her adding to his woes. Besides, he would think she was a bunny-boiler of the highest order if she declared her love after one night together. Or he'd think she was hopelessly unsophisticated and gauche.

Neither was an attractive proposition.

"Would you mind keeping an eye on the toast while I start packing up my gear?" she asked.

"Gear. What kind of gear does a dancer have?"

"Wouldn't you like to know."

She slipped from his arms and out of the room.

"That was the whole point of me asking, actually."

His words followed her as she walked up the hallway to the spare room. She grinned, consciously letting go of the melancholy that had gripped her for those few moments in the kitchen. She'd decided to enjoy Leo, and enjoy him she would.

Humming to herself, she entered the spare room, shutting the door long enough to retrieve the garment bag hanging from the hook on the other side. Throwing it on the spare bed, she turned to her dress, ready to stow it ever so carefully in the bag for the trip to the dance studio.

And froze.

For a moment she forgot to breathe as she stared at the shredded satin of the dress's once-bodacious skirt. Instead of three deep, tiered ruffles with black fringing, there was nothing but a mess of red-and-black threads that trailed down to the carpet, ending in a tangled ball of thread and fabric.

"No. Oh, my God."

Sick and shocked and dizzy, she sat on the bed, unable to tear her stricken gaze away.

Her dress was ruined.

CHAPTER SEVEN

RACHEL'S HEARTFELT EXCLAMATION echoed up the hallway to the kitchen. Leo glanced over his shoulder and frowned, waiting for her to say more, but he didn't hear a sound.

"Everything okay?" he called.

He was busy buttering the toast, but there was something about the silence from the other end of the house that drew him into the hallway.

"Rachel?"

"I'm…in here."

He followed her voice to what was obviously a second bedroom. The moment he saw her face he knew something was badly wrong.

"What's the matter?"

She gestured weakly toward the dress hanging on the outside of the wardrobe door. At least, it *had* been a dress. Now it was closer to a mop, the bottom third of it a tangled mess of shredded red-and-black fabric.

"The cat. The neighbor's cat got in. I must have left a window open somewhere…"

He was no expert, but it was immediately obvious to him that the skirt was beyond repair. The cat had clearly had a very good time.

"Okay. Okay." He sat down beside her. He was used to dealing with emergency situations, but there wasn't a section on ballroom dancing–costume disasters in the fire department manual. "Let's just think this through."

She was very pale. He could *feel* the shock and the panic and the disappointment vibrating through her.

"I'll have to call Greg and cancel. We'll have to pull out." Her voice was flat. Controlled. She was being a trouper, trying to take it on the chin.

"What about another dress? You must have something."

"Nothing that would be even close to suitable."

"What about the dress you wore last time?"

"Borrowed. And she lives on the other side of town." She stood. "I'll call Greg."

She left the room. Leo stared at the ruined dress, wishing there was some way he could magic it back into one piece. Rachel hadn't said it out loud, but this dance meant a lot to her. He'd seen her face as she'd danced Friday night—it was as though she'd been lit from within. She'd found something that made her heart sing, and best of all, she was great at it. He knew exactly how that felt, because he was a great firefighter, and there was nothing he'd rather do than hold the line with the rest of his crew. Even though it was dangerous. Even though people died.

It was who he was. It was who he wanted to be.

He went very still as he registered his own thought. Then he bowed his head for a brief moment. So. He'd made his decision, then. He'd go back. He'd pick up his ax and take his exams and continue doing what he did best. Despite Cameron not being at his side.

He lifted his head, his gaze gravitating to the ruined dress once more. An image flashed across his mind— Rachel, whirling across the dance floor on Friday night in a gauzy black skirt and black stockings.

He stood, striding to the door. He found her in the living room, phone in hand, tears sliding silently down her face.

It was so like her to take herself off somewhere to cry. She would never, ever ask for anything for herself or draw attention to her own needs. Witness last night, when she'd taken him into her arms and her bed, despite the line in the sand she'd already drawn. He'd needed her, needed her calm and her warmth after a harrowing day watching Carrie be brave at the fund-raiser. She'd understood that and given him everything he'd asked for and more.

He'd been so torn up, so conflicted over being back at the station house, over how good it was to see the rest of his crew. One minute laughing at a joke, the next racked with guilt because Cameron was absent, the ghost at the feast.

His only thought once he'd made his escape was that he had to see her. He'd driven out of the city and parked in front of her house, but the memory of their kiss, of what she'd said, had stopped him from going inside.

So he had walked. And walked some more. Until he was wet and miserable and unable to stay away.

She hadn't hesitated to take him in, to give him what he'd needed, and now it was his turn to reciprocate.

Anything to take away the misery in her eyes, to make her smile again.

Anything.

"What about the skirt you were wearing the other night?"

She shook her head, using the back of her hand to wipe away her tears. "It's just a skirt. I need a whole outfit." She sniffed, lifted her chin. "It's over. I have to accept that. Maybe next year I'll know better than to leave a window open when Claudius is around."

She started to dial. He took the phone from her hand.

"So what if we put the top of the competition dress and your practice skirt together? Wouldn't that be an outfit?"

She frowned. "I don't even know how I would do that. I'd have to find some way to finish the hem of the bodice... The competition starts in less than three hours."

"Then we'd better hustle, hadn't we? You've got a sewing machine, right?"

She blinked at him. "Leo... It's too hard."

But he saw the hope in her eyes. He hooked an arm around her neck and dropped a kiss onto her mouth. "Lucky we're both so smart and stubborn then." He swatted her on the backside, just hard enough to make her blink. "Move it, soldier."

She frowned, but she went to the hall cupboard and pulled out a sewing machine. "I guess I could use what's left of the old skirt as a sort of bias binding around the bottom of the bodice," she said when she returned. "Then I could stitch the skirt to the bodice."

He had no idea what a bias whatever was, but he liked that she was thinking now, and not giving up. "Great. That sounds perfect. Tell me what to do and I'll do it."

The next hour passed in frantic activity. Together they worked to separate the bodice from the shredded skirt, then, under her instructions, he cut strips of fabric from what was left of the skirt. She used big looping stitches to hold things in place before sewing the makeshift band to the bottom of the bodice.

"Your mother would tell me to do it again if she saw

this, but we don't have time to make it better," she said, running a dissatisfied hand over the puckered seams.

"Sweetheart, you have legs all the way to the moon. No one is going to notice a crooked seam. Trust me."

She blushed and rolled her eyes, but he could see she was starting to get excited again. It was another ten minutes before she'd stitched her rehearsal skirt to the bodice and announced herself happy with the result.

"Great. Into the shower, tell me what I need to pack for you."

He'd been doing his best not to mention the time, since it was in increasingly short supply, but when she glanced at the clock she leaped to her feet.

"Crap. It takes an hour to get there. And I haven't done my hair or makeup or anything."

He steered her into the shower. "Panic while you wash. You can do your makeup in the car. What do you want me to pack?"

She shucked her robe and leaned in to turn on the shower. "Um… A change of clothes. I don't care what it is. I'll have to go in the dress."

He couldn't help pausing to admire her in all her glory. Clothed, she was gorgeous. Naked…

"Leo," she said, pushing him toward the door.

"I'm only human."

She kept issuing orders while she showered, then she flung on underwear and fishnet stockings and finally the salvaged dress. They both examined her reflection critically in the mirror. He could tell she wasn't happy, that this wasn't how she'd wanted to present herself.

"You look great," he assured her, despite the fact that even he could see that the detail and color in the bodice was not matched by the very plain skirt.

"It'll have to do."

Inspiration struck while she was throwing makeup and hair spray into a tote bag—he called his mother. Five minutes later, they were in the car, heading toward the highway out of town.

"What are you doing?" Rachel asked, her expression comically panicked when he detoured via Main Street and stopped in front of his mother's store.

"Two seconds." He leaned on the horn and his mother raced out, a bulging shopping bag in hand.

"I grabbed everything that looked like it might work. Just give me back what you don't need. And good luck, Rachel. We can talk about you keeping such a juicy secret another time…"

"Thanks, Mum." He stepped on the gas then, tossing the bag into Rachel's lap.

She opened it and made an appreciative noise. "Oh, these are perfect."

He'd remembered his mother had a display bin full of artificial roses at her store. When he'd called, he'd explained the situation and his mother had risen to the occasion, filling the bag with big red roses and ribbons and other bits and pieces he didn't have names for.

"Leo, thank you. What a perfect idea. Who knew firemen were so creative."

"You make a single crack about me being in touch with my feminine side and I'm pulling over," he said.

"I wouldn't dare. I'm too busy being grateful."

He happened to glance across at her then, and the way she was looking at him, the gratitude and warmth and affection in her eyes… His chest got tight all over again, but for a completely different reason this time.

Making Rachel Macintosh happy was the kind of work a man could very easily find himself getting addicted to.

THEY MADE IT to the studio with ten minutes to spare. Leo let her out at the front door and drove off to find somewhere to park, and Greg rushed out to greet her.

"Thank. God. You made it. And you look gorgeous."

She glanced down at her makeshift dress, complete with a skirt that was now dotted with half a dozen red artificial roses that she'd stitched on as Leo drove. In between doing her hair and makeup, naturally. It was not the dress she would have chosen to wear, but it wasn't an embarrassment, either.

Thanks to Leo.

"I need to go to the bathroom," she said, even as she craned her neck to locate Leo.

"He can find his way into the building. He's a big boy," Greg said, dragging her inside. "We're going to have a little chat later about you keeping him a secret for so long, too, by the way."

It seemed she would be having quite a few little chats in the near future.

She still hadn't laid eyes on Leo when the first dancers took to the floor. She fidgeted nervously, dividing her attention between the dance floor, the door and Jack's last-minute instructions.

Then she saw Leo's head at the back of the crowd. He was pushing his way through to where they were waiting. His gaze did a slow track down and then back up her body, his mouth curling into an appreciative smile.

"Great dress, sexy legs," he said.

"Thanks. You should meet my seamstress. He totally rocks a pair of dressmaking scissors," she said.

Jack nudged her in the ribs. "Two minutes."

"Okay. Thanks." She took a deep breath, nerves suddenly jangling as adrenaline zipped through her.

"I'm going to go sit over there," Leo said. "So I can

get a good view of you wiping the floor with the rest of these suckers."

He kissed her cheek carefully so as not to smudge her makeup before turning away. She watched him until he was swallowed by the crowd, a fierce surge of longing knifing through her.

This morning she'd told herself she'd be content to take whatever she could from Leo, that she'd settle for a short bit of joy and love and laughter if the only other option was nothing at all. But she didn't want a little, she wanted a lot. She wanted it all.

She wanted Leo to call her sexy legs and to ogle her in the shower every day.

She wanted to lie in bed and talk about books with him on lazy weekend mornings.

She wanted the right to look at him and know in her heart that she was his and he was hers.

She wanted his time and attention and interest for always, not just for a night or a week or a month.

And she had no idea if he wanted those things from her. She had no idea what was going on in his head or heart. His mother had warned her he was a bad bet. Her own gut had confirmed it.

And yet today he had moved heaven and earth to get her here. He'd talked her out of despair, found solutions for her and believed he could make them happen. Because this mattered to her. Because he wanted her to have this moment.

It wasn't every day that a man braved the terrors of dressmaking for a woman, after all. A man who was used to hacking his way into buildings with an ax. But he'd done that for her. That had to mean something, didn't it?

"Okay, kids, you're up. Do me proud. And remember—little steps. And smile like you mean it," Jack said.

Greg led her out into the center of the floor. Her stomach did a slow roll as she registered the lights, the crowd, the man with the video camera off to one side. If she and Greg made it through this round, they would go to the state level.

She scanned the crowd, searching for one dark head. And there he was, a small smile on his mouth. Watching her. They locked eyes and he gave her a slow nod. She could almost hear his voice in her head. *Wipe the floor, sexy legs.*

Greg cleared his throat and she broke eye contact with Leo and took up their starting position.

Concentrate, Macintosh.

The music started, and she and Greg began to move. Back and forth, in and out, making good use of the space. Her makeshift skirt swished around her legs. Sweat trickled down her spine. She flicked her hips and strutted her stuff and let Greg lead her where he would.

And just as it had the other night, that lovely sensation of rightness bubbled up inside her. Her fingers tingled with it. Her chest was filled with it. She felt beautiful and strong and desirable. She felt invincible, a siren, a heroine, a vixen.

She lived the dance, felt it in every cell, every bone. And then the music stopped and it was over and she had to restrain the urge to let her head drop back and whoop for joy.

Greg hugged her, grinning ecstatically. "Baby, baby," he said, shaking his head. "I don't know what you had for breakfast, but I want me some."

She was too busy searching for Leo to respond. Because she suddenly realized there was something she needed to say to him. It didn't matter that it was too early, or that he might think she was unsophisticated. It didn't matter that his mother had warned her off.

What mattered was that she loved him, and as she'd whirled around the floor, it had hit her that she would be doing them both the greatest disservice in the world if she denied him the chance to know her love.

Because she was a *catch*. She was smart, and she was fun, and she cared deeply about people. She had a great job and she burned up the dance floor and she had so much love to offer the right man. The only reason for not declaring her love was that she was afraid.

Afraid that he would reject her. Afraid that someone as golden and perfect as Leo wouldn't want someone as mousy and quiet as her. Afraid that the only reason she'd been allowed into his world at all was that he was off balance and injured and low. As she searched the room for his familiar face, she forced herself to acknowledge that the root of all those fears lay in those overheard comments from long ago. Such was the lingering legacy of that night.

Her heart did a leap in her chest as she found his familiar face. She squared her shoulders, deliberately remembering the glorious, life-affirming buzz she'd experienced as she danced her heart out. Reminding herself of those handful of moments when she'd been saucy and bold and invincible.

The past was the past. She was better than it, and so was Leo. And more than anything, she wanted a future with him.

Heart pumping madly, she pushed her way through the crowd toward him. He forged his own path. They met halfway, just as the music came up for the next couple.

"That was fantastic. If you guys don't win it'll be an international incident," Leo said, leaning close and shouting to be heard.

He was smiling, one hand reaching out to draw her closer. Such a natural, instinctive gesture of possession. So full of affection and comfort and familiarity. It gave her the final push she needed.

Screwing up all her courage, she looked him in the eye. "I love you," she yelled over the music.

His fingers tightened around her waist, but he didn't look away. "Good," he said.

For a moment she wasn't sure she'd heard properly. "Good? Is that all you have to say?" It wasn't quite what she'd hoped to hear.

"I could say more, but I don't want to offend anyone's delicate sensibilities." He grinned then, a joyous, boyish grin, and pulled her closer, ducking his head so that his mouth was right next to her ear. "I could say that you have made me realize that I have a long way to go before I can even hope to be as good a person as you are. I could say that when I'm with you I feel as though I'm home. I could say that lying skin to skin with you last night was the most erotic, essential act of my life."

Heat rolled through her, followed by a wave of love that made the backs of her eyes prickle with imminent tears. He touched his lips against the soft skin beneath her ear, and she felt the whisper of his breath against her cheek as he spoke again.

"I could say all those things, but right now I'll settle for saying I love you, too, Rachel Macintosh. More than I have ever imagined I could love anyone or anything."

She threw her arms around him, not caring where they were or who was watching. She pressed her face into his neck and drew in great gulps of air full of his scent.

He was hers. He loved her. *He was hers.*

His hand landed on the nape of her neck, large and warm, and for a moment they simply held each other. Then the music came to an end and she reluctantly let him go. His eyes were suspiciously damp when she met them, and her mouth curled into a tremulous smile.

"You're not crying, are you, tough guy?"

"Firemen don't cry," he said.

He kissed her then, in front of everyone, and she didn't care, because she was exactly where she needed to be—in the arms of the man she loved.

EPILOGUE

OLIVIA MILLER STOOD on the top step of Hollymeade, squinting against the glare of the sun off the snow. Her feet were starting to turn into ice blocks, but no way was she going inside. Not until Eric came home.

She'd been waiting for this day for over a year, surviving on Skype calls and letters and emails, dread creeping over her every time the phone rang too late or too early.

But they'd made it. Eric had landed, he was safe, and he'd done his last tour of duty in Afghanistan. He was all hers, at long last.

She heard the sound of a car engine and her heart skipped a beat. She stood on her tiptoes and craned her neck to try to do the impossible and see around the bend in the driveway. She'd wanted to meet him at the airport—had, in fact, been there at the crack of dawn this morning—but a last-minute snafu with his flight had meant he'd been hugely delayed. She'd left after four hours, convinced he wouldn't be home until tomorrow. He'd called just as she'd reached Hollymeade. She'd wanted to turn the car back around, but he'd insisted she stay put and that he'd find his own way home.

Stubborn man. Stubborn, brave, beautiful, kind, sexy...

Her chin started to tremble and she sucked in a deep breath of cold air. She would *not* ruin this homecoming by greeting him with puffy panda eyes. There would be plenty of time to cry all over him when he was here with his arms around her.

The sound of the car engine grew louder. She started down the steps, dizzy with excitement.

She had so many things to tell him. Like the fact that the house on the lake they'd always loved was suddenly on the market, the asking price well within their careful budget. And the fact that her mother had given her the most incredible gift twelve months after her passing, returning her cousins to her. Ella, Jo and Rachel, her childhood soul sisters...

She still couldn't quite believe that they would soon be here, and that they were about to spend the next few days finishing the quilt that her mother had started more than a year ago and charged Jo, Ella and Rachel with finishing.

So like her mother, to still be looking out for her, even though she was no longer here to do so in person. Her mother had understood that Olivia had always regretted the distance that had grown between her and her cousins, and she'd found the perfect way to bring them together again—a quilt. A quilt to hang on the wall of her and Eric's new home. A quilt that would forever symbolize her mother's love and the ties of friendship and family.

A car appeared around the bend in the driveway. She stopped on the bottom step, both hands pressed to her chest. Waiting.

The car stopped, and the door opened. And there he was, tall and broad and handsome in his uniform. Tanned from the harsh Middle Eastern sun, and lean from a year of hard work.

She broke into a run, heedless of the ice and snow-slicked ground.

"Careful, Liv," he called out, but he was laughing, his arms already open to catch her.

She launched herself when she was still a few feet away, hitting him so hard he staggered back a step. But his arms closed around her, big and strong, and she clung to him, the tears she'd been holding back suddenly choking her.

"Liv. Liv," he said, his voice rough. He was crying, too, but she was sure he wouldn't be ashamed of his tears, because while he was big and tough, he was also tender. Her poet-soldier.

Her Eric.

They pressed their cheeks together so hard it hurt, and then they kissed and she tasted his tears and her own.

"I love you. I love you so much," she said.

"I love you, too, Liv. To the moon and back."

They both laughed then, and took a moment to draw back and wipe away some tears and simply look at each other. There were new lines around his eyes, lines Skype hadn't revealed to her, and it was a little startling how blue his irises were against his tan.

"You cut your hair," he said, lifting a hand to touch a strand of her newly cropped blond hair.

"It was getting too long."

"It looks good."

"You look good. Good enough to eat."

He laughed, his eyes darkening, his expression becoming distinctly wolfish. He flicked a glance toward the house as he pulled her in for another kiss.

"There's no one home, right? It's just us until everyone else gets here?"

She grimaced apologetically. A year was a long time, after all. "My cousins are coming this afternoon. I didn't get a chance to tell you about it. They'll be here any minute now. But they'll probably want to rest up after their flights. Well, Ella and Rachel will, anyway."

"They'd better."

He kissed her then, the old magic burning between them. Without saying a word, they started for the house, leaving his luggage in the car. They could collect it later.

Afterward.

And hopefully her cousins would be late. Really late.

They made it inside before he pinned her against the wall and started unzipping her coat. She fumbled at the buttons on the front of his uniform, drunk with the lovely familiar-strangeness of it all. Oh, she remembered this. How good it was between them...

He was just sliding her jacket off her shoulders, his mouth still locked with hers, when they heard the distinct sound of a truck engine, followed by the *thunk* of doors opening and closing. He groaned against her mouth, breaking their kiss to rest his forehead against hers.

"I'll make it up to you. Over the next fifty years," she whispered.

"I'm going to hold you to that."

He kissed her one last time, then tugged her jacket up her arms. She watched as he carefully zipped her back up, her heart swelling with affection and love and adoration.

"Okay. You're decent," he said.

"I love you, Eric Grant."

"And I love you, Olivia Miller."

Together they opened the door, and there they all

were, standing at the bottom of the steps—Jo and Rachel and Ella.

It hit her suddenly that this was going to be a very special few weeks—a wedding, a celebration and a reunion. And all at Christmas.

It was the best present she'd ever had. Heart brimming, she went to greet her cousins.

* * * * *

REQUEST YOUR FREE BOOKS!

2 FREE NOVELS PLUS 2 FREE GIFTS!

ⓗ HARLEQUIN®

SPECIAL EDITION

Life, Love & Family

YES! Please send me 2 FREE Harlequin® Special Edition novels and my 2 FREE gifts (gifts are worth about $10). After receiving them, if I don't wish to receive any more books, I can return the shipping statement marked "cancel." If I don't cancel, I will receive 6 brand-new novels every month and be billed just $4.74 per book in the U.S. or $5.24 per book in Canada. That's a savings of at least 14% off the cover price! It's quite a bargain! Shipping and handling is just 50¢ per book in the U.S. and 75¢ per book in Canada.* I understand that accepting the 2 free books and gifts places me under no obligation to buy anything. I can always return a shipment and cancel at any time. Even if I never buy another book, the two free books and gifts are mine to keep forever.

235/335 HDN F45Y

Name _____ (PLEASE PRINT)

Address _____ Apt. #

City _____ State/Prov. _____ Zip/Postal Code

Signature (if under 18, a parent or guardian must sign)

Mail to the Harlequin® Reader Service:
IN U.S.A.: P.O. Box 1867, Buffalo, NY 14240-1867
IN CANADA: P.O. Box 609, Fort Erie, Ontario L2A 5X3

Want to try two free books from another line?
Call 1-800-873-8635 or visit www.ReaderService.com.

* Terms and prices subject to change without notice. Prices do not include applicable taxes. Sales tax applicable in N.Y. Canadian residents will be charged applicable taxes. Offer not valid in Quebec. This offer is limited to one order per household. Not valid for current subscribers to Harlequin Special Edition books. All orders subject to credit approval. Credit or debit balances in a customer's account(s) may be offset by any other outstanding balance owed by or to the customer. Please allow 4 to 6 weeks for delivery. Offer available while quantities last.

Your Privacy—The Harlequin® Reader Service is committed to protecting your privacy. Our Privacy Policy is available online at www.ReaderService.com or upon request from the Harlequin Reader Service.

We make a portion of our mailing list available to reputable third parties that offer products we believe may interest you. If you prefer that we not exchange your name with third parties, or if you wish to clarify or modify your communication preferences, please visit us at www.ReaderService.com/consumerschoice or write to us at Harlequin Reader Service Preference Service, P.O. Box 9062, Buffalo, NY 14269. Include your complete name and address.

HSE13R

◆ HARLEQUIN®

SPECIAL EDITION

Life, Love and Family

A COLD CREEK CHRISTMAS SURPRISE

When Haven Whitmore is injured on
Ridge Bowman's ranch, Ridge steps up—and falls
for her. Whether this tantalizing twosome can make
it work will depend on whether they can put to rest
the Ghosts of Relationships Past.

Look for the conclusion of
The Cowboys of Cold Creek miniseries
from RaeAnne Thayne next month,
from Harlequin® Special Edition®!

Available wherever books and ebooks are sold.

www.Harlequin.com

HSE65781

Christmas cheer brings...love?

Aaron Holder doesn't mean to sound like old man Scrooge. But Maeve Buchanan's bubbly holiday cheer brings it out in him. It's a sudden act of Christmas kindness that finally draws them together, though will they admit their true feelings even when they meet under the mistletoe?

A Valley Ridge Christmas

by **Holly Jacobs**

AVAILABLE IN DECEMBER

HARLEQUIN®

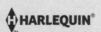

More Story...More Romance

www.Harlequin.com

HSR71893

All she wants for Christmas is...

When they come home for Christmas,
three military heroes have visions in their
heads of things far sexier than sugarplums.
But the women they love want more than
just one very good night....

Pick up

A Soldier's Christmas

by *Leslie Kelly, Joanna Rock*
and *Karen Foley,* available November 19
wherever you buy Harlequin Blaze books.

Red-Hot Reads
www.Harlequin.com

HB79780

SPECIAL EXCERPT FROM

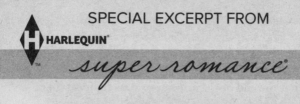

HARLEQUIN®

super romance®

This might be the best Robbie Burns' Day ever
for Kristin Hart. Why? Because the gorgeous
consultant, George, who her company hired
joined her at her family's celebrations. And now,
the night is coming to a close.... Read on for an
exciting excerpt of the upcoming book

The Sweetest Hours

By Cathryn Parry

"I hope that you got all you need from us today," Kristin said,
as she walked George out.

He turned and smiled at her, descending two steps lower
than her on the stairs. His eyes now level to hers. "I did."

His hand touched hers, warm from the dinner table inside.
His fingers brushed her knuckles. Kristin was glad she hadn't
put on mittens.

"Kristin," he said in a low voice.

She waited, barely daring to breathe. Involuntarily, she shiv-
ered and he opened his coat, enveloping her in his warmth. It
was a chivalrous response, protective and special.

"Is it bad that I don't want this day to end?" she whispered.

"No." His voice was throaty. The gruff…Scottishness of it
seeped into her.

His eyes held hers. And as she swallowed, he angled his head and…and then he kissed her. He was tender. His lips molded gently over hers, moving with sweetness, as if to remember her fully, once he was gone.

The car at the end of the drive flashed its lights at them.

He straightened and drew back. Taking the warmth of his coat with him.

"I have to go." He looked toward the car. "Maybe some day I can tempt you away. To Scotland."

Maybe if she were a different person, in a braver place, she would dare to follow him and kiss him again…. But she wasn't that fearless.

"Goodbye, George," she whispered, touching his hand one last time.

"Kristin?" His voice caught. "I hope you find your castle."

And then he was off, into the winter night, the snow swirling quietly in the lamplight.

After this magical night, will George tempt her to Scotland? And if he does, what will Kristin find there? Find out in THE SWEETEST HOURS by Cathryn Parry, available December 2013 from Harlequin® Superromance®.

Copyright © 2013 by Cathryn Parry

HSREXP1113

Love the Harlequin book you just read?

Your opinion matters.

Review this book on your favorite book site, review site, blog or your own social media properties and share your opinion with other readers!

Be sure to connect with us at:
Harlequin.com/Newsletters
Facebook.com/HarlequinBooks
Twitter.com/HarlequinBooks

HREVIEWS